JAHAJI

An Anthology of Indo-Caribbean Fiction

edited by

Frank Birbalsingh

TSAR
Toronto

We acknowledge the support of the Canada Council for the Arts for our publishing program. We also acknowledge support from the Ontario Arts Council.

"Sushila's Bhakti" was published previously in *Out on Main Street* (Vancouver: Press Gang, 1993); "Pooran, Pooran" in *A Day in the Country and Other Stories* (Leeds: Peepal Tree Press, 1994); "Swami Pankaj" in *Grain* (Spring 1999); "Far from Family" in *Sweet Like Saltwater* (Toronto: TSAR, 1999).

Cover illustration courtesy of the Thomas Fisher Rare Book Library, University of Toronto.

Canadian Cataloguing in Publication Data

Main entry under title:

Jahaji : an anthology of Indo-Caribbean fiction

ISBN 0-920661-88-2

1. Short stories, Caribbean (English). 2. Caribbean fiction (English).
3. East Indians – Caribbean Area – fiction. I. Birbalsingh, Frank.

PR9205.8.J33 2000 813'.010889140729 C00-931973-5

Printed in Canada by Coach House Printing.

TSAR Publications
P. O. Box 6996, Station A
Toronto, Ontario M5W 1X7
Canada

For Christine

Contents

Introduction

Jahaji is a follow-up to *Jahaji Bhai,* which appeared in 1988 when the very idea of Indo-Caribbean identity appeared suspicious and the classification of Indo-Caribbean literature seemed superfluous if not subversive. Yet 1988 marked one hundred and fifty years since people from India first immigrated to the Caribbean, and one would think that that was long enough for their distinctive, ethnic features as an immigrant community to be accepted in their new environment. During a similar period of time, European immigrant groups from Ireland and Europe, for example, settled in the United States and were accepted as American while retaining some degree of individual ethnic or cultural identity. Jews and Africans have been in the United States for longer and can claim similar acceptance, although no one would dispute their difficulties in achieving integration. Some may even question this claim, but the model of American multicultural integration is nevertheless useful to initiate a discussion of Indo-Caribbean identity and literature. The identity and literature of these American groups results partly from ethnic or cultural factors and partly from the historical circumstances of their immigration, for example, slavery and racism in relation to African Americans. In much the same way, the identity and literature of Indians in the Caribbean —Indo-Caribbeans—is influenced by their ethnicity and historical circumstances in the region.

Although Indians may be found in many different territories of the Caribbean, the large majority settled in English-speaking territories like Jamaica, St Vincent, St Lucia, Grenada, and particularly Trinidad and Guyana; so that while the comments that follow may be true for the region as a whole, or for the English-speaking Caribbean in general, they apply most of all to Guyana and Trinidad. Like the rest of the region, the English-speaking territories were first inhabited by aboriginal peoples such as Caribs, Arawaks, and Ciboneys, and other groups such as Macushis and Wapisianas in the mainland territory of Guyana. The advent of Columbus, however, brought Europeans who conquered the region at the end of the fifteenth century, and eliminated virtually the entire aboriginal population in the islands. The Europeans set up plantations for growing a variety of crops including cotton, coffee, cocoa, citrus and later and most importantly, sugar cane. It was as a producer of sugar that the Caribbean (or West Indies) first gained international attention, when huge profits were made from its sugar plantations during the eighteenth century.

At first the plantations employed indentured labourers from Europe, but from the beginning of the sixteenth century to 1834, they relied principally on slaves from Africa. This period established the broad outline of Caribbean or creole culture as based on a structure of race, colour and class, with the European (white) plantation owners forming a small but dominant group, a larger group of brown, mixed blood (European African) clerks and skilled artisans forming the middle class, and the large majority of the population made up of black workers at the bottom. After the slaves were emancipated in 1834, plantation owners brought in replacement workers from countries such as China, Madeira and India. Indians were by far the most numerous of these new workers, and between 1838 and 1917 more than four hundred thousand Indians came under contract or indenture, where other workers numbered no more than a few thousand each.

The terms of indenture required Indians to work for a period (usually five years) before either returning to India or remaining in the Caribbean. Almost three quarters chose to remain, and their descendants today form about twenty percent of the nearly five million population of the English-speaking Caribbean. Three hundred thousand Indians settled in Guyana and Trinidad alone, and the remainder were distributed in small, insignificant numbers over several islands. Thus the anomaly of Indians forming a minority in English-speaking territories generally, and a majority or almost so in Guyana and Trinidad where their large numbers allowed them to grow and outnumber or equal the freed Africans.

Indo-Guyanese today form fifty-one percent of a total Guyanese population of 825,000, while the other major ethnic group, Afro-Guyanese, are forty-three percent. Similarly, Indo-Trinidadian form forty percent of a total population of 1,058,320, while Afro-Trinidadians are forty-one percent. Since most people agree that the electorate in both territories tend to vote along ethnic lines[1], these statistics give a clear political majority to Indo-Guyanese, and almost equal status to Indo-Trinidadians; but the effect of these figures is not reflected in the results of elections held during the past few decades. The People's National Congress (PNC), which was led for most of the time by Forbes Burnham (1923-1985), an Afro-Guyanese, won six consecutive elections from 1964 to 1985, although it was predominantly African and opposed by a "majority" Indian movement, the People's Progressive Party (PPP), led by Dr Cheddi Jagan (1918-1997). Similarly, the People's National Movement (PNM), which was led for most of the time by Dr Eric Williams (1911-1981) in Trinidad and Tobago, and normally taken to represent Afro-Trinidadians, won six consecutive elections from 1956 to 1981 despite opposition from the Democratic Labour Party (DLP) which was identified with Indian interests.

Such political marginalization cannot simply be attributed to the Cold War and international or American disapproval of the left wing Indo-Guyanese leader Dr Jagan, who was suspected of communism, for Indo-Trinidadians suffered similar electoral losses although Indo-Trinidadian political leaders were not suspected of communism. What is significant is that Indian political marginalization coincided with independence in Trinidad and Tobago (1962) and in Guyana (1966). Independence was perceived as the political expression of creole cultural hegemony, historically claimed by Afro-Caribbeans for the English-speaking Caribbean as a whole, and asserted, for example, by the poet Edward Brathwaite whose poetic trilogy *The*

Arrivants[2] and his essay "The African Presence in Caribbean Literature"[3] both stress African cultural survivals and reconnections. Rex Nettleford too has written of the "centrality" of people of African ancestry "to the shaping of the new Caribbean ethos."[4] Yet, while African centrality was long acknowledged by distinguished commentators in the region, and even by the colonial government, it could not be fully expressed in political terms during the colonial period. Having gained an opportunity for expression after independence, however, it quickly recognized a threat from Indo-Caribbean political aspirations. It is the containment of these aspirations that has combined with existing historical factors to generate themes such as marginalization, insecurity, and homelessness that have become part and parcel of Indo-Caribbean experience and literature.

One historical factor is that the indenture system was temporary in purpose, merely a convenient device to stem the economic haemorrhaging of Caribbean plantations following the emancipation of African slaves. Indians did not come to the Caribbean, like the puritans to North America or British settlers to New Zealand, in order to establish a new home, or create a better civilization: for most of them, at least during the first few decades of indenture, when many were lured by false promises of quick riches, the region was simply a temporary residence before they could return home to India. Little wonder then that Neil Bissoondath, in his short story "Insecurity,"[5] written as recently as in 1985, presents an Indo-Caribbean character who, although several generations removed from indenture, nevertheless regards his native Caribbean island as a mere "stopover" before he moves on to some other destination. Little wonder too that the central preoccupation in the finest example of Indo-Caribbean fiction, indeed of all West Indian fiction, the novel *A House for Mr Biswas*[6] (1961) by V S Naipaul, is a fundamental sense of placelessness, marginalization and homelessness.

The physical conditions of indenture, too, induced disorienting feelings of insecurity, fear and panic. Herded like cattle on so-called "coolie ships," the immigrants were treated little better than human merchandise, as indeed their predecessors were, the African slaves who were also transported in ships across the Atlantic during the infamous Middle Passage. In truth, the voyage made by the Indians, from the east coast of India, westward around the Cape of Good Hope and across the Atlantic, was a good deal longer than the direct Atlantic crossing of their African counterparts. But not by its length alone was the voyage disorienting: it enforced loss of caste and custom, and cut the immigrants adrift from all that they knew and cherished in their homeland. The term "jahaji bhai," Hindi or Urdu for "ship brother," was invented as a designation of the new relationships which the immigrants had forged with shipmates in their attempt to compensate for broken ties with family and friends they had left behind in India. *Jahaji*, as the title of the present volume, represents a new sense of human togetherness invoked among Indian indentured immigrants by their shipboard experience.

The circumstances of indentured Indians on arrival in the Caribbean represent a third factor that accounts for themes of insecurity, alienation and homelessness at the heart of Indo-Caribbean literature. The strenuous bodily exertions required of this first Caribbean encounter is one thing. Far worse, though, was the disorientation Indians experienced because of the initial unsuitability of their languages, customs, religions, dress and culture in an English-speaking, Christian society with feudalistic mores based on African criteria of race, colour and class. There was simply no room in such a society for people with strange customs and dress, illiterate in English, and "pagan" to boot. The only justification of their presence was, quite literally, their labour; and that is how they were regarded—as labourers or coolies who were assigned a social position as outsiders, incompatible and mismatched.

No single word catches the flavour of Indo-Caribbean experience more completely than "coolie," which was applied to Indians on their first arrival in the Caribbean and has remained attached to them despite their subsequent emergence from plantation thralldom into careers as business people, financial entrepreneurs, land owners, politicians, authors, sportsmen and skilled professionals of all kinds. The word originally derives from the Tamil "kuli" (having to do with hire) and so signified a porter, jobber or carrier, especially one from India, China or other parts of Asia; it was therefore correctly applied to Indians upon their arrival in the Caribbean. But only the peculiar dynamics of creole society could ensure its continuous and indiscriminate application to Indians (interestingly, not to Chinese) so many generations after the beginning of indenture.

Dr Eric Williams, historian as well as politician, describes the situation in Trinidad around 1911: "There is no question that the Indian occupied the lowest rung of the ladder in Trinidad"[7]; and in a single phrase "the scorned and ostracized coolie,"[8] the Trinidadian politician Albert Gomes (1911-1970), himself of Portuguese or Madeiran ancestry, confirms the prevailing attitudes towards Indo-Trinidadians around World War Two. The Guyanese novelist Edgar Mittelholzer (1909-1965), who belonged to the mixed-blood or coloured middle class, frankly admits to anti-Indian in the period between the two world wars: "It was my class that looked down upon the East Indian sugar plantation labourers ('coolies' we called them, whether they were labourers or eventually became doctors or barristers or Civil Servants.)"[9] And to confirm the staying power of "coolie," Lucretia Stewart, a presumably unbiased British traveller, writing of a visit to Trinidad some time after 1970 states that: "Indians are dismissively called coolies behind their backs."[10]

The structure itself of colonial government helped to maintain the coolie stigma. Caught between competing interests of the whites and blacks (freed Africans) who voiced entirely justifiable demands for social and political change, the British administration walked a diplomatic tightrope trying to steer a middle course in maintaining order. In this situation, it is not hard to imagine how severely the massive Indian influx into Guyana and Trinidad tested the skill of British governors, who regarded Indians both as a source of economic necessity in helping the white planters and as a cause of embarrassment in so far as they were seen to compromise black demands for change.

As early as the 1850s, when Governor Francis Hincks of St Vincent objected to Indian indenture because it "would underbid Blacks in the labour market and likely produce race animosity,"[11] he inadvertently put his finger on what would later become a central dilemma of Indian experience in the Caribbean: whether Indians were a blessing or a curse; whether they saved the region from economic ruin by rescuing the sugar industry or strengthened imperialism by compromising the bargaining power of blacks for higher wages. What made things worse for Indians was that, in the latter case, they could be seen as scabs or strike-breakers, repugnant, not only in cultural or economic, but moral terms as well. It was another wedge driven into relations between Africans and Indians in Guyana and Trinidad. These were the seeds of racial division, planted by the system of indenture itself and watered by policies of colonial government, that sprouted so menacingly after independence with riots and killings in Guyana, and civil unrest in Trinidad and Tobago. The postindependence (African) political dictatorships or at any rate the African-dominated governments in both territories, must also be seen as products of the same colonial history.

One effect of these postindependence ethnic governments was to drive tens of thousands of Indo-Guyanese and Indo-Trinidadians into exile in foreign parts, mostly Britain, Canada, and the United States. Although this diaspora was part of a larger, postindependence immigration of all ethnic groups in the Caribbean, the scale and intensity of Indo-Caribbean participation are striking: one can estimate Indo-Caribbean diasporic numbers at about 350,000 and the total Indian population currently resident in the Caribbean at about 850,000. Relations between this diaspora and home, and between the diaspora and their host societies, are new and potent themes in Indo-Caribbean literature, as is the conflict between different generations of the diaspora. As for its literary impact, suffice it to say that of the sixteen stories included here, thirteen are by authors living in the diaspora.

From Samuel Selvon (1924-1994) who began writing in the 1950s to Shani Mootoo in the 1990s, Indo-Caribbean literature has been nourished by interaction between Indian political destiny in the Caribbean and the six factors enumerated here—the initial temporariness of the indenture system, its harsh and psychologically unsettling conditions, the coolie status of indentured Indians, the cynical "divide and rule" policies of colonial government, the ethnic divisions that emanated from all that went before, and the formation of a diaspora in the countries of the North. But if all this suggests bitter and unending racial rivalry between Indo- and Afro-Caribbeans, it is interesting that the Caribbean has experienced nothing like the murderous casualties inflicted by ethnic rivalry in Rwanda, the Balkan countries, and other parts of the world. On the contrary, Walter Rodney in *A History of the Guyanese Working People 1881-1905*[12] cites several examples of active cooperation and collaboration between Indo- and Afro-Guyanese workers over many decades, while S S Ramphal, in *A Heritage of Oneness*, argues for ethnic unity by perceiving an "unbroken chain between African slavery and Indian indenture"[13] in Guyana. Ramphal's conclusion is that slavery/indenture is "a common experience of human bondage" (22), and since racial rivalry is generally agreed to be less serious in Trinidad than in Guyana, one may safely assume some level of racial cooperation there as well.

As a region the historical (colonial) development of the Caribbean is unique. It is not like South Africa where a white, fascist regime brazenly exploited a black majority during the apartheid era, or like Australia and New Zealand where colonial governments persecuted native minorities for centuries. Nor is it like Asian and African nations that suffered European and colonial oppression for a time, and after independence came to loggerheads, as India with Pakistan, or the Ibos against the federal government of Nigeria. Two things confirm the unique history of the Caribbean islands: one is that their indigenes were exterminated and replaced by fresh waves of immigrants; the second is that the main function of the region was not to supply the needs of its people but those of their victimizers. And now that the victimizers have gone, only victims are left. As the poet Derek

Walcott writes with knowing ruefulness in "Ruins of a Great House": "The rot remains with us, the men are gone." That is why it is hard to believe that one set of victims could persecute another, for surely they would be restrained by their "common sense of human bondage."

But however much Forbes Burnham and Eric Williams may be products of a unique colonial history, there is the hard fact of Burnham's brutal dictatorship, his enforcement of corruption into every facet of national life, his ruinous economic mismanagement, and his creation of a brain drain that still cripples Guyana. There is also the disturbing fact that Burnham received little or no condemnation from other Caribbean heads of state: on the contrary, he was publicly approved by Eugenia Charles, prime minister of Dominica, for his role in Guyana's political history. This is the contradictory context which makes Indo-Caribbean identity (and literature) appear either as suspicious or chimerical, if not subversive; for it has emerged in a freshly settled region that is still imperfectly understood and is merely one generation away from the misrepresentations, distortions and illusions of colonial rule. Caribbean identity itself is under question: the doubt is not whether it exists, but whether it is creole in the sense of still being predominantly Afro-Caribbean or in the sense of incorporating a wider range of ethnic components.

Brathwaite's poetry performed a valuable service in the 1960s, when it corrected the mistaken colonial view of the African role in Caribbean culture as something to be despised, derided or denied. Brathwaite confirmed African connections and roots as an authentic, historical aspect of Caribbean culture and identity. The only debate now is whether enthusiasm over this correction led Brathwaite and others to go too far in proclaiming an Afro-centric view of the Caribbean, one that regards the entire English-speaking region as predominantly African, thus justifying the political marginalization of Indians in Guyana and Trinidad and Tobago.

The point of view in this volume is that multiple Caribbean cultures, each consisting of distinctive ethnic elements, are in a continuous process of indigenization or creolization. African elements are further along the process because they have been in the Caribbean longest, except for the aboriginals and Europeans. In most English-speaking territories, this predominantly Afro-Caribbean model undoubtedly prevails, but not in Guyana and Trinidad, where the large influx of Indians has altered and is continuing to modify historic African predominance.

Like African American literature that is both African as well as American, Indo-Caribbean literature is both ethnically Indian and broadly Caribbean. The moral values, religious rituals and customs in *A House for Mr Biswas*, for instance, are distinctly Indian, and have little in common with Afro or other Caribbean values and rituals, but the novel is unmistakably Caribbean in its social context of cultural displacement and insecurity, and in its aura of political and economic powerlessness, shifting improvisation and restless groping for fresh identity. The ethnicity of Naipaul's novel is confirmed by George Lamming when he writes: "it is only through this novel that many areas of the non-Indian Caribbean, including Trinidad, got some glimpse of the movement and the substance of life within that Indian world."[14] To regard *Biswas* as Indo-Caribbean is no more separatist than regarding Alice Walker's novel *The Color Purple*[15] as African American, since both novels are distinctly attached to their ethnic communities while, in a national sense, remaining fully Caribbean in one case, and fully American in the other.

Indo-Caribbean literature may be defined as writing either by or about Indians in the Caribbean, and the earliest examples are official documents, travel accounts, biographical sketches, ethnographic commentaries and some fictional or semi-fictional narratives by Europeans about indentured Indians in the second half of the nineteenth century. There are, for example, two or three accounts of voyages by "coolie ships" written by English ship captains or other personnel. One example is a journal or diary kept by Edolphus Swinton, captain of the ship *Salsette*, which sailed on 17 March 1858 from Calcutta with 324 Indian indentured immigrants bound for Trinidad. One hundred and twenty Indians died at sea, and Captain Swinton's opening entries capture the desperate conditions that prevailed in this early, shipboard stage of Indo-Caribbean experience:

> March 17th, 1858. Left Calcutta for Trinidad; several coolies sick.
> 18th. An old woman died of cholera; she was rejected on coming on board but 18 men would not come without her.
> 19th. Several coolies sick.

Once the immigrants had landed, the first examples of writing about them again comes from European administrators or missionaries. In Guyana Rev J G Pearson's *The New Overseer's Manual* (1890) gives practical hints for dealing with Indian workers, and Rev J D MacKay's *Under the Southern Cross* (1904) dramatizes the conversion of a Hindu to Christianity. Perhaps the best known of these European accounts is by John Edward Jenkins, an Englishman, who visited Guyana and wrote a travel narrative, *Notes on a Journey through British Guiana* (1871), a polemical work, *The Coolie, His Rights and Wrongs* (1872), and a novel *Lutchmee and Dilloo* (1877). Although Jenkins shows some sympathy for Indians, he and his fellow European writers betray standard Victorian assumptions about race, colour, and religion which make for a rather limiting or incomplete image of Indian customs, conditions, attitudes and conduct.

The first examples of writing by Indians are letters sent by the newly arrived immigrants to their families in India. Professional letter writers existed, but none of their letters survive, nor any of the replies that must have been received from India. In any case, these letters would have been in various Indian languages. The first letters that have survived are those written by the immigrants in English and sent to the local press. Such letters first appeared in Guyana in the 1880s, and Bechu is by far the most accomplished practitioner in this genre. Although his letters appeared mostly in the *Daily Chronicle*, the following example is the opening sentence of a letter which he addressed directly to the Secretary of State for India, Lord George Francis Hamilton MP, on 27 April 1899:

> My Lord,
> It being the highest as well as the most dearly cherished privilege of every British-born subject without regard to class, creed, or colour to approach Her Most gracious Majesty the QUEEN-EMPRESS when it is certain that to appeal to the Authorities on the spot would involve too much of personal reflection on those whose connivance has entailed a shameful reproach to the administration of justice, permit me though only an indentured immigrant, who came to this colony in the ship "Sheila" in 1894, to address YOUR LORDSHIP on a matter which affects the welfare of a large number of my countrymen who like myself have had the misfortune to come to Demerara, the political system of which colony has very appropriately been divined and defined by Mr Trollope under a happy inspiration as "despotism tempered by sugar."[16]

The polished elegance of Bechu's florid, Victorian style, including rhetorical flourishes and educated references to Anthony Trollope's writing, is simply unbelievable coming from the pen of a lowly, indentured Indian immigrant. One can imagine more run-of-the-mill letters, in broken English, about day-to-day events and complaints or grievances. But Bechu was clearly exceptional: his writing is notable as an example of Indian achievement and possibility, and for its revelation of the conditions of indenture from the unusual point of view of an educated indentured immigrant.

Other letters exist from ordinary, destitute, helpless and unlettered Indians. Normally such letters were sent to the Protector of Immigrants who was appointed to oversee Indian interests. One example is a letter from Nathew in Frontier Estate, Jamaica, on 9 December 1934:

> Dear Sir,
> I write you this few lines to let you know that the wife sufferin with rheumatism pain. So Dr EG Gordon say, and I am suffering with Tubercolis and I think to take the children to the girls home, because I can't manage to care them . . .[17]

Such letters and replies from the Protector of Immigrants provide much insight into the day-to-day affairs of indentured Indians, and their often tragic circumstances in a new environment in which they felt displaced and disadvantaged.

Another notable literary achievement during this early period comes from Joseph Ruhomon (1873-1942) who, unlike Bechu, was born and educated in Guyana. Ruhomon was a journalist and lecturer who is best remembered for his lecture "India: The Progress of Her People At Home and Abroad, And How Those in British Guiana May Improve Themselves," delivered in October 1894 and published in installments in the *Daily Chronicle* beginning 7 October 1894. Clem Seecharan confirms that Ruhomon is "the first Indian intellectual in British Guiana,"[18] and his lecture is "the first extended piece ever to be published by an Indo-Guyanese . . . indeed, the first by an Indian in the Caribbean." The lecture exhorts Indo-Guyanese to pull their socks up by pursuing moral, intellectual and educational self development:

> The great majority of our people are weak and ignorant. Stretch forth to them a helping hand. The East Indian race in British Guiana has not yet begun its history as a race. Its past has been chaos and darkness. Our people 'shall' be great and 'must' be great in the future . . . (64)

Ruhomon writes within the same Victorian literary conventions as Bechu, although with rather less staid, periphrastic formality. He admits that Indo-Guyanese are behind Afro-Guyanese in self-development, and should follow them, as well as Africans and

Indians in adopting the model of scientific progress and Christian morality established by their British rulers.

Yet another Indo-Guyanese Ayube Edun is notable as the author of *London's Heart Probe and Britain's Destiny*[19], the first book-length work by an Indo-Caribbean author, and the first work by such an author to be published in England. Edun's book is undated, but its description of the author's visit to England in 1928 suggests that it was published soon afterwards. *London's Heart Probe* provides observations on conditions in England during the Great Depression and serves as a platform for the author's opinions and speculations on just about everything. Edun claims in his introduction that his book has "probed with the lancet of Rational-Practical-Idealism into the heart of British Civilization." Even if it does not do that, *London's Heart Probe* illustrates typical preoccupations of an enterprising, self-educated and civic-minded Indo-Guyanese who was also a trade-union leader, about thirty-five years after Ruhomon's ground-breaking pamphlet.

As one might expect in this early period, the writing of Bechu, Ruhomon and Edun is strongly influenced by nineteenth-century, British social democratic ideals. Such was the dominance of empire and the sway of British political, intellectual and moral habits, that although these three men champion the welfare and progress of indentured Indians, they do so firmly within an imperial framework: Bechu and Ruhomon remain stoutly Christian; Bechu refers to himself with evident pride as a "British-born subject"; Edun proclaims himself a "Britisher"; and all three pay more than lip service to the manners, conventions, codes and statutes of British civilization. For all that, Bechu, Ruhomon and Edun must be saluted as pioneers in giving literary expression for the first time to Indo-Caribbean subjects from an Indo-Caribbean point of view.

Up to the 1930s, Indo-Caribbean literary expression consisted chiefly of nonfiction prose. Imaginative literature—fiction, poetry, or drama—scarcely existed except for the odd poem or story that might appear in magazines. Fictional treatment of Indo-Caribbean life, which was first seen from Europeans, now started to appear from Afro-Caribbean writers—A R F Webber (Tobago and Guyana), H G DeLisser (Jamaica), and more sketchily from the Trinidadians—C L R James, Ralph DeBoissiere and Alfred Mendes. In general, these references are similar to the exotic fictional versions of Indian indenture given by European writers before 1900. This is true, for instance, of Webber's novel *Those That Be in Bondage: A Tale of Indian Indentures and Sunlit Western Waters* (1917)[20] which is notable on two counts: for being the first novel by a native of Trinidad and Tobago, and for being the first novel about indentured Indians by a native West Indian. But despite its subtitle, and the appearance of two or three Indian characters, very little of Webber's novel actually deals with Indians, and what there is consists of openly racial stereotypes of Indians as passionate, hot blooded, unrestrained, primitive, and lying by nature. Webber writes as follows: "Indeed it may be said that 'to lie' is the East Indian immigrant's vital breath" (27), and again the phrase "the native chicanery of his race" (27) appears in reference to the Indian driver Abdool Karim; and when Karim gets into a fight with Bibi Singh, a woman, the author comments "for these primitive natures exhibit none of the chivalry which is usually found in more developed minds" (26).

Similar descriptions are found in DeLisser's novel *The Cup and the Lip*[21], which was first published in installments in 1931 and 1932. DeLisser's Ramsingh is a crude Indian plantation labourer who is exceedingly thrifty, greedy and jealous, while his wife Marie is just as fiercely passionate, treacherous, spiteful, and cunning; and when Ramsingh discovers his wife's infidelity, he savagely attacks her with a machete, chopping off her head and hacking at her body. Ramsingh is in a state of delirium from ganja, and when he is finished with Marie, he attacks a bull, which gores him to death. No wonder that DeLisser often resorts to animal imagery to describe the savage brutality of such people. One of the European characters sees in Marie "a kinship with the tigress from her ancestral Indian's jungles" (123) and Marie's body is also described as "that of a snake rearing itself to strike" (147).

But perhaps the culmination of creole fictional representations of Indians is in the novel *Corentyne Thunder* (1941)[22] by Mittelholzer. The hero Ramgolall is a miserly Indian cow-minder who prefers to starve himself into sickness rather than pay for medical attention. Ramgolall and his daughters live in simple-minded ignorance in rustic surroundings that allow only for basic, coarse manners; they can be described as primitive, which is the general view of Indo-Guyanese that prevailed during the 1930s, as Mittelholzer himself admits in his autobiography; but in fictional terms this view is too generalized, one dimensional, not rounded enough, and Ramgolall, like other characters in fiction by European or creole, middle-class writers, is too incomplete or lacking in convincing, individual traits—a mere caricature.

Up to the 1940s, in Guyana at any rate, there was no significant imaginative writing by Indians. Occasional stories can be found in annual magazines like the "Christmas Annual" and "Christmas Tide," but they tend to be imitative and unrealistic, while the poetry in *The Anthology of Local Indian Verse* (1934) relies heavily on the diction, subjects and rhythms of nineteenth-century English poets like Shelley and Swinburne, rather than on the poets' own local, Guyanese experience and speech. The first significant example of imaginative writing by an Indian about Indo-Caribbean experience comes from Seepersad Naipaul (1907-1953) of Trinidad in the form of a collection of stories, *Gurudeva and Other Indian Tales*, that was published in Trinidad in 1943. Seepersad, father of Vidia (V S) and Shiva Naipaul (1945-1985), worked as a journalist on the *Trinidad Guardian*, and his stories were republished posthumously in England in 1976, with a foreword by V S that catches exactly the unexpected wonder of Seepersad's achievement as a writer: "I do not know how, in such a setting, in those circumstances of dependence and uncertainty, and with no example, the wish to be a writer came to my father."[23] Wherever the wish came from, Seepersad writes mainly about

Indo-Trinidadians Hindus and displays an insider's familiarity with the sacred books, rituals, customs, rivalries and personal traits of the Hindu community in Trinidad. Gurudeva, in the title story, exhibits typical traits of emotional volatility and fecklessness: he hears tales of valour and has an urge to rebel against authority and become a bad-john. Predictably he ends up in jail. If Seepersad's stories do nothing else, they provide the first authentic record that we have of Indo-Caribbean life in imaginative literature.

The wonder of Seepersad Naipaul's literary achievement seems all the greater when we realize that he also initiated a literary dynasty, in the form not only of his two sons (V S and Shiva) who both became distinguished authors, but also through his grandson Neil Bissoondath (son of Seepersad's daughter Sati). In view of the social and educational disadvantages of Indo-Caribbeans up to the 1930s and 1940s—the 1931 census reported that forty-three percent of the Indian population in Trinidad was illiterate in English—the literary achievement of the Naipauls, and especially of Vidia Naipaul's reputation as one of the finest living writers of English, seems quite spectacular.

The achievement of the Naipauls reflects a concerted effort by Indo-Trinidadians and Indo-Guyanese to overcome their social and educational disadvantages between the 1890s and 1940s. In Guyana an East Indian Institute was founded in 1892, followed later by the British Guiana East Indian Association, which briefly produced a journal *Indian Opinion*. In 1937, an Indian group formed the British Guiana Dramatic Society. In Trinidad, an East Indian National Association was formed in 1898, and the more radical East Indian National Congress in 1909. Another boost to Indian education was given by Presbyterian missionaries from Canada who built schools and colleges attended mainly by Indians in Trinidad and Guyana. A Presbyterian Theological College was established in Trinidad in 1892, followed by a Teacher's Training College in 1894, and Naparima College, a secondary school, in 1900. Similarly, the Canadians established the Berbice High School in Guyana. By the end of the first century of indenture, that is to say by 1938 in Guyana and 1945 in Trinidad, there was definite growth in Indian social and cultural self-awareness and education, as we can see from the publication of *A Centenary History of Indians in Guyana* by Peter Ruhomon in 1938 and *The Indian Centenary Review* published by a committee in Trinidad in 1945. In Trinidad, an Indian newspaper called T*he Kohi-Noor* existed since the early 1900s, and during the period between 1920 and 1940 more than eight weekly publications, for example *The East Indian Patriot* and *The East Indian Weekly*, were in circulation at one time or another.

As the end of the colonial period approached, however, great changes lay in store for the entire English-speaking Caribbean region. The decade of the 1950s was pivotal, politically, because it provided the final stage of anticolonial agitation before independence, and culturally, because it was the decade when the English-speaking Caribbean first gained international recognition as a source of imaginative literature. The writers who had appeared before 1950, for example H G DeLisser, C L R James, Claude McKay, Alfred Mendes, and Ralph DeBoissiere were scarcely known within the region itself, much less abroad. Then, in the 1950s, several writers appeared in London, England, and were recognized as introducing a vibrant addition to new literatures in English, what is today known as postcolonial literature. Some of these pioneer West Indian writers were Edgar Mittelholzer, George Lamming, Roger Mais, John Hearne, Jan Carew, V S Reid and Andrew Salkey, but the group also included Samuel Selvon (1923-1994) and V S Naipaul.

If two names out of so many suggest that the Indo-Caribbean role in the literary awakening of the region was small or insignificant, that is misleading, for the literary contribution of Selvon and Naipaul is out of all proportion to their numbers. Naipaul's contribution needs no elaboration since he is internationally regarded as one of the major novelists of the last century. What might be noted is the extraordinary transformation from Seepersad Naipaul's first major example of Indo-Caribbean imaginative literature in 1943 to his son's *Biswas* less than twenty years later. It is also notable that V S Naipaul came from an orthodox Hindu family and that his essential perceptions of displacement and homelessness originate from a context of Indian cultural marginalization within Trinidadian creole society.

Selvon is altogether different in that he was more creolized than Naipaul, and his early fiction at least was motivated by a sentiment for West Indian nationalism which was strongest in the 1950s and 60s when a worldwide movement of decolonization was creating new nations out of Britain's subject territories in the Caribbean. Selvon's first novel *A Brighter Sun* (1952) is a landmark event in this respect since it considers, for the first time in Caribbean fiction, the possibility of Indo- and Afro-Trinidadians cooperating in the building of a new nation. In other ways too, Selvon proves to be a seminal, pioneering figure in Caribbean literary history: he invented a narrative medium based on creole rather than standard English, and he was the first to seriously consider West Indian immigrants as a subject of fiction in his ground-breaking novel *The Lonely Londoners* (1956).

In the 1960s, as the development of West Indian literature continued apace, Indo-Caribbean contribution to it was maintained largely by the enormous productivity of Naipaul and Selvon as well as by the arrival of Ismith Khan (Trinidad) who produced two novels—*The Jumbie Bird* (1961) and *The Obeah Man* (1964) and Peter Kempadoo (Guyana) who is also the author of two novels—*Guiana Boy* (1960), and *Old Thom's Harvest* (1965). By 1966 Trinidad had produced three major novelists and Guyana none. Kempadoo's fiction is distinguished mainly by its use of Guyanese creole speech, and lacks the degree of political, philosophical or technical sophistication found in the writing of Naipaul, Selvon and Khan. There are other Guyanese writers like Sheik Sadeek and Rajkumarie Singh, examples of whose work may be found in *Jahaji Bhai*, but they are no more distinguished than Kempadoo. Even today, with the emergence of a good many Indo-Guyanese writers in the diaspora, Guyana has not produced literary figures of the stature of Selvon, the Naipauls (Seepersad, V S, Shiva, Neil Bissoondath), Ismith Khan and H S

Ladoo. One explanation may be the greater effectiveness of the educational work of Canadian Presbyterian missionaries, which started earlier and was more concentrated in Trinidad than Guyana. Also the plantation structure was such in Guyana that it tended to seal off the Indians more completely from contact with the rest of the population than in Trinidad. This may have further restricted Indo-Guyanese from ready access to education, the English language and creolization.

It is also curious that one hundred and sixty years after indenture, although the Indo-Caribbean contribution to West Indian fiction is second to none, no major Indo-Caribbean poet has yet emerged. While it is elusive to derive answers to literary creativity from sociological evidence, it is remarkable that an Afro-Caribbean poet—Derek —won the Nobel prize for literature in 1992, and another—Edward Brathwaite—is one of the more renowned poets writing in English today. Perhaps Afro-Caribbean poets have had longer and more direct access to a literary, creole medium that has been strongly influenced by an African oral tradition with resources of proverbs, ribaldry, banter, repetition and other technical devices. This again raises the controversial question of the centrality of Africa in Caribbean culture. The strongest evidence of this centrality is the creole language that is spoken by everyone in the English-speaking Caribbean. But as stories by Elahi Baksh, Rooplall Monar, Narmala Shewcharan and Sasenarine Persaud will show in the present anthology, an Indo-Guyanese creole has emerged with striking influences of Hindi in vocabulary, idiom and rhythm. This confirms the dynamic and fluid nature of the linguistic and literary situation in a region of almost legendary racial and cultural mixing.

As mentioned before, the centrality of Africa to Caribbean culture cannot be disputed up to the time of African Emancipation, because Africans then were a clear majority of the population in every territory. "Creole" then did mean Afro-Caribbean. But after 1838, the influence of Indians on the ethnic equation in Guyana and Trinidad created a remarkable change. No doubt the implications of this change will take time to sink in, especially in the minds of Jamaicans, Barbadians and those in smaller islands where the population is still more than ninety percent African. But as George Lamming observes about Indo-Trinidadian farmers who produce fruit and vegetables for all Trinidadians: "If labour is the foundation of all culture, then the Indian in Trinidad was part of the first floor on which the house was built" (47). Since Indo-Guyanese produce even more fruit and vegetables than Indo-Trinidadians, Lamming's observation certainly applies to Guyana as well. Thus, if Lamming is correct, the contribution of Indians to Caribbean culture, at least in Guyana and Trinidad and Tobago, is equal to that of any other ethnic group.

So far as literature is concerned, the Naipauls, Selvon, Khan and the younger writers who appear in this volume prove beyond any doubt that Indo-Caribbean literature—writing about Indo-Caribbeans by themselves—is among the best in the region. What is more encouraging is that writing by Afro-Caribbeans about Indians which, up to 1950, appeared limited to racial stereotypes and stock generalizations, is now far more accurate and reliable, for example, the novel *Crick Crack Monkey* (1970) by Merle Hodge (Afro-Trinidadian), and the magisterial *The Shadow Bride* (1988) which is almost as authoritative a study of Indo-Caribbean life as *Biswas*, by Roy Heath (Afro-Guyanese). These two examples suggest that for all the cultural displacement and ethnic division of colonial and postcolonial history, the positively multicultural nature of Caribbean society is evident in Guyana and Trinidad, and it is simply preposterous to regard the idea of Indo-Caribbean literature either as superfluous or subversive.

This anthology *Jahaji*, is concerned only with Indo-Caribbean fiction. It consists of sixteen stories, all of which, with the exception of the first, "Pooran, Pooran" by Ismith Khan, are by authors who did not appear in *Jahaji Bhai*. Since most of the authors in *Jahaji* became well known after 1988, when its predecessor *Jahaji Bhai* appeared, the pieces in this volume should give some idea of the development of Indo-Caribbean literature, both in scope and quality, during the past twelve years. The presence of Ismith Khan establishes continuity in Indo-Caribbean imaginative writing, which can be said to have begun with Seepersad Naipaul in 1943, but really took off with Selvon in 1952.

Like its predecessor, *Jahaji* cannot claim to include all Indo-Caribbean writers of fiction who are currently active, or even all of the very best. V S Naipaul is not included , nor is David Dabydeen and other second-generation writers like Mahadai Das or Krishna Samaroo. Yet the volume does claim to be representative to the extent that it includes some of the most active younger writers, including those like Christine Singh and Marina Budhos who have grown up in Indo-Caribbean diaspora communities and have little first-hand experience of the Caribbean. There are three types of authors represented: those like Sharlow Mohamed and Rajnie Ramlakhan who live in the Caribbean and write about situations around them; those like Cyril Dabydeen and Sasenarine Persaud who have emigrated and write both about memories of home and their new environment; and the youngest group who, in the case of Marina Budhos and Christine Singh, are either American or Canadian in culture or nationality but have at least one Indo-Caribbean parent. The strongest difference between *Jahaji Bhai* and *Jahaji* is exactly this focus on immigration and the fate of the Indo-Caribbean diaspora.

"Pooran, Pooran" dramatizes the historical context of Indo-Caribbean literature in much the same way that Selvon's story "Turning Christian" did in *Jahaji Bhai*: it captures the harsh, rural living conditions of the earliest indentured immigrants, as well as their first experience of change as reflected in the educational opportunity which Pooran has of attending secondary school in the city; it also reproduces a dichotomy between old and new, country and city, the life of faith or religion and the power of scientific rationalism. At the same time the story is a masterpiece of evocation; no one who has lived in the mid-twentieth century Caribbean will fail to recognize the scents, sights and sounds, as well as Pooran's feelings on his journey by train to school each morning. "The Propagandist" is equally evocative, although set in Guyana rather than Trinidad; but its main appeal is an elegiac note inspired by the passing of colonial innocence. Not that the author regrets the demise of colonialism: he rather expresses skepticism about the political maturity or independence that is to follow. That is why our hero—Ramkissoon—is both sinner and saint, victimizer and victim, and seems to possess an ambiguity similar to the "heroic blackness" that Herman Melville elicits from the contemplation of another postcolonial milieu—the mid-nineteenth century United States.

Although a story about Chinese Caribbeans may seem irrelevant within an Indo-Caribbean anthology, "The Marriage Match" reflects features of racial and cultural mixing, dynamics of coordination between race and class, and the emergence of intergenerational conflict within a creole, social environment that is identical to the social background in most stories here. Chinese, after all, were indentured immigrants in the Caribbean, like Indians, and many of the food, games, films and events in "The Marriage Match" arouse compelling associations with Guyana that would be readily recognized by most Indo-Guyanese. But the main appeal of the story is a sense of pathos, Chekhovian in flavour, that arises from a dramatic interplay between obviously limited, local, colonial conditions and the psychological foibles or personal conflicts of the characters.

The next two stories "Swami Pankaj" and "Bruit" are set in Trinidad and fuse typically Naipaulian techniques such as caricature, farce, irony and repartee, with comic resources of Trinidad creole speech to produce a keen satirical edge. Swami Pankaj is an unacknowledged agricultural genius with longings for his ancestral home (India) and religion (Hinduism), but although he is presented as somewhat deluded and therefore a figure of fun, his portrait conveys the message that his deluded longings and restless wanderings are in reality exaggerated versions of genuine feelings shared by many Indo-Caribbean people. While the focus of "Swami Pankaj" is mainly on the personality of the hero, "Bruit" relies less on character study than on boisterous, clownish and farcical high jinks mixed with religious satire. The religious charlatanism and social background in

"Swami Pankaj" and "Bruit" are strongly reminiscent of Naipaul's first novel *The Mystic Masseur*.

"The Insiders" and "Common Entrance," both by Trinidadian women, dramatize Caribbean social manners mainly through dialogue. Through the simple expedient of a job interview, "The Insiders" offers astute insights into complicated relationships between race, class, colour, commerce and education in Trinidad in the middle of the last century. These insights are produced by crisp and entertaining dialogue, and by extensive interior monologues that serve as commentary on the dialogue. "Common Entrance" is another story about childhood and the impact of education in colonial Trinidad; its real achievement, apart from comedy, is its revelation of stock Indo-Caribbean attitudes towards gender.

"Janjhat: Bhola Ram and the 'Going Away' Plan" is unusual as the only story here to employ an oral, creole narrative medium throughout. The medium is a rural Indo-Guyanese variety of creole that adds immensely to the authenticity of the author's depiction of Indo-Guyanese life in the 1980s, during the Burnham dictatorship, when food shortages and currency restrictions were the order of the day, and political injustice was manifested in numerous ways that drove all Guyanese, Indians as well as Africans, to seek refuge in emigration. But the story's description of a culture of fear and flight is accompanied by a comic narrative that eschews any suggestion of pity and grief. On the contrary, instead of pity what we get is a narrative of vigour and vitality, and characters embroiled in a tragi-comic free-for-all of competitive deviousness, connivance, manipulation, and zany skullduggery, all in the interest of survival.

"Blame" is a short but powerful tale with a dark, haunting atmosphere that seems fitting from a Guyanese writer who, whether he knows it or not, benefits from a literary inheritance of brooding, historical melodramas by Edgar Mittelholzer, and impenetrable, metaphysical parables by Wilson Harris. Sexual suggestiveness, Freudian hints, the unreliable workings of memory, and an isolated colonial setting are all joined smoothly into a meditation on blame; and if there is blame there should also be wrongdoing or violation, sin or crime, and, no doubt, guilt. But guilt for what, except for life itself?

"Mai, Mai, Mai" is like "Janjhat" both in its oral narrative, and its use of an Indo-Guyanese creole medium: but whereas "Janjhat" offers a "pure" translation of creole speech, "Mai, Mai, Mai" employs a more anglicized version that nevertheless succeeds in capturing much of the raw, earthy quality of its original. The plot of "Mai, Mai, Mai" is enmeshed in the intricate network of an extended Hindu family over three generations and displays a maze of cross-cutting interrelationships and a convoluted mixture of family unions, divisions, rivalries, alliances and suspicions that are reminiscent of the Tulsi family in *Biswas*. To include so much in a short story is a masterly feat of compression.

Like other stories here Cyril Dabydeen's "Going to Guyana" is also about immigration. As one character says in "Janjhat," it is not so much that she wants to emigrate from Guyana, she simply wants the visa to be able to "go and come." The central event in "Going to Guyana" is the return to Guyana of a planeload of Guyanese immigrants from North America. But while Dabydeen reports typical attitudes inspired by the frenzy of immigrant to-ing and fro-ing—cynicism, anger, impatience, disillusionment—he elicits Naipaulian themes of physical placelessness, political insecurity, psychic instability and postcolonial chaos; and while his story relates consecutive events in a conventional manner, it also contains postmodernist narrative elements of discontinuity, dislocation and a mythic quality that seems to link Arabella firstly to Africa, and secondly, just as mysteriously, to Magdalenburg, scene of the first African slave rebellion in Guyana in 1763. "Buckee" is yet another immigration story narrated largely through dialogue and interior monologue, like "The Insiders." Its Guyanese speech and characters also place it in the same category as other Guyanese stories here, but its psychological study of motives such as jealousy and revenge tends to set it apart.

The final four stories deal with the problem of identity in the children of Indo-Caribbean immigrants who live in northern countries. "Far from Family" considers the problem in an unnamed northern country, "American Dad" in an American context, "The Job Interview" in a British milieu, and "Sushila's Bhakti" in Canada. In "Far from Family" a Trinidadian boy Feroze, who lives with his uncle's family in a northern country, is consumed by curiosity about his dead father and his family's past, but his uncle's evasive answers merely heighten his perturbed sense of confusion, loss, expectation and wonder. "American Dad" and "The Job Interview," both ironically named, relate the mental and psychological struggles of their main characters in coping with their racial and cultural inheritance, Indo-Caribbean on one hand, and American or British on the other.

With a distinctly feminine touch, the author of "American Dad" sensitively communicates the young, female narrator's genuine perplexity and vacillation over her role, in New York, as daughter and student, immigrant and citizen. The narrator's childish pranks and sense of mischief are seen to blend naturally with her perplexity, and the result is a touching portrait both of the narrator and her father. In the process, their story conveys revealing commentary on the cultural confusion and psychological complications that are the inescapable baggage of the economic rewards of immigration. "The Job Interview" investigates darker recesses of similarly confusing or unsettling feelings produced in second-generation immigrants by skin colour, an unmistakable badge that marks them out as foreign in the only place they know as home. If a sense of Indo-Caribbean exile prompted in V S Naipaul's writing perhaps the most affecting jeremiad about homelessness, placelessness, alienation and exile in the latter half of the twentieth century, it is no wonder that a sense of Indo-Caribbean diasporic exile in northern lands should inspire similar themes in Naipaul's spiritual heirs.

Because of the earnest doubts and uncertainties that her Indo-Caribbean heritage inspires, the heroine of "Sushila's Bhakti," the final story in *Jahaji*, truly deserves the last word in the volume.

Sushila sees herself as "floating rootlessly in the Canadian landscape," which leads her to question her family history; but all she discovers are further questions: "What is my point of origin? How far back need I go to feel properly rooted?" These are exactly the questions that are answered in V S Naipaul's fiction, and his answer is to face up to rootlessness, placelessness and homelessness, not merely as a specifically Indo-Caribbean curse, but as the curse of Cain that brands all humankind. But the answers of one generation may not serve the exact needs of a later one, which is what justifies the contributors to this volume in either reformulating old questions in their own way or asking new questions of their own. In this sense, whether its contributors ask the right questions or not, or whether they find answers or not, *Jahaji* provides evidence of continuity in Indo-Caribbean experience and of the effort of Indo-Caribbean writers in resisting the forces of fragmentation that have loomed so large in this experience.

NOTES

1. The elections that the PNC "won" between 1968 and 1992 were rigged. These "victories" were only possible if large numbers of Indians supported the PNC. It is known that Indians did not support the PNC in 1957, 1961, and 1964, when elections were held under British supervision, nor again in 1992 when the elections had international supervision, so the alleged Indian support only occurred when elections were run by the PNC.
2. Edward Brathwaite, *The Arrivants* (NY: Oxford, 1973).
3. Edward Brathwaite, "The African Presence in Caribbean Literature," *Daedalus* 103, 2 (1974): 73-109.
4. R Nettleford, "Afterword," in V L Hyatt and R Nettleford, eds., *Race, Discourse, and the Origin of the Americas: A New World View* (Washington and London: Smithsonian Institution Press, 1995), 280.
5. Neil Bissoondath, *Digging up the Mountains* (Toronto: Macmillan, 1985), 68-77.
6. V S Naipaul, *A House for Mr Biswas* (London: Andre Deutsch, 1961).
7. Eric Williams, *Inward Hunger: The Education of a Prime Minister* (London: Andre Deutsch), 21.
8. Albert Gomes, *A Maze of Colour* (London, n.d.),.12.
9. Edgar Mittelholzer, *A Swarthy Boy* (London: Putnam, 1963),.155.
10. Lucretia Stewart, *The Weather Prophet* (London: Vintage, 1996),.16.

11. See Arnold Thomas, "Portuguese and Indian Immigration to St. Vincent (1885-1890)" in Frank Birbalsingh ed., *Journal of Caribbean Studies* 14, 1 and 2, (1999, 2000): 46.

12. Walter Rodney, *A History of the Guyanese Working People 1881-1905* (Baltimore and London: Johns Hopkins University Press, 1981).

13. S S Ramphal, *A Heritage of Oneness* (London: Commonwealth Secretariat, 1988), 23.

14. George Lamming, "The Indian Presence as a Caribbean Reality", in Frank Birbalsingh, ed., *Indenture and Exile* (Toronto: TSAR, 1989),.47.

15. Alice Walker, *The Color Purple* (London: The Women's Press, 1983).

16. See Clem Seecharan, *Bechu: Bound Coolie Radical in British Guiana, 1894-1901* (Jamaica: University of West Indies Press, 1999), 152-153.

17. See V Shepherd, "Poverty Among Indian Settlers in Jamaica" in Frank Birbalsingh ed., *Journal of Caribbean Studies* 14, 1 and 2 (1999, 2000):115.

18. See Clem Seecharan, Joseph Ruhomon's "India: The Progress of Her People at Home and Abroad, and How Those in British Guiana May Improve Themselves," unpublished manuscript, 18.

19. Ayube Edun, *London's Heart Probe and Britain's Destiny* (London, n.d.).

20. A R F Webber, *Those That Be in Bondage: A Tale of Indian Indentures and Sunlit Western Waters* (Wellesley: Calaloux Publications, 1988).

21. H G DeLisser, *The Cup and The Lip* (London: E Benn, 1956).

22. Edgar Mittelholzer, *Corentyne Thunder, Eyre and Spottiswode* (London, 1941).

23. Seepersad Naipaul, *The Adventures of Gurudeva and Other Stories* (London: Andre Deutsch, 1976).

Acknowledgements

Thanks are due as follows: to contemporary historians for illuminating the Indo-Caribbean past, in particular, Basdeo Mangru and Clem Seecharan; to the editors and writers of *In Celebration: 150 Years of the Indian Contribution to Trinidad and Tobago* (1995), and *They Came in Ships: An Anthology of Indo-Guyanese Prose and Poetry* (1998) for recording growth in Indo-Caribbean culture; to colleagues in the Ontario Society for Services to Indo-Caribbean-Canadians (OSSICC) for sustaining Indo-Caribbean studies in Canada since 1986; and to Nurjehan Aziz of TSAR for counsel and support in publishing. Special thanks for editorial, word processing, and proofreading assistance to Adriana Hetram who, to my surprise and delight, turns out to be the granddaughter of the late Doodnauth Hetram, who taught me Latin at Queen's College in British Guiana from 1951 to 1956. In the end, however, thanks alone are insufficient for the kindness and generosity of authors without whose contributions *Jahaji* would not even exist.

Pooran, Pooran

ISMITH KHAN

The wheels of the donkey cart cut deep into the asphalt, softened by the afternoon heat, on the main road, as Ramdath turned off into a dirt path, both sides of which were lined with spreading Saman trees, whitewashed from their bases to about the height of a man. The lawns were deep green, without a single bald spot, and were as well kept as the police station surroundings. He tied the donkey to one of the whitewashed stakes which lined the sides of the halt, and looked down the tracks. "Train not come in yet," he said out loud, taking a large red handkerchief out of his old felt hat. First he wiped his forehead, then ran the handkerchief through his hair, around the base of his neck, then through his slightly bearded face. At a quick glance he looked like an old man, but underneath his growth of hair and week-old beard, there was the tautness of young skin and his eyes flashed quickly. His body, although frail and somewhat bent, seemed worn, not with the days and nights, but with long hours, from his childhood on, of stooping and crawling through the sugarcanes from under the pelting strings of the sun, clearing away the cane trash, heaping up the earth around the roots when rain washed away the soil. His long fingers, which looked as if they should have been flying across the strings of a sitar, had thickened, grown callused and hardened by use and wear and time, strengthened by tearing and mending. They were not as beautiful, nor as slender as they had once been, but twice as strong and heavy. Ramdath was proud of his hands—yet he felt that his son should not spend his life in the sugarcane fields.

He walked around two lengths of rail, pierced deep into the earth, across which was bolted an eight-foot board, painted black with the words TUNAPUNA HALT written in square, exactly spaced letters. The halt was a small house that stood on an elevated square of ground, edged off by a rim of foot-wide cement, about two feet above the road bed.

He waited for the country silence to suddenly wake up from its afternoon slumber, to spring into a strange busying of activity and commotion when the train pulled in with sounds of opening and slamming of the heavy wooden carriage doors, voices talking, laughing, shouting, the loading and unloading of crates, large round baskets of vegetables, ground provisions, fruit, and live chickens tied six together by the feet, squawking and croaking.

It ran through his mind how opposed he had been to the idea of Pooran's going to the city to learn strange things, things which he did not know enough about to judge; and how it was Leela, his wife, who had really been responsible for the decision. "Let boy go down to Sadhu . . . learn Bhagvad-Gita, Ramayana . . . learn 'bout life," Ramdath had said. Although he had not changed his mind, he couldn't quite remember how he became reconciled to Leela's urgings to send their son to the city college.

Just then the small train came rattling in, its levers slip-slopping in and out of short, thick tubes, swishing up and down, turning its wheels past the platform. Someone blew a shrill whistle, then some city workers came off, jackets hung over their arms, their neckties loosened; at the far end, vendors from the city market were unloading their leftover goods. Ramdath saw a boy about Pooran's height and build get out of the third-class carriage whom he did not recognize at first. The boy was dressed in black serge shorts, knee-high grey socks, white shirt, and a college necktie. "Dat is Pooran, or no?" he said to himself. As the boy approached, he suddenly remembered the outfitting they had got him a week ago in the city. "Ay, Pooran . . . Pooran, dis side." Pooran had no difficulty recognizing his father, but Ramdath was overwhelmed with the transformation now that he saw his son in the college uniform. "King George College," he said, under his breath, his veins standing out on his temples, a thin smile across his face.

"Babooji," Pooran said to his father, "de teacher say we have to forget everyt'ing we learn at home, an' learn only what he say."

"Teacher is a smart man, boy. Babooji teach you how to plant cane, Leela teach you how to dress, comb hair; teacher have 'um different sometin' for you to learn . . . You listen good to teacher."

Of course his father was right, the boy thought. How often had he heard him say, "If you want mango, you can't plant orange." Pooran hopped onto the rear of the donkey cart while Ramdath sat at the edge of the front and tugged at the reins. The cart wheels crunched through the path to the main road; it was strewn with white pebbles from the nearby river bed, before the rainy season came, to give the muddy road more body. After a short distance, they turned off the Main Road onto a dirt path. This was overgrown on both sides with all kinds of weeds, including the occasional mango sprout which had caught root, slender and tall, standing above all the other weeds of the wayside. The donkey leaned forward as it pulled upward on the incline leading to the carat hut in which they lived. When the cart stopped, Pooran flipped himself off the rear and started to unload the sugarcane tops which the donkey would be fed that night, while Ramdath was unhitching the animal.

"Don't bother to do that . . . now you going to college . . . Go inside, Leela mus' be anxious to hear 'bout college."

Squatting on the smooth greyish earthen floor around the kerosene lamp, the three figures cast shimmering shadows against the sides of the hut as they ate supper that night. The flavour of curried fish oozed out of the silk smooth floor they sat on, its pungent odours seeped out of the trash of which the roof was made. The evening was filled with the flavours of the fish as it was first fried, then the frying of onions in the magic spices, and the roti which Leela fixed in an open charcoal fireplace. Ramdath broke off a piece of the bread, putting a small bit in the curry, and swept it through the thin sauce until it was soaked, then placed it in his mouth. The three ate the first mouthfuls without looking at each other through the pale, flat tongue of orange flame which reflected beads of perspiration on Ramdath's forehead as he added more chillies to the curry than Leela had already fixed it with.

"What you learn in school today?" Ramdath asked, ready to discuss whatever Pooran might mention.

"Science," he replied.

"Yuh hear dat, Leela? . . . Yuh hearin' what de boy learnin' so quick? . . . Science, dat is good t'ing. Sadhu say to learn all kind t'ing. Wot dis science teach you today?"

If he could only put into words the whole state of confusion and bewilderment he was overcome with . . . Mr Hopkins, the laboratory, hundreds of bottles –

"Now I want you to look closely at this, because it is what we all looked like at some time or another," Mr Hopkins had said as a glass slide with a speck of jelly was circulated among the boys. "Over here you see everything that goes into the making of that substance." He waved his hand to the shelves on the wall which were lined with bottles. "What you see on the slide is a cell, it is the essence of life. Your shoes, your clothing . . . the food you eat . . . and even you, my dear fellows, are made up of cells." During this speech, he had not so much as looked at the class. His eyes focused at a point in mid air, away from the class. "There are thirty-two of you in this room, and you invariably come here with different explanations of who you are, what you are, and what makes you the way you are . . . Now it's my job to see to it that you know the correct answers to some of these questions. There is no substance whose composition is not contained in these elements." He waved his heavy hand across the bottle-filled shelves. "Yes, I repeat. Even you, my dear fellows, are no exception to this."

For the first time he looked squarely at the class, his bushy eyebrows lifted, carrying his eyes from row to row of the boys who sat hypnotized and motionless. "Good," he answered the silence which fell upon the room, a tight grin across his face, as though he had won a point over some opponent at whom he now scoffed. "Good," he repeated with an expression of delight and ridicule. "Now that we understand each other, shall we proceed?" But his question was not intended for reply.

Pooran felt that they had not understood each other at all. "He can't make trees and flowers out of those bottles, and cane, and people . . . " He felt that all of life was a lie—that Ramdath, Leela and the Sadhu, the holy man, had filled his head with stories which he would now have to cast off, and he meant to ask them when he got home what Mr Hopkins meant; but looking about him in the hut, he knew that he couldn't, that they wouldn't understand, because he had not himself understood, and had only a feeling of loss and despair. He remembered Leela telling him a long time ago how the big gods and the little gods had built the world and all that there was in it, and given it to men to take care of, to make beautiful, and do good things. It was they who made the rain, and the sun and the moon, they who made the sugar cane grow, who made people, and took them to another world when they became old and tired of their bodies. Like the holy man, who would perhaps become a drifting pink cloud in the evening when he died, or maybe he would be a fish in the river where he broke bread and threw it on its surface each evening. The holy man had found his name, Pooran. In his Great Book he had identified him by the exact time and hour of the moon and stars in the heavens. His was a unique destiny, one which had been rolling through the eons of time and would continue until he had fulfilled his task in the world. Then he would be one with the gods who made it all in the beginning.

Ramdath got up suddenly and went to his room for his pipe. Then Pooran went to his room. Leela went to the kitchen and started scouring the bronze platters with a cake of soap and ashes from the fireplace until they were bright as a mirror, and when everything was put away for the evening, Leela and Ramdath sat with the kerosene lamp between them talking about Pooran, the things he would need, as time went by—new clothes, new shoes, books each term–

"What Sadhu say dis morning when you see he?" Leela asked.

"Sadhu say good for de boy to learn everything, but he can't learn Bhagvad Gita in college, can't learn 'bout life. Must learn Gita, grow big man who understand plenty—more than college teacher he-self," Ramdath said.

"You tell Sadhu, Pooran learn Gita later. Next time you go dat side, you tell'um, Ramdath," Leela said, as she ran her wiry fingers through her hair, stopping from time to time, dipping them into coconut oil in a clay bowl, rubbing it into her scalp.

Ramdath cupped both his hands, locking them together with a black stained pipe inserted between two fingers. He placed a piece of cloth around the pipe and spread his moistened lips against the top of his hands, sucking in the bite of black tobacco smoke through his hands into his lungs. His cheeks sank on either side of his face, giving him the appearance of a man ten years older than he was. Then he blew out the lamp, and they went into their room.

The wind rustled outside, carrying with it faint smells of coriander; a full moon played hide and seek between the clouds; the cricket calls quickened. All blended into Ramdath's consciousness until they were one, as he lay in bed, wondering if the world outside had changed as much as it seemed to have done. A picture of his son's sudden appearance at the halt earlier in the day floated before him, and he stretched his limbs as far as they would reach, taking in a deep breath of satisfaction and pride. He reasoned that this happiness must be something within him. The sadhu had said words to this effect, but for the first time he really understood what the holy man had meant when he said that happiness is "inside you." Yet, he wondered whether he was doing the right thing by sending Pooran to college. Wasn't he deliberately trying to reach out for something for Pooran? Something beyond the calling of his birth? Was this the kind of doing that made for the "happiness inside you" that the sadhu would approve of? The more he thought, the more confused he became.

The next morning, and many following, came and went with Pooran setting out on foot for the Tunapuna halt. The Tunapuna halt, the waiting for the train, clean new clothes—Pooran liked it all. Every morning he would try to get a seat near to the window so that he could see what was happening at the halts and stations. The tiny train ran to the city, brushing past overgrown bamboo patches, rattling over the clear waters of the streams where the train grated over bridges. Every day there were children about his age, waving at the train, carrying bundles of cut grass on their heads, or milk pails from which they sold the clean white contents to village people who waited in front of their huts with bronze containers when they heard the milk vendor's cry. There were small chicken pens enclosed by wire netting outside some of the huts and, here and there, a beautiful flower patch, or a bright green lettuce patch in someone's yard.

As the train whistled through the sunlit morning countryside, he thought of the place from where he had heard the same train-whistle sound so many times, where a tiny stream came to rest in a still basin. The train crossed the stream about a mile before Tunapuna, and he remembered how, wading in the water down below, he had looked up and seen the bottom of the engine and its carriages as they went by. Now he felt sad as he looked out of the window, wishing that he were one of the children outside watching the train go by, instead of being in it with a fixed schedule and destination each day. The train would roll into the big dark railroad station of the city any minute now, he thought, knowing that he would forget this feeling as soon as the crowds started moving, and moving him along with them. Then he would be in the college with its desks and laboratories and smells of ink.

At the end of the morning, as the clock in the ghostlike tower struck twelve, a stream of bicycles drained out of the four entrances of King George's, leaving only an emptiness behind. It was an emptiness that mocked and lingered with the wind through the corridors, that drifted into the lived-out classrooms and crawled into the desks, filling them with a tiredness of wear and use that all places accustomed to life acquire when their actors leave. It moved in and out of the wastepaper baskets, tossing about bits of crumpled paper; looking at the shells of fruit and candy wrappers; staring at the refuse and names of men perhaps long dead, engraved upon the honour rolls that lined the walls. Each day at twelve, after everyone had left, Pooran breathed in this emptiness when he took out the paper-bag lunch which Leela fixed in the morning. He opened the bag, taking out first an orange and a mango, then, wrapped in a piece of brown paper, a roti into which was folded a blend of spinach leaves which Leela had collected along the wayside. He spread the fried spinach into one long trail across the roti, rolled it into a cylinder, then bit into it. Just then the door flung open and Pooran, surprised, let his lunch fall on the desk. His cheeks still swollen with the first mouthful, he stopped chewing and looked first at his desk, then to the door. He saw the roti slide slowly open, exposing the row of wilted spinach leaves, and John Glenford and Harry Sharpe, two of his classmates, coming into the room.

John Glenford walked over to the desk on which his lunch lay. "What ees eet?" he said.

"It's his lunch," said Harry. "Come on now, let the chap alone."

"It's his lunch, ees it . . . it's cardboard and grass . . . that's what this native boy is eating, cardboard and grass. He, he, ha, ha, ha."

"Stop that!" Pooran shouted, "Stop that!" as Glenford took a pencil and poked in and out of the spinach leaves, piercing tiny holes into the roti with his pencil point.

Just then the door opened again, and before Pooran could see who it was, a heavy voice pounded the quiet walls of the classroom. "What's going on here? . . . Stop what?"

"Nothing, sir," said John Glenford.

"Yes, that's right . . . Nothing, sir," added Harry Sharpe.

Mr Hopkins, the science teacher, had heard them shouting. "All right, get out of here, you two, and leave that boy alone."

The two boys walked out defiantly. Mr Hopkins, in a sympathetic tone of voice, turned around to Pooran. "You're in my class–" But there was no one else in the room. Pooran had already slipped out.

It was not until two days later that he saw Mr Hopkins again in the lab, and though Pooran thought that everything had been forgotten, Mr Hopkins, whom the boys referred to as "that mad man in the Science Block," had been made more aware of Pooran's presence in his class as a result of the incident. He studied the boy through eyes the colour of the nitreous grey liquids that settled down in thin layers of ocean-bottom silence. Above them his shrubby grey eyebrows seemed filled with the mystery of the fumes trapped in the glass-stoppered bottles on the laboratory shelves. Below them the strong stubbles of hair on his nose looked as if they thrived on the rarest substances from the out-of-reach, out-of-use bottles on the top shelves. His laughter was crooked, tugging his mouth to one side, two frontal teeth crossing each other, making a triangular snout of his upper jaw . . . a laughter which spelt humiliation and disgrace to any boy who had not prepared the morning's lesson. It was John Glenford's turn that morning, the boy whose home, it was rumoured, boasted two running fountains, with many-coloured fish swimming in them.

"Get out of the room, you jackass–" The class winced as Mr Hopkins bellowed. His remark pelted itself at the boy, changing the colour of his face as though he had been physically slapped, then ranged back and forth, back and forth, against the tiers of seats and desks of the classroom. In this dead silence, no one in the class dared speak. All coughing, clearing of the throat, or shifting of the feet below the desks had to be postponed for some other time . . . not now. A drip . . . splurt . . . drip . . . splurt of a faucet from the far end of the room became the focus of irritation, and the whole class seemed to be straining its concentration to shut it off. It was as if they felt some responsibility for the singular daring of the tap in interfering with this silence.

John Glenford made his way slowly, leaning forward, pressing through the six other boys who sat in the same row. "Get a move on, lad," said Mr Hopkins, his voice more calm than before.

Glenford started down the steps of the tiered classroom. At the bottom of the steps, there was a resounding clatter of books, pencils and lunch box as he tripped, falling headlong in front of Mr Hopkins' shirt pocket, almost pulling him to the ground. Convinced that the fall was faked, or at least resulted from the boy's sullen swaggering as he descended the stairs, Mr Hopkins was only more irritated. The class, in the meantime, carried on its pretense of nonexistence, all ears and eyes, but expressionless. The moment's clatter could be heard thinning down into silence, settling itself for another cascade of louder and heavier humiliations from Mr Hopkins.

"Get out of the room, sir, and stand on the base of the flag pole on the front lawn where all can see what a naughty fellow you are." Glenford walked slowly out of the room, gait defiant. "Faster, lad, faster," Hopkins growled. "And when you get there, you're to stand with your hands in the air." He went out of the room into the corridor where he could follow the boy with a closer eye.

Inside the classroom, the pupils whose seats permitted them to watch the various moves were passing on a blow-for-blow account. "Is he crying?" "No, he isn't." "Not crying as yet." "Bold sort of chap." "Rather." "Did he look back?" "No, he's on the lawn now." "Think someone will see him, and tell his father?" "That Hippie is rather cruel sort, anyway, don't you think?" "Shhh, . . . here he comes now."

"And if you continue to play the ass, I shall give you weights in your hands to run around the block with, sir," Mr Hopkins said before entering the room, by which time the class had already returned to its serenity, as if it was completely unaffected by the whole morning's episode.

For the first time Pooran was glad that he did not live in a big house with acres of lawn, and gravelled driveways. He felt a kind of camaraderie with Mr Hopkins, which grew as the days went by. Together they would pollinate and cross-pollinate flowers, they would mix things together, and watch their reactions, fumes and foam and all. He had pictured Mr Hopkins doing just such things in the late hours, in the Science Block, with only the crickets and fireflies and gnats about—creatures unaware of this strange man's thoughts—a man who could make or break their whole lives as he wished; heavy wristed, with thick fists, the same width where they joined; he seemed put together in separately ill-proportioned parts. Together they two would make the green of the grass, they would breathe life into things, together they would make the rains come down.

Later that morning, one of the boys called Mr Hopkins over to see something under a poui tree. It turned out to be a puppy, its stomach swollen like a balloon, its hind legs dragging behind. Apart from its stomach, the protruding ribs and other bones of the animal made it look more like a skeleton than a living dog.

"Legs must have been broken and knitted back badly . . . Take it back to the lab, shall we? . . . Oh, Pooran . . ."

Mr Hopkins and Pooran went into the lecture room, where the class had met earlier, and opening one of the upright lockers, the teacher took out a large cube-shaped trough and placed it on the laboratory bench with the sinks and faucets.

"Get out a pair of tongs and wad of gauze," he said to Pooran, as he left the room.

"Are you hungry, doggie?" The dog licked his hand with a whitish tongue that felt like a warm, soft sandpaper. "Mr Hopkins is going to fix you up all right so you won't have to drag your legs anymore," Pooran whispered to the dog as he patted it from head to tail. "With all those bottles and burners, there is no substance which is not contained in these elements." He looked at the shelf where Mr Hopkins had waved his hand with the assurance that the secret of creation, of life and death, were contained in the mysterious bottles labelled in Latin.

Mr Hopkins came into the room, a small can in his hand, the writing on the label bleached out. He unscrewed the cap and soaked the gauze to dripping. "Now take hold of the gauze with those tongs," he said, as he placed the dog in the trough. "Quickly . . . press the gauze against its nose, and try at all times to keep it pressed firmly," he said, as he tried to keep the dog from moving. "We'll pickle it tomorrow."

The dog was trying desperately to move its nose away from the gauze; it pawed at the tongs with quick, sharp slaps, its claws scratching them, and fraying the gauze. Pooran was amazed at the sudden vigour and movement, which the dog had not seemed to possess up to this movement.

"We'll pickle it tomorrow . . ." The words suddenly ran through his mind again: he was killing the dog . . . Its hind legs began to shiver, and the clawing at the gauze was becoming more and more feeble, and it began to make sharp, whining sounds, as if it were pleading for its life. Mr Hopkins abruptly took the tongs out of Pooran's hand, as he was allowing the gauze to slip away from its position.

"I wonder if we couldn't save it at this point," Pooran thought. "When is it past life? . . . Is it now . . .?" He watched the dog's legs shiver less and less. Its whines were now tiny, guttural whisps of noise, and he knew that the dog was past the fine borderline of life and death . . . that now the dog was dead. His temples grew warm, and the blood began pounding the sides of his head; he ran out of the laboratory while Mr Hopkins still jabbed at the dog with the forceps.

That evening his thoughts raced from the lab to the picture of the dog dragging its hind legs through the bright bed of yellow flowers of the poui tree, to Mr Hopkins saying that, "Of course we can put it together here in the lab. It's not any different from the compounds we find in everyday living . . . Call it life, if you will, the formula is given as . . ." and then he felt weak and tired out and went to bed that night without saying anything to his parents.

As he lay on the pallet of coconut , he felt his body tightening and loosening, tightening and loosening, and as the scenes forced themselves upon his mind, he tried to silence them, to shut them out, but they came like waves rolling up on the seashore, and each time he tried to run ahead, they caught up with him, and swept him off his feet, smothering the breath in his chest. The flavour of whatever was in the can with the bleached-out label lingered in his mouth, and he wanted to brush it out from between his teeth, to scrape his tongue free of the acid flavour of the laboratory. He wished he could take his insides out and calm them, like smoothing out clothes on an ironing board, to take his brain out and hold it under the rushing flow of water from the public standpipe, to wash away the rusty thoughts, the rancid, rusty, rotten thoughts of breathing life into things with Mr Hopkins, and as he thought these things, he felt that the different parts of his body had heard, had understood, and were now trying to help push their way out, that they were locked in a struggle about his throat, harder and harder, tightening, screwing up his neck to bursting, not sobbing out loud, not making a sound. Then he cried . . . he cried, and it was early morning, the first morning of the rainy season.

He listened to the pitter-patter of the raindrops on the thatch roof, and he breathed with it. He knew that soon it would be running down along the patches of the thatch, and already the fine shrill trickles were filling the small dug-out canals around the hut. The old man was smoking his clay pipe in the next room, and he could see the light glowing, then darkening, smouldering, then die, through the burlap curtain between his room and his father's. He felt the hut expanding, then contracting, as the old man sucked on his pipe, and he could taste the raw flavour of the damp leaves of black tobacco. His consciousness and his thoughts entwined themselves with the tobacco smoke, and the song the rain sang, and they melted away in each other . . . and he slept.

Morning awakened with smells of eggplant frying in coconut oil and smoked herrings in the embers of the earthen fireplace, and he could see Leela squatting in front of it, blowing gently into the embers through a hollow bamboo stalk, and Ramdath standing at the back of her, staring blankly into the embers, making a circular motion with a hibiscus stem against his teeth, spitting out its juice and broken fibres. As he looked at Ramdath and Leela again, he knew how it was in the beginning, that Mr Hopkins was wrong. He knew that the little gods and the big gods had put the world together one morning . . . with the smell of smoked herrings, and the taste of hibiscus stem, and odours of eggplant frying in coconut oil. And as he thought these things, he heard his own voice in the midst of this first morning of creation when he spoke: "Babooji, can I go with you to plant the sugarcane fields? . . . I don't want to go back to learn any more in the big college."

Ramdath felt the strange pleading in his voice. Another generation of his ancestry had tumbled through an opening in the clouds, plunged through the maze and mire of the fields of insane sun and withered skin that he and his fathers knew. He looked at Leela; on her face the expression of horror which a face acquires by looking into eyes that have seen something horrible. Then he looked at Pooran.

"All right, then . . . You will go with me to the sugar cane fields."

The Propagandist

ELAHI BAKSH

Living here in Canada for so long, I had not thought of him much. Yet hearing that he had been left by his wife to bleed to death cranked up both memories and tears. His name was but we called him the Propagandist, only that, and nothing more. If there was a first name, we never heard of it; and we were not even sure whether Ramkissoon was his real name. Nor did we ask: it was enough that the *Ram* in his name meant "God." Maybe Ramkissoon was godlike according to the traditions of the Hindu indentured labourers—coolies, later known as Indo-Caribbeans, Indo-West Indians, whatever–who began coming from India to Guyana more than one hundred and fifty years ago. About *Kissoon*, I do not know; if I am not mistaken the word is Hindi for "a peasant." So if Ramkissoon the Propagandist was a godlike peasant, that was good enough for us in a young and green British Caribbean colony like Guyana.

I was a mere boy then, and he a grown man, a "born coolie," as he often proudly proclaimed, pounding his bare chest with his fist as he walked, or rather swayed, making his drunken way home from the village rumshop. His skin had been cooked golden brown in the blazing sun during long years of cutting and loading sugar cane on a plantation owned by Briggs and Company, the British-owned company, and this labour had made Ramkissoon heavily muscled, square shouldered, solid in build; and being of medium height, he looked squat, with a full, handsome head of long and thick black hair that was always heavily greased with coconut oil. His cheeks were round and babylike, but this dubious hint of innocence was quickly contradicted by tough tanned skin and fleshy lips that hid gaps in his jaw where two of his lower front teeth had been knocked out by an unknown assailant in some brawl.

Ramkissoon did not live on the residential quarter of the plantation with its array of tiny, same-styled, same-painted wooden houses, but on adjacent, probably squatter's land where, with his own hands, and the helping hands of friends, neighbours and relatives, he had built a small wooden cottage with two rooms and a kitchen for himself, his wife Joyce, and daughter Daisy. The cottage stood on a long, narrow strip of land, most of which consisted of a garden of leafy, green vegetables that could easily feed his semivegetarian household for generations to come. Although Ramkisssoon claimed credit for such productivity, and although I did sometimes see him forking in the garden, I suspect it was Joyce and Daisy who deserved the real credit, for mostly I saw only them weeding, watering, cutting, digging, cleaning and reaping. But no one dared dispute Ramkissoon's proprietorship of house, land, garden, and all.

Joyce was just as sturdy and browned, and even a couple of inches taller than her husband. Her long, luxuriant, black hair was all that she had in common with other women in the district who tended to be shorter, slighter, skinnier and more sinewy than her. Her name was also different: "Rajkumarie"or "Jasmattie" yes, but "Joyce" no. "Joyce" was more common among blacks—Afro-Guyanese, scarcely any of whom could be found on the plantation, although they made up the bulk of the population of the neighbouring village. Joyce also matched Ramkissoon in raucousness, for she could curse and swear like any man, and in the quarrels that frequently blazed between neighbour and neighbour, she could outshout anyone, male or female, black, brown or in-between. One did not look to her for delicacy. Once I saw her stoop down to have a pee in broad daylight, in the empty pasture land that connected our district to the village. As she sat on her haunches, her rumaul turned rakishly backward on her head, she drew her skirt tightly around her knees to form a screen from prying eyes, and looked for all the world like some great, plumed bird peacefully perched on a nest of warm eggs, in the middle of a silent field of unwaving carrion-crow bush with tufts of soft, bright yellow flowers. What fired my youthful imagination, since I saw her take nothing off before settling down, so to speak, was that she could not have been wearing drawers!

When exactly Ramkissoon became the "Propagandist" I do not know. My family lived only five houses away from him at the time, my father being a schoolteacher who was frequently transferred from one school district to the next, which is why we chose to rent a house from one of the squatters in Ramkissoon's district. I suppose our house was rather special for being a teacher's house, also for having newspapers; and Ramkissoon appropriated some of this special quality by borrowing our newspapers, often several days old, whenever the spirit took him, either to read to Joyce and Daisy in their own home or, more often, to pontificate to an audience of fellow sugar-cane cutters and labourers, seated around the bridge that connected our district to the main plantation road. It was probably during one of these sessions when he was expounding the intricacies of world affairs and expatiating on momentous issues of peace, war and cricket, that some reckless soul might have questioned what Ramkissoon said, only to be abruptly silenced by having the question summarily dismissed as "propaganda."

It was a completely new word for us, and by its length and weight alone, it was somewhat mysterious. None of us knew what it meant; but after some time, when we realized that anyone who disagreed was automatically deemed guilty of it, we solemnly concluded that the word was bad. For those who were slow or stubborn, Ramkissoon's dismissive air of dogmatic certainty soon drove this point home; and since no one wanted to be guilty of something bad, all future queries were instantly stifled.

"Propagandist" was first applied to Ramkissoon partly in jest, partly out of respect, and partly in good-natured ridicule, strictly among ourselves, when he was out of earshot; but it soon became common parlance, and was eventually accepted by Ramkissoon himself, in good spirit, as a mark of respect rather than ridicule. If I was pushed to give chapter and verse I would say the name first emerged when Ramkissoon was stung by the arrival from England of a new, British director for all the Briggs sugar estates in Guyana. This man—Sir John MacDonald—was something of a socialist, which was also a new word for us, and he introduced initiatives such as better housing and social and recreation centres for the sugar workers. Yet nothing made Ramkissoon more angry than these initiatives, which he vehemently denounced as mere propaganda. It struck me as strange indeed to denounce MacDonald's initiatives when they were evidently good rather than bad.

At any rate, I never pretended to understand the Propagandist. And I was not alone. So there must be truth in the saying: "One-eyed man is king in blind man's country," for it was galling to see that a man whose main qualifications, in a manner of speaking, were brute strength and boisterousness, was being honoured as a reliable commentator on the current affairs of Guyana, the Caribbean and the world. I doubt he could read a sentence straight through without halting, although I never tested this myself by venturing close to his audiences. I knew it would put him off, what with my going to high school and all that. So he persisted in vigorously expounding his dubious erudition to all who cared to listen, for good measure occasionally throwing in a few Hindi words that he had picked up either from Indian films or from the few older people among us who still retained memories of India or Indian languages.

We were all avid filmgoers, and not for the Propagandist alone did these films summon up the vision of India as a land of fabled princes and princesses riding on milk-white steeds as they conducted serenely happy lives bathed in luxury and attended by splendidly attired loyal retainers. India was a specialty of the Propagandist. Also Indian cricket. To hear him talk you would think he was a bosom friend and confidant of every Indian cricketer or administrator who ever lived!

Yet all he knew was learnt from our borrowed newspapers. Here at least, since I had read the very papers that he had, I could catch him out, as I once did when he claimed that Lala Amarnath, the Indian cricketer who had captained India against West Indies in 1948-49, had once punched an umpire during a Test match because the umpire had made a decision with which he (Amarnath) disagreed. Not that I said anything. Why spoil a good story! Even though the story was untrue—Amarnath disputed the decision, but he didn't punch anyone—it had the intended effect: it commanded attention and won admiration both for Amarnath and the Propagandist.

I mention cricket because the Indian cricket team toured the West Indies for the first time in early 1953 when the Propagandist was at the height of his popularity. The Indian cricketers were themselves regarded as film stars by most Indo-Guyanese. In some cases, Indo-Guyanese who had never seen a proper cricket match in their lives made the long journey to the city of Georgetown simply to catch a glimpse of these cricketers who, if they were not film stars, were at least true Indians, original models of which we Indo-Guyanese felt ourselves to be mere debased replicas. In that sense, the Propagandist was preaching to the converted when he proclaimed the superiority of Indians over all other cricketers including our own home-grown ones from the West Indies.

You would think that as a Caribbean or West Indian by birth, he was morally bound to support West Indian cricketers. But the truth is that, as Indo-Guyanese or Indo-West Indians, although we never admitted it, many of us were wracked by guilty ambivalence if not open disloyalty on the subject. We only pretended to be shocked by the Propagandist's partiality towards India while we joined in instinctively with the humour of his racist jokes putting down West Indian cricketers who were mostly Afro-West Indian like the villagers next door. We cheered and egged him on when he demanded with sneering and conclusive rhetoric: "Since when yuh hear monkey can play bat and ball?" It was a standard colonial jibe— labelling Africans or people of African descent as less than human.

Whether Ramkissoon deliberately wanted to pick a quarrel, or simply craved a wider, more challenging audience, I do not know, but I soon noticed that he had taken to going directly into the village to broadcast his preposterous claims for Indian cricket. Talk about Daniel in a den of lions! Just as we were schooled in racial stereotypes, the Afro-Guyanese villagers were conditioned by their own racial and social prejudice against us coolies. Many of them, after all, were office clerks, civil servants, policemen, schoolteachers, administrators and professionals of one kind or another. They at least could read. On top of that, cricket was mother's milk to them.There was no hint of ambivalence in their loyalty. They were passionately, patriotically and unreservedly West Indian. This time, I felt in my bones, this time surely Ramkissoon had gone too far. Blood was bound to flow.

But, wonderful to relate, our hero always returned safely from each visit to the village. Whether his survival was due to the forbearance of the villagers, or his magical skills of manipulation, I admit with admiration and awe that he had come through these village visits apparently unscathed. It was after one such visit that he seemed eager and almost triumphant, when he came to our house asking me to search for an old newspaper that stated the Indian cricket captain Vijay Hazare had previously scored a century in each innings of a Test match against the mighty Australian team. This must have been one claim too many, and an irate villager had taken the plunge and bet him ten dollars that it was false. He had come to me for proof, and promised to make it worth my while. What he was claiming was a very rare feat. At the time only one West Indian cricketer—the immortal George Headley—had achieved it; and it incensed the villagers, every bit as Afro as Headley, to be told that this rare achievement had been equalled by a coolie cricketer like Hazare. Much as I resented the villagers' prejudice though, and secretly hoped they might be proved wrong, I honestly could not recall any such feat by Hazare.

I had no real urge to go back through our bundle of old newspapers, but after I remembered the Propagandist's exact words, "Man ah gun gie yuh someting. Try fuh me nuh man," I decided to have a go. I read each day, for several days, after I came home from school, but could find nothing. Meanwhile, as the days passed, the Propagandist became increasingly impatient. "Yuh fine anyting yet? Remembah. Ah gat someting fuh yuh, yuh know." Frankly, after being reminded of this so often, I was getting impatient too. But he was in no mood to take no for an answer. Besides, I was more and more intrigued by the "someting" he had to offer. I needed quick money for something else that I had in mind. So I slinked back to the first article about the arrival of the Indian team in the West Indies; and there, to my unbelieving eyes, right at the end of the very article, which began by saying how weak India was but ended acknowledging that the Indian team did have a few star players like Umrigar, Mankad and Hazare, was exactly the information about Hazare's feat that was wanted!

My first impulse was to deliver the good news immediately. But I hesitated. Since I had already told the Propagandist that the article did not exist, would this now prove that he was a better reader than me? How he would gloat! It would be madness to play directly into his hands like that. It was not as if I didn't have plausible excuses: I could say that some of the newspapers were lost or that they were used as wrapping paper. He would never know. But I also longed to see those Afro-Guyanese swallow their racial pride. And all the time—I don't want to sound greedy—I could not forget the usefulness of "someting" for what I had in mind. I did not study mathematics at school for nothing. The bet had produced stakes of twenty dollars. If I got even five percent of that, it would still be one dollar—at the time, a windfall for a schoolboy. Indeed, why expect five percent only? My effort was certainly worth more since, without it, Ramkissoon would not only get nothing but lose his ten dollars as well. It was more than reasonable to expect generosity. Why else would he keep reminding me about "someting?"

When I took the paper to him the Propagandist was beside himself with joy. He smiled from ear to ear and swore triumphantly in anticipation of his winnings: "Wait till dem mudder ass black man hear dis!" he shouted, holding the newspaper in both hands and reading the passage about Hazare out loud, over and over again. "Ah goin to shub it up dem ass!" he screamed, waving his arms and pacing around in restless excitement. Nothing or no one could hold him back. He was complete lord and master in the gallery of his own house: "Dem mudder scunt tink coolie good for nuttin nuh? Ah goin show de fuckers dem!" He was about to go on when Joyce intervened: "Man stop cussin nuh," she pleaded, "yuh nah see picknee dey roun here." It wasn't anger. She was too delighted herself for that. Not that the Propagandist cared whether men, women, children or animals were around when he was in a drunken state. But now he was sober and deliriously happy, and could afford a rare concession to reason: "Ah true, ah true," he said to Joyce briefly; then addressing me directly, "nah min' bay, nah min;, you remembah wha ah de tell yuh. Yuh guh get someting." That was all the confirmation I needed before I dashed home almost as happy as he was.

Like an agouti sprinting out of the bush I reached home in no time at all. After I calmed down, I assessed my prospects, going over the details, calmly, carefully, over and over again. Two dollars out of the total stakes of twenty could not be considered unreasonable. Being the sort of villain he was, he might give me only one, which would be mean, although I would still accept it. What I had in mind all along, and why I had stuck with the Propagandist thus far was that I badly wanted a cricket bat, not one of the proper ones for adults, but the smaller version that cost about eight dollars. I had already saved three dollars and fifty cents to buy one, and if I could raise a little more on my own my father had promised to add the rest and get me the bat. This is really why I had persevered with the Propagandist. It was all up to him now. If he came through, I had it all sewn up.

Days passed. One week. At first, I sat each day on our front steps from where I could easily see anyone passing by. Then it began to rain heavily, day after day, until all the drains, trenches and canals had become swollen, and little water snakes could be seen washed up on dams. A fortnight passed, and still not even a glimpse of the man.

Suddenly, like a bolt from the blue, it hit me: what if he gave me nothing? He could not be forced to keep his promise. In any case, what proof did I have of it? I had told no one. Just as well, mind you, for if people knew, and he reneged, they would all say what a fool I was to trust such a wretch. Then, just as my dilemma was reaching fever pitch, he rattled the chain on our front gate one day when I had just come home from school and was still inside the house. I shot through the front door, then slowed down trying to appear as casual as possible. His greased hair glistened and his pockets bulged. "Eh, eh bai," he called out from the gate as I made my way down the steps, "come nuh,yuh see, ah remembah de someting ah de tell you bout. Propagandist doan forget yuh know. Come." As I opened the gate, he pointed to his pockets and said, "Yuh see, ah gat de black man money right hay," and pulling a coin out of his right pocket he said, "hey, hey, someting fuh yuh." He deposited a twelve-cent coin in my palm and walked quickly away.

It was an old sixpence coin that was going out of use at that time. The shock blinded me, and I virtually staggered back into the house. Surely he had made a mistake and would soon come running back to say so. But I dared not look back. And he did not come. No wonder we Indians have a reputation for meanness and blind, unfeeling avarice that some of us liked to call thrift! Whatever this was, it was definitely not thrift. It was greed of monumental proportions —deliberate, calculating, selfish, scandalous greed. Twelve cents out of twenty dollars! The bastard! It couldn't even buy me a tennis ball, much less a cricket bat. If I hadn't known the meaning of propaganda before, I certainly learnt it that day. It was not merely something bad but bad, bad, bad, and the name was a perfect fit for Ramkissoon.

I was consumed by disgust, shame, hatred, hostility, revenge. I couldn't take such a blow lying down. It was unspeakable to expect ten percent and get less than one percent! I had to get even. I enlisted help from friends, and we considered many plans. But it was not easy. Whatever we did had to be secret to be safe. We knew better than to risk tangling physically with the Propagandist. But like mice who couldn't bell the proverbial cat we only came up with impractical schemes. One plan was to secretly open the back gate of his garden and let in wandering cattle to graze his plants down flat; but he had a chain and padlock on the gate. Daisy was a possible target. She was after all an only child, and something of an estate beauty—tall, willowy, nubile, with long plaited black hair. Older boys ogled and whistled at her whenever she passed by. They did worse, if their accounts of what they did to her were true. There were claims of "holding Daisy down" in the very pasture land where I had spied on her mother peeing. These boys used to eye her flour bag panties hung out on the clothes line in the garden. They longed to get their hands on them. But how? Every strategy drew a blank. And to tell the truth, I didn't want Daisy drawn into it. She had done me no wrong. It was all a waste of time. Eventually, I had to give up.

Meanwhile, as the weeks passed, and the Indian cricket tour came and went, the Propagandist was shameless and brazen enough to act as if nothing had happened. He still came to borrow newspapers, but now, quite often, I lied and said that my father had taken the papers away to his school. Even if it was feeble and didn't exactly quench my thirst for revenge, it was at least a response. Then election fever came, and the Propagandist was once more in his element. Although I didn't fully understand why at the time, the election was a truly exciting event—the first in which the country would vote under universal adult suffrage. We had always been ruled by white people and I didn't see how this election would change that, but to judge by the way people were carrying on, we were in for a big change. The British were going to be kicked out, it was said. By whom I wondered? Perhaps by Dr Persaud and his People's Freedom Party, the PFP, the major political party in the country. It could not have been by the two or three smaller parties, or by any of the numerous independent candidates. The only thing was that some members of the PFP were suspected of being communist.

It goes without saying that the Propagandist did not know the difference between a communist and a catechist; but as the election approached, and the frequency of speeches and rallies accelerated, he was to be heard fuming and fussing, hectoring and lecturing, discoursing learnedly about both the benefits and perils of communism. He made it look as if he had been waiting for the election all his life. Our political meetings carried an aura of entertainment as arrangements were set up, people gathered and local helpers busied themselves. The candidates all came from Georgetown, and they treated each visit like a holiday excursion to the countryside where they could be indulgent, loud, outspoken, trenchant, extravagant, humorous. There was rivalry as each candidate tried to outdo the other by making bigger promises or dishing out more scorn and abuse, it was also good humoured, contributing to the general spirit of festivity. And amidst it all, secretly and furtively, when no one was disposed to watch, the Propagandist had inveigled himself into each candidate's clique of helpers, and established his credentials as local bigwig, a power broker, who could deliver votes at the drop of a hat.

In our constituency of Indians or coolies the PFP clearly had an advantage since the party had an Indian leader and mainly Indian members. Their main problem was the communist smear. One independent candidate Paul Harrichand, a fat pudgy lawyer with thick, horn-rimmed glasses, attacked the PFP with relish: "My friends," he pleaded, "doan let them fool yuh. They come as friends to tempt yuh. But once yuh in their clutches, yuh cyan get out. They got yuh." He warmed specifically to the communist theme: "Do yuh know what Russia is like today?" No one seemed particularly interested. But that was no deterrent. He went on: "Russia is a big jail. Everyone is a slave there. Is that what yuh want—to become slaves?" He paused, looking pleased with himself.

His direct, provocative approach perked up his passive listeners and provoked a low murmur, which he mistakenly regarded as a gesture of approval. He therefore plunged forward about absence of human rights and denial of freedom in the Soviet Union. "Do you want to be slaves?" he repeated. "Yes" replied at least a dozen voices in unison. Surprise. Shock. Did he hear correctly? The murmurs grew louder, and soon a loud bellow was heard: "Propaganda! Dat is propaganda." We all knew the voice. It had a familiar authority. The last thing poor Harrichand expected was disagreement from a bunch of illiterate plantation labourers. He paused and did what he could to collect himself. "Propaganda?" he asked weakly. "Yes, propaganda" answered the voice—robust, peremptory and aggressive. As a criminal lawyer, Harrichand relished argument. "Do you know what is propaganda?" he yelled back. "Yes" replied the crowd, egged on by the Propagandist and his cronies. But Harrichand paused again. Perhaps aggression would be counterproductive. He turned to conciliation: "My friends, what I am telling you are facts. This is not propaganda. Believe me." The crowd was becoming restive. They were not used to debate. "Believe me." Harrichand pleaded. "Yuh can read what I say in any newspaper." But the crowd was becoming noisy, and no one was listening. The speaker had lost their attention. People were chatting openly and gaily. Some drifted away, and with them so did the meeting itself.

The crowd dispersed into little straggling groups wandering or dawdling under the clear night sky. It was a clear beautiful, half moon evening with a gentle, cooling breeze that encouraged people to linger and laugh. I was surprised to see the Propagandist hunched and huddled with some of Mr Harrichand's helpers, giving every impression that they had something to hide while everyone else was chatting openly, joking and laughing. Since he had broken up the meeting, why would the Propagandist collaborate with the very people whose effort he had obstructed? Soon I noticed that he and his helpers moved off towards Mr Harrichand's car where the exhausted speaker sat disconsolately in the driver's seat, no doubt bemoaning his fate and despairing of his political fortunes. But the Propagandist did not speak to Harrichand. Instead he was given a cardboard box that must have been quite heavy since he had to put it on his shoulder in order to carry it. Then he and his cronies marched swiftly away. Whatever was in the box seemed to be exactly what they were waiting for. After Mr Harrichand and his helpers drove off, most of the crowd disappeared, and my friends and I hung around for a while before going home. Later, as we passed the Propagandist's house, we could hear loud sounds of music and revelry that were unusual for a Friday night in our district. It sounded rollicking. No doubt the Propagandist and his cronies were celebrating their success in breaking up Harrichand's meeting.

There were several other political meetings involving other candidates, and parties were taking place in the Propagandist's house two or three times a week. I had not realized that politics could provoke such merrymaking. The Propagandist was at every meeting I attended, and after most of them he took away a brown cardboard box from each candidate's car. He seemed to get louder and more raucous at each meeting, as he and his friends heckled and harangued with increasing abandon. I confess I used to stand over in the Propagandist's section of the audience to better enjoy the heckling and humour, for although all candidates delivered a serious litanies on imperialism, oppression, exploitation, injustice, colonialism, freedom and worker's rights, in every case, no matter what was being discussed, it would prompt scurrilous remarks, ribald jokes, irrelevant jibes, and always seemingly jubilant shouts of "propaganda" from those in that section. One evening a candidate who had become incensed by the constant heckling from this section of the audience shouted back hotly and angrily: "What I said was not propaganda. Do you know what propaganda is?" Total silence. It was not the Propagandist himself who had heckled, but as their self-appointed leader, everyone now turned to him for an answer, and he obliged, muttering so that the candidate could not hear clearly: "Yuh mudder's scunt, yuh tink because yuh read two, tree book yuh know everyting." Giggles and laughter spread all around. "Me nah know bout propaganda, but me know bout shovel though." More chuckling and joking. The candidate stood in silence, looking perplexed, while he strained to hear, feeling more and more as if he was being excluded from his own meeting. The Propagandist continued: "Me ah shovel man. If ah drop couple shovel cross yuh backside, yuh gun see real propaganda today." Outlandish laughter, sneering catcalls, whistling, boos, barracking. The candidate struggled to restore order, but the damage was done, and his meeting soon folded up in disarray.

On the night of what must have been the very last meeting before the election, I was so incensed by the Propagandist's antics that I followed him as he made his way to the candidate's car at the end of the meeting, and I saw him receive a brown paper bag with bottles in it. As he grabbed the bag I was close enough to hear him say reassuringly to the candidate's helpers: "Tell de boss, doan hut he head. Dis place gat plenty vote, and every man jack gun vote fuh he." Bottles and votes! Daily eating and drinking. What a dim-witted rogue and silly peasant slave I had been all this time while the Propagandist had taken gifts of liquor from each candidate and made the identical promise of political victory to each! I can only imagine that his strictures against the candidates in public were intended to deceive the candidates' helpers by showing equal disapproval in public for all candidates and cementing his solidarity with his fellow workers.

In the end justice prevailed, thank God, and the PFP candidate—the only one probably who had not bribed the Propagandist—won in our constituency, while the PFP gained a landslide victory in the country as a whole. As for the candidates who were duped, they deserved it. Two did so badly they lost their deposits. For the rest of us, all too soon, it seemed, the election had come and gone. We would now have to wait and see what benefits it might bring. Of one thing we were sure: it had already brought immense benefits to one man —the Propagandist —who, with his friends, over the three or four weeks of campaigning, had enjoyed gallons of rum and delicious curry feasts which Joyce and Daisy were reluctantly forced to prepare at all hours of day or night.

The end of the election was the end of an era: nothing in Guyana would ever be the same again. The old serpent of politics had made its fatal entrance into our young and green Caribbean garden of colonial innocence; and we would pay dearly for it. As for myself, my father was transferred from the district soon after the election and I seldom saw the Propagandist or my friends again. They quickly faded from my mind. Or so I thought. Perhaps my grievance against the Propagandist would never fade. I had to admit that as the serpent had brought knowledge and self-awareness to our country, so the Propagandist had brought a more mature knowledge of the ways of the world to me.

Reluctantly, after all these years, I see that now. At the time, however, I felt I was truly done with the Propagandist and all his dastardly works after I finished high school and went to Canada. If I shed tears for him now it is because news of his death has brought back everything and made me see my indebtedness to him. That is why, although I only have the story in pieces from different people, I can tell exactly what happened on the evening of his final flourish. He sauced up that Saturday afternoon after receiving his pay, and staggered home just after nightfall, demanding dinner and whatever else. But Joyce had not cooked, thinking he would be out late. (By that time, of course, Daisy had married and long left home.) The usual ructions ensued between him and Joyce and they came to blows. Then, choosing the right moment, Joyce ran into the bedroom, locked the door and left him screaming, swearing and threatening, drunk as a lord in the gallery outside. When she woke up in the morning he was lying dead on the floor of the gallery with his right arm caked in blood. What he had done, besides raving and ranting, was to smash his arm through the glass door of the cupboard that held their drinks. The cut he sustained was much deeper than he probably realized in his drunken state. So he quietly bled to death while Joyce was locked in her bedroom, unknowingly asleep, a few feet away. Inevitably, doubt about her unknowingness remained and she would never live it down; his family firmly believed that she had killed him: that she must have heard the glass breaking and callously left him to die.

Like his family, I too am inclined to wonder. How could he disappear just like that—Ramkissoon who was both a godlike peasant and the invincible Propagandist, incurable scamp, incorrigible rogue, inveterate bully and unscrupulous fraudster —who included among his victims a twelve-year-old boy who had helped him win a bet! That, maybe, is what still rankles. Do I then weep out of guilt that I have not forgiven him after so long, and over such a trivial thing? Surely not. After all, that world—our world of colonial Guyana—has long vanished, and I am far away, safe and sound in Canada where I am unlikely to meet the Propagandist and his kind again. But as I contemplate this cold, northern refuge, somewhere inside of me is a thought that has been struggling to get out, probably for a long time: the world that drove him to death has also driven me into exile, and I can no longer deny an indissoluble bond between him and me, one that links much more than the two of us together.

The Marriage Match

JAN SHINEBOURNE

"Arrange a marriage match," Alexander Choy told his mother.

Schoolteacher Elizabeth Waldron wrote the letter on their behalf.

His mother came late one afternoon and stayed from beginning to end to witness the writing. Her eyes were black as the ink, and she observed closely each stroke and loop of the moving pen until the page was full of words.

It was four o'clock in the afternoon. They were sitting in the Waldron family kitchen. Elizabeth had come in from teaching all day to find Clarice Choy waiting patiently for her on the front landing. Before writing the letter, she had put some plantains and other ground provisions to boil. Now, with the kitchen moist with steam from the cooking pot, she reflected as she wrote that Alexander could have written the letter himself. After all, she taught him to read and write. His handwriting was just like hers, full of italic flourishes. But it was the Chinese custom for the mother to negotiate.

"Mrs. Choy, what do you want me to say about Alexander?"

"Nothing 'bout Alexander. Say to come hey three week time, she an' daughtah. Say it nice, write nice letter."

So she wrote:

Mrs Clarice Tsue Choy,
Plantation Rose Hall Village,
Canje District,

Berbice County.

5th of March 1944

Mrs Enid Li
4 Light Street,
Albertown,
Georgetown,
Demerara County.

Dear Mrs Li,
I trust that my letter will find you enjoying the best of health and God's Blessings.
May I extend my gracious thanks to you for your letter of 15th of February 1944 instant and enclosure of the photograph of your eldest respected daughter Ruth Felicity Li with whom you ask to arrange a marriage match with my eldest son, Alexander Theophilus Choy.
I have the greatest pleasure in informing you that I will be pleased to receive a visit from yourself and your daughter at a time befitting your convenience to be arranged at the above address.
Please inform me in advance the date of your impending visit in order that our family can make the proper arrangements to receive you.
Thanking You In Anticipation,
I Remain,
Your Humble Servant,
Mrs Clarice Choy

Instead of a cash payment for the letter, Elizabeth accepted the promise of a Christmas cake to be baked and delivered on 24 December. The Choy family were famous for their baking. Ovens were a luxury. The overseers brought special ones from England. Local people used wood-fired ovens or stoves that used as much as a gallon of kerosene to do one round of baking in four hours—expensive and time-consuming. Alexander had built a large wood-fired clay oven where he was to be seen every Friday shoveling trays of Creole and Chinese cakes into the blasting hot oven: cassava pone, pine tarts, patties, rock buns, salara, cheese rolls, tennis rolls, and blackeye cake. It was customary for a large audience to gather in their front yard each Friday under the shading guinep tree to gossip, play cards and dominoes, and consume the cakes fresh, hot and just from the oven, washing it all down with his mother's homemade iced mauby and sorrel drinks. At Christmas, the oven took ten two-pound fruit cakes at one go.

The letter was dispatched to Georgetown without Clarice's other children, Winston or Eleanor, knowing about the match. However, they spied the photograph where Alexander had placed it near his bed, next to photos of film stars Claudette Colbert and Jane Wyman. They asked about the girl in the photograph and learnt about the matchmaking.

In Georgetown, Mrs Li also kept the letter secret from her three girls, Lilith, Evelyn, and Rebecca. Fortunately, the postman delivered it to her rented room in Light Street after they left for school or else she would have had to open it for them to read. She tucked it into her bosom and headed towards Brickdam for the Chinese Association where she worked. She stopped in at Brickdam Cathedral to ask Father Del Pino to read the letter. He not only read it, he told her to be sure to arrange a Catholic wedding for Ruth. She had not given any thought to whether to use Chinese or Catholic customs to marry Ruth. She decided to cross that bridge later.

Rain fell early that morning but the sun was out now and drying everything. Yesterday's heat and dust were gone. The oleander and bougainvillea looked beautiful, with their leaves, branches and flowers beaded with sunlight and rainwater. People were enjoying the coolness in the air. At work she sang over the ironing and wondered why. After all, it was not easy to raise four girls without a son or husband to help you face the world. There was more dowry to be scrimped and scraped, more matchmaking to be done for the other three. But a good marriage for Ruth was important now. She needed it more than any of the girls because she was the only one to be fostered.

In the evening Mrs Li walked back to Albertown tired, but with the letter still near her heart.

A week passed with her setting off each morning with the letter in her bosom, intending to visit Ruth and tell her about the marriage match. But each afternoon, she failed to do it. Finally, Ruth came home on her weekly visit and then Enid broke the news and revealed the letter. It was a shock. They never knew their mother asked the Chinese Association to select a family in Berbice or that she asked Father Del Pino to write them. One by one, the girls rebelled.

Lilith said, "Mother, this the twentieth century. We are not living in the dark ages anymore. People do not have arranged marriages anymore. You only marry the person you love and choose."

Evelyn said, "Mother, we are Guianese now. We are Christian. I am not having a marriage match."

Rebecca said, "Mother, please do not pick my husband. I will pick him myself."

Mrs Li went on the warpath. Limited rations of meat with meals, more callaloo than usual in the egg soup, the furniture to be polished twice if it did not shine enough, dusting three times a week instead of two, and no visits to the cinema that month. And lecture after lecture about the meaning of being Chinese: the Chinese were the most industrious people in the world; the Chinese invented everything from paper to counting to gunpowder to silk; the world would be nowhere without the Chinese; the Chinese were the oldest civilization in the world; Confucius, the Chinese philosopher, invented the civil service and civic society. They had never heard their mother talk like this. After all, she was born in Guiana; her mother came from China and left her orphaned to be raised by Catholic nuns, without any Chinese customs; she had raised her own daughters as Catholics. What did she know about Chinese customs? Since when was it so important to be Chinese?

Enid never told her daughters that she listened regularly to the public lectures on Chinese culture held at the Chinese Association. The Chinese community in Georgetown, being so small, knew her business. By way of helping her to bring up her four daughters, they gave her a generous salary for her services as cook and laundress, and the wives of the professional men liked to leave her anonymous parcels of food, books and clothing.

Three weeks after the letter arrived, the girls found themselves on the train to Berbice with their mother. It was the first time they had visited another part of the country. They took the six AM train, with the intention of returning on the six PM, They made a pretty picture—this petite Chinese woman and her four beautiful young daughters dressed in their Sunday best and smart hats, as they boarded the train in Carmichael and Lamaha Streets.

The train sped across the flat land. Village after village appeared and disappeared—Plaisance, Buxton, Beterverwagting. You could see straight into people's backyards as the train passed through. There were coconut plantations, cattle farms, rice fields and American army jeeps on the public road. Wherever the train stopped hucksters crowded round and tried to sell their trays of roti and curry, fried plantain and cassava, fried fish and bread with pepper sauce, phulourie, sugar apples, sapodillas, sugarcakes, koni and even black pudding and souse. By the time they reached Mahaicony, it was almost eight and the train was full of passengers. Everyone was talking at the same time. On and on the train sped through Abary, into the west coast. The girls forgot their reason for going to Berbice—Enid too. She was enjoying herself eating all the different foods they bought. She ate roti with souse and sipped coconut water through a straw to cool the sting of the ball-of-fire-pepper on her tongue.

British Guiana was such a big country, you had only to travel across the endless horizon and acres of sky to forget your problems and think they were really smaller than you thought. It occurred to

Lilith that her mother was unsure the arranged marriage was the right thing and they stood a chance of making her change her mind. She told her sisters so and they agreed. They began to feel so optimistic they stuck their heads through the window to let the breeze play with their hair but their mother ordered them to stop after they leaned right out to try and pluck bananas off the trees. At Rosignol, they crossed the river in a steamer and got so excited, they made their mother lose her temper and order them to sit still and be quiet.

In New Amsterdam, Elizabeth Waldron met them at the stelling and explained that she had written the letter and acted as a go-between for Mrs Choy since her English was not good. Mrs. Li began to feel nervous. That Mrs Choy spoke poor English must be a sign of how Chinese she was. Maybe she would think they were too Creole. Maybe the Choys did not come to British Guiana as labourers and would look down on her because her parents did. Maybe the Choys were Punti and would not like her being a Hakka. Worse, maybe she would not like Ruth when she saw her, even though the Chinese Association told her she was not full Chinese but East Indian too. Maybe Mrs Choy would change her mind once she saw the whole family together, all female, with no man to look after them, their father having died when they were still small.

On the bus, Ruth began to cry, and this set off her sisters. As far as they were concerned, their mother was about to foster her a second time. When the bus stopped in Rose Hall, a miserable family emerged. Enid had to take only one look at Mrs Choy to see she was in the presence of a genuine Chinese. She was dressed in black silk pajamas and silk sandals, and her hair was swept back in a bun, not cut short and permed in the English style like hers.

Enid felt a little better to see that there was also no husband and father in the Choy family; but there were two sons, Alexander and Winston. Enid had longed for a son but got four girls. The Choys were lined up along the stairs. Their mother instructed them to bow to their visitors. Enid bowed back, but not the girls. They just wept and clung to Ruth, making a complete fool of her. Clarice Choy looked so annoyed, Enid felt more and more ashamed, but she said nothing, only did her best to keep her dignity.

They sat down to a Chinese meal. Immediately, Ruth knocked over the Chinese vase full of hibiscus flowers. It shattered on the immaculately polished floor. Clarice said nothing as she retrieved the broken pieces. Shirley arranged the flowers in another vase. After that, Alexander and his teacher tried to maintain some conversation. He made attempts to encourage the visitors to eat but the broken vase hung like a ghost over the meal, depressing them. The studio photograph of Ruth was wooden and formal and made her look like a doll, but in the flesh she and her sisters were the most beautiful girls he had ever seen. He had fallen in love with Ruth the instant he saw her. His heart could not stop pounding or his blood racing. Even though she was weeping, she did it in a sad, not pathetic way. It was obvious how much she loved her family. It meant she would love him and their children too. Her face told him she was strong as well as soft—just what he wanted in a wife. For all their show of fear and timidness she and her sisters were only trying to make their mother do what they wanted. He had no doubt he wanted to marry Ruth.

When it was time to clear the table, the Choys showed the Lis to the verandah. Clarice and Shirley served them coconut water, and soft and delicate pink and white sugarcakes. There was a good view of the village, with the dark green canefields and cocoa brown canal running parallel on the wide horizon. The breeze blew in from the canefields and it was warm and scented with the perfume of cane and freshwater. There was more space here than in the crowed streets of Georgetown. There was a good-sized kitchen garden around each cottage and wide parapets along the paths where the men were playing cricket. It was Sunday. People were resting at home in their hammocks or forking and planting their gardens. There was the intoxicating smell of East Indian and Creole cooking in the air. They could hear a baby crying and the voices of children—perhaps boys climbing trees or plunging and swimming in the canals or the girls playing gutty or skipping.

While they took in all this, they could also hear the sounds of the Choys clearing the table, washing up, and when their voices rose the occasional sentence which they could put together well enough to hear that Winston and Shirley did not like them because they were not "real" Chinese, they were Hakkas, and worst of all, they were Creole; because they did not show them the proper respect of bowing, of taking care to appear glad to meet them, and because they broke their best piece of Chinese China and did not offer to replace it. Enid burned with shame. She wanted to replace the vase but knew she might not find or afford one. She felt worse when her daughters asked her to explain the meaning of Hakka and Creole and what it was to be a "real" Chinese. She pretended not to hear their questions but Elizabeth explained to the girls some of the history of the Chinese in British Guiana. The Choys did not come to BG as indentured labourers, who were all mostly of the Hakka group. They were Punti and came voluntarily, as free people, and therefore saw themselves as better then the rest. They had not lost their original Chinese ways so easily and looked down on everything Creole and on mixing with the other races. Elizabeth told the Li family not to worry, that the Choys were not really prejudiced, it was just the anxiety of Alexander getting married and having a wife that was making Winston and Shirley insecure; in time, they would get over it. Elizabeth explained that Alexander was getting older and was anxious to marry, and of all the photographs of all the girls the Chinese Association had sent, Ruth's was the only one he had fallen in love with.

It did not reassure Enid. She knew her girls. She knew that now that they knew how prejudiced the Choys were, they would be even more determined and fight against Ruth marrying into this Chinese family. So, she decided that before Clarice Choy returned to cancel the match, she would do it first. She was thinking about how she would say it, when Alexander's voice carried clearly on the breeze, declaring that Ruth was the only girl he was going to marry and if necessary, he would abandon his own family and follow her to Georgetown.

Alexander was the favoured son. What he wanted counted. They all heard Clarice tell him to ignore his brother and sister, the match would go ahead. But Enid was proud. Before the Choys could return to the verandah, she told her daughters she was calling off the match. Ruth was as proud as her mother. She was not going to let her family come all this way to be insulted either. Canje was not a bad place. It was big and spacious. It was a good place to raise a family. It was somewhere her sisters and mother could visit to get away from Georgetown. It was time their luck turned. Who knows, perhaps Alexander would do so well, they would live in their own house and she would be able to look after her mother in her old age. He was very good looking. He seemed soft hearted and kind. His bakery was also doing very well. He was a breadwinner. He was his mother's favorite. He would defend her against Shirely and Winston. He could be the best husband she would get.

It was a shock for Enid when Ruth declared she was willing to accept Alexander. And so when the Choys returned to the verandah the two matriarchs bowed very deeply to each other and their offspring were compelled to follow suit.

Elizabeth helped complete the formality of agreeing upon the dowry, the financial contributions each side would make to the wedding expenses, and a consultation with a Chinese fortune-teller to set the best date for the wedding.

Alexander and Elizabeth accompanied the Li family back to the stelling, but they went so far as crossing the river with them so that Alexander could take Ruth's hand and help her on to the six o'clock train.

Swami Pankaj

RABINDRANATH MAHARAJ

For most of his life, Pankaj lived with the dream that when he retired from his job as a farmer—the most popular farmer in Trinidad, he liked to boast—he would move to somewhere in the Himalayas region and spend the rest of his days meditating. Those who knew of this ambition had already, as a kind of preparation, began calling him Swami or Swami Pankaj.

My wife and two teenaged daughters were not so sympathetic. I could see that they were annoyed by Pankaj's constant complaints and by his gloomy, mystical moments. I could not blame them; they didn't know Pankaj in Trinidad. They didn't know him planting his cabbage and pakchoi and bodi on a piece of land less than a lot wide and selling the produce for a penny or two in a wooden stall in front of his house. They didn't know him saving and saving, expanding his farm to one acre, then five, then one hundred. They didn't know him winning the Farmer of the Year award, year after year, and university students visiting his farm and mentioning him in all their papers and write-ups.

My memory of Pankaj in Trinidad is more of the later period, when he was already recognized for the techniques he had developed to get rid of the red beetles which had ruined nearly all the coconut plantations in the island and for counteracting the papaya mosaic virus which had left the papaw trees of neighbouring farmers useless and diseased. Pankaj's coconut and papaw trees were always healthy, lustrous and laden with fruit. The other farmers paid sly visits to his farm, carefully noting the chemicals he used and the way he would throw everything in a steel drum, fold up his sleeves, push his hand in the drum and carefully mix the yellowish liquid. Graduate students from the Tropical College of Agriculture in St Augustine also came with their notepads and pens but Pankaj resisted them all. He Resisted even the officials from the Ministry of Agriculture who descended on his plantation with letters authorizing them to collect the data for their reports. They, too, were disappointed, stumbling back into their shiny new cars and complaining about "peasant mentality."

In the meantime, Pankaj's estate flourished and year after year he won the Farmer of the Year award. I lived about five miles away from Pankaj and on Friday evening after work, I would stop at his estate and fill my car with pineapple and papaw. I would comment on the size and texture and taste of his fruits, but I never asked any questions. That pleased him a lot. Sometimes, he would tell me, "Look, take a few extra papaw. Is the best thing for digestion." At other times, if he was in the mood, he would mention that he was thinking of selling his estate and moving to the Himalayas. Although I would say, "Yes, Swami," or "I see your point, Swami," I never really fell for that Himalayas business. He looked happy enough in Trinidad and his estate was booming.

So I was surprised, after all those years, to receive a letter from my brother stating that Pankaj was moving to Canada and needed someone to stay with for a few days. Pankaj stayed with us for exactly eleven days, then rented a one-bedroom apartment for two months, and finally purchased a small semidetached just one block away from where I lived in Brampton. Then, in a most unexpected turn, he started driving a cab with the Omni Cab Company, owned by a short, fat man from India. I think he liked the idea that, although we worked for different cab companies, we were both taxi drivers. In Trinidad I never asked him many questions, but when he was newly arrived in Canada I was curious about what had caused him to leave and end up here. And his replies were always satisfactory. He told me that he was forced to postpone his swami ambition because of an illness he had developed in Trinidad. The doctors could not properly diagnose his illness, but they revealed that it was most likely from years of exposure to chemicals. They felt that he could be treated better in Canada or America. He chose Brampton, because one of the ministry officials, a graduate of some university in Ontario, mentioned that parts of Canada, like Brampton, were becoming just like India, with Indian businesses and Indians walking all over the place.

Even Pankaj's job as a cab driver for Omni Cab Company fitted in because the company was owned by an Indian. Pankaj made it absolutely clear that this Canadian phase was only a stepping stone to the Himalayas. In some respects, Canada agreed with him and he often mentioned to me that his doctors had given him the right advice. He stopped wheezing, he no longer suffered from short breath and he didn't feel as tired and dizzy as before. More than the treatment he was getting here, he felt that it was the nice, clean, cold Canadian air.

But he was not happy. Every time he visited us, I would see that. I knew that he had taken the job as cab driver, not—as my wife believed—because he had overstepped his ambition and purchased an expensive house or because he needed money to pay for the medical treatment he was receiving, but rather because Pankaj was not the kind of person to be idle for too long. And more importantly, because the company was owned by an Indian. From India. Maybe somewhere around the Himalayas. But things were not working out. The owner, according to Pankaj, was a cheap, money-hungry scamp. As far removed from a swami as one could imagine. There were too many rules. Pankaj didn't like that. Pankaj argued frequently with the owner. The owner didn't like that.

One Sunday, when he was off-duty, he took me for a ride in his cab. We went to Niagara, where there were miles and miles of apple and grape and plum farms. While he was driving, he kept staring at the fruit trees. "That is how farms should be," he told me. "Well organize and maintain. Not like the little garden and them we had back in Trinidad with everything mash-up and mix up together. Look how neat and clean everything is. No disease, no rotten tree, no waste."

He looked so happy during the trip. I asked him, "Why don't you open up a farm right here in Canada?"

He shook his head. "The doctors advise me against it. They tell me to keep away from that line of work."

"Well at least you have the cab job."

Mentioning that was a mistake. He told me very bluntly that the owner was a jackass of the highest order. After a while, he cheered up. "But I feeling better now. I might be able to leave soon."

"Leave the cab company?"

He continued driving as if he didn't hear. Then he said, "Leave for the Himalayas."

As Pankaj's dissatisfaction with the owner increased, he began speaking more and more about his swami ambition. He avoided the topic about his recent life in Trinidad, except to tell me once that his wife had died two years ago and that none of his children—little jackasses, he called them—wanted to leave for Canada with him. Understanding his reluctance, I didn't press him.

He needed no such prodding about the Himalayas. During his visits, he showered us with stories of ordinary men and women who had journeyed to the mountains and after ten or twenty years of meditating, had developed a number of mystical abilities. Swamis who could eat fire, swamis who could sleep on nails, swamis who could survive for months on nothing but air. He mentioned several of these swamis by name, as if he knew them personally.

Whenever these accounts unfolded, I would see my wife frowning and wait for my two teenaged daughters to leave in a huff. After one visit, the eldest told me, "That man is absolutely crazy, daddy. We shouldn't have him around visiting."

How could I explain? How could I make them understand that twelve years ago, just before I left for Canada, I, like so many others, had been gripped by the idea that a simple man, not college or university educated, could develop techniques to counteract diseases that had puzzled so many? As it was, I felt his desperation; I suffered with him.

I knew that they were angry when he began visiting us, not in his everyday shirt and pants, but in salmon-coloured kurtas and dhotis. And I knew that they were angry when, unexpectedly, his manner of speaking began to change, to fit more with his image of a swami. Once, while we were strolling through the park, he pointed to some seagulls and told me: "Those birdijis are so wery wery lucky. Not a single care in the entire uniwerse." At that time he had already started speaking in the sing-song way of Indians from the subcontinent. Then he told me about a swami who was levitating when he encountered a flock of birds. The swami, who understood their language, overheard them saying that it was so strange that a creature without wings or feathers could fly. And he told them that when you know you can do something, then that thing becomes possible just by knowing you can do it. But the slightest doubt that came in his mind, he explained, would cause him to drop on his head like a stone.

I may have been the only person sympathetic to this transformation that had taken hold of Pankaj. He was fired from his job with the Omni Cab Company when, during an argument, he told the owner that he would be reborn as a hippo in his next life. I had to smile when Pankaj related that, but he was in a serious mood. "All the signs are coming together. It is getting very close now." Then he told me a story about a swami who could distinguish different kinds of personalities just by sniffing at the owners. "Just one smell," he shot up his index finger, "and this swami would know all that there was to know."

I suppose that I had become used to Pankaj's talk about swamis and the Himalayas and I didn't pay any extra attention to him then. But less than a week later, he called me over the phone and said that there was "a matter" he wanted to discuss. He asked if I could come over.

I put on my coat and boots. I didn't tell my wife and daughters where I was going. The day was pleasant enough, not very cold, so I decided to walk the block. While I was walking to his house and enjoying the cool air which was responsible for Pankaj's recovery, I wondered about his "matter" and whether he had decided to return to Trinidad, now that his problem with wheezing and short breath and giddiness were gone. When I saw the sign on his lawn, I felt that my suspicions were correct.

Pankaj didn't really have a lawn though, because the majority of his yard was occupied by parallel rows of purple and red and yellow flowers. They were of all shapes, some like bells, others stars and a couple like tiny hearts. And in the middle of all this was a sign: "House for sale."

I knocked on the door. Pankaj was in grey pyjamas and fluffy slippers.

"Please do come in," he said acting surprised, as if he was not expecting me, and shaking his head from side to side. As usual, I was struck by the number of plants he had managed to fit into his living room. They hung from walls, they climbed over shelves, they twisted around lamps, they peeked from behind chairs. Pankaj was pleased by my staring. "My only wice." And like so many times before, he lectured me on the names and properties of every single plant. African violet, philodendron, Boston fern, English ivy, caladium, tropicals. Midway through his lectures, he stopped. "It is now yours."

He had been talking about a guava plant which he had sneaked in his suitcase when he had left Trinidad.

"But I can't." I remembered that it was his favourite plant.

"Oh, don't be saying such and such a thing." He removed the pot from the centre table, pressed the leaves against his nose and then held out his hands. "Here, take it."

"Thank you, Pankaj." I felt uncomfortable with this unexpected gift.

"No need for all this thanking business." He waved a hand. "You can be taking any one that you like."

"Oh no, no. This is okay. I am not really a plant lover."

Pankaj looked at me sternly. "I am knowing a plant lover when I see one."

I tried to change the subject. "Are you leaving for Trinidad?"

He looked hurt. I thought he was going to cry.

"The sign on the lawn—"

Pankaj got up, took a deep breath and clasped his hands behind his back. "I am sailing for India."

"Sailing? In a ship?"

I felt that I was saying all the wrong things. I decided to keep quiet. I looked at Pankaj still standing with his hands clasped behind his back. His eyes, halfway closed, were gazing at the wall. I followed the direction of his gaze and observed the framed picture of a swami whose eyes were also halfway closed. They seemed to be halfway gazing at each other. It was a touching scene in a way. I felt that it was time to leave.

"His name is Swami Purohananda. He is the smelling swami."

I remembered Pankaj's story. And the swami with his eyes halfway closed, with a little smile on his face, really seemed to be smelling something. It looked like a pleasant scent.

"My favourite swami. I am always recalling something that he said. Would you like to hear the werse?"

"Sure Pankaj."

"Wherever we go, we leave a piece of ourself."

"That's very profound, Pankaj."

He unclasped his hands and turned around. "We are forever leaving smells. Good smells. Bad smells. In-between smells. They remain behind. Did you know that?"

I shook my head.

"I wonder what smell I left behind in Trinidad?"

I began to smile but then I realized that Pankaj was not speaking to himself. He wanted an answer. "Pine and papaw." That didn't satisfy him. "And chemicals." I tried to remember the name of some weedicide or fungicide. "Benlate. Gramazone." He was getting slightly angry with me. "And some sort of swami smell. Like incense and ghee and pitchpine wood." It only made him angrier.

"And what good would that sort of smell do in Trinidad? Anybody will appreciate it? All these jackasses who try to trick me into telling them how only my papaw and only my coconut tree never get any disease?" I had heard this boast before, but this time Pankaj continued. "They thought they was smart, but I was smarter. All the little trick they would come up with. But I never tell a soul. Not even my own worthless children. You know why?"

"Why Pankaj?"

"Is because nobody ever help me. They laugh at my little backy garden, they laugh when I expand to five acres, they laugh when I say I going to plant one hundred acres total. But they stop laughing when only my tree remain healthy. And all the time they was expecting me to fail." I realized then that Pankaj was no longer speaking like a swami or even an ordinary Indian from India. "They expect me to fail because I was too small. I was stepping outa my shoes. 'What wrong with that kissmeass Pankaj?' they used to say. 'Oh he think he is some damn French-Creole or what, with all this plantation stupidness. Take care he don't bring in a few slaves to work in the estate just now.' And the rest them used to laugh gil-gil and say that they only waiting for him to end up with his foot in the air like a dead cockroach." He came and sat next to me. "But they never understand me. None of them."

He gazed at the guava plant in my hands. I felt that I should give it back to him. "I was the enemy, not because I do harm to anybody, but because I didn't fail. They couldn't understand that. And that is why I never tell none of them that the only way to avoid the papaw mosaic disease was to cut off the top of the plant when it was only one foot high. Then cut off all the secondary branches when they spring up. Excepting one. And that one branch never get the disease. It take me years to discover that. Day and night. Night and day, I was trying something different. It was the same with the coconut trees. Day and night. Night and day. But I never give up. And then I discover that the only thing that could keep away the red beetle what used to live in the heart of the tree was to mix up some garden salt with Aldrex and car oil, tie everything in a piece of sugar bag and put in it the centre of all the leaf. Right in the heart. Kill the beetle one time and keep away all the others. Just two time a year. And no disease again. So simple-simple and nobody ever think of it before me. None of them university people with they thick notebook and none of them government people who was afraid to dirty up they clean shoes in the mud."

It took a while to realize that Pankaj was actually revealing his secret to me. The secret he had held for all these years. It was too much.

"I could tell you something?" He leaned close to the guava plant. "Sometimes I feel that it was really all the bad-mind that used to get me sick, not the chemicals and them." He was talking softly and his lips were moving but not his teeth. I felt worried for him.

"You think this is a good move that you are making, Pankaj? Going to India?" He leaned back on the sofa. I saw that he was looking once more at the framed picture of the swami. I pressed on. "I mean Canada seems to agree with you."

For a minute or so, he remained silent, his eyes never leaving the picture. Then he said, "If you don't have any dreams, you might as well give up."

"But you've established yourself here. The house. Your health—"

"Is why I never ever give up," he continued, as if he didn't hear me. "Because my dream was no little-children-stupidness that disappear at the first sign of any problems. That only make it stronger. I walking around with it inside me all these years." And Pankaj told me a story about a swami dedicated to discovering the true meaning of life. From city to city this swami travelled, from shrine to shrine. Sometimes he spent months in the jungle before he reached another city. He saw famines, floods, miracles, kings, beggars, and saints. But he kept on walking, searching, searching. Then, one night, when he was asleep under a banyan tree some dacoits killed him and stripped him of the little clothing he had.

I waited for Pankaj to complete his story but he was staring at the picture again. I got up. There was something I had to ask. I didn't know how my voice would sound. "Why did you tell me your secret Pankaj?"

He looked as if he didn't understand.

"The secret about the papaw and the coconut trees?"

He remained serious, then a little smile came on his face. "Because of your smell."

"My smell?"

He nodded. "Your smell tell me that you is an honest person. A honest person who too frighten to see the dream hide away in the back of his mind." He was still smiling. He may have been joking but my eyes began to burn. I had to leave.

"Thank you, swami." I hurried to the door.

A little more than a week later, Pankaj left for India and I never got the chance to ask him about this swami who had been searching for the true meaning of life. But sometimes, on the weekends, I take little drives to Niagara to admire the rows of pears and plums and grapes. And looking at them, I imagine Pankaj sitting alone in some cave, his eyes halfway closed and a little smile on his face.

Bruit

SHARLOW MOHAMMED

Outside the country of St Augustine, if the traveller were to follow the old Southern Main Road for two miles or so, he would be sure to come up on a side street with a broken sign post. Hanging from a clownish angle, the writing says "Caca Village." There is also a rather long, white arrow as if to indicate that the village lies deep within the pitched street. If the traveller was a linguist he would know that "Caca" was shortened from the word "carcass." And if he were to follow his linguistic curiosity, he would learn not only how the village derived its name, but how a particular type of pollution altered the lives of the once peaceful villagers. Mr Abdul was the first pioneer. In the thirties, he set up a sugar cane plantation of twenty acres, and the cultivation of this enterprise brought in labouring families to settle. Indians and Africans then called the village Abdul Village. Now, in the seventies, the children of Abdul were happy to abdicate their title. In fact, it was Sybia, the last of Mr Abdul's daughters, who gave the village its new name.

At the end of Abdul Village lived Mr Sookpalee and his wife, Sunardai. They had children enough to fill a dozen. Sunardai so loved the new song by Sundar Popo that whenever she heard it on the radio she would rush to raise the volume, so that her next-door neighbour, Rastafarian George Mac Williams, was often serenaded by the full blast of "Kaise Bane." Sunardai, short of stature and heavy in weight, so loved this song that she daily urged Sookpalee to buy a new record player. Oil had begun its conversion to black gold, and Sookpalee so loved his spouse that Sunardai's wish was soon granted. Each morning, noon and night, I-man George heard: "Kaise bane, oh kaise bane, phoulowrie bena chatney kaise bane. . ." George's occupation was that of a tout for the whe-whe man, and these days George was finding it difficult to keep his accounts straight. "Kaise Bane" kept gurgling in his mind, and this morning, as another neighbour hailed out. "Good morning, George," he replied, "Kaise bane." Then he shook his Rasta locks as if to clear his head of the chatney song. "Listen to I and I, Rajiv," said he. "Ah can't take no more 'Kaise Bane.' Every day. . . every day, whole day Sunardai pounding meh head." Rajiv was a student at the university. He noted the frustration on George's face and said: "Talk to Sunardai, George. Tell her she's disturbing your life." "Sunardai not disturbing my life, she ruining my life. I done talk to her. I talk to Sookpalee too, but some people just hard of hearing." At that moment, Sunardai was heard spinning "Kaise Bane." Rajiv shook his head in sympathy with George. But the fellow left muttering: "I and I going to fix it, man. I saving Jah penny."

As a whe-whe tout, George had already learnt the ropes and was able to hedge on his marks, that is to say, if at the end of the day his collection could cover the winnings of several marks, he could forego playing them and keep the money for himself; and should the mark be played, the collection obviously would pay the winner: George couldn't lose.

Some six weeks later, I-man George stopped counting his pennies. He had a fine taste for household articles and, in the city, he chose his music set and selected his records. On his way home, he shouted out to Rajiv. From his gallery, Rajiv saw the wide grin; even George's dreadlocks seemed to be grinning this morning. With his Rasta fist raised in the air, George was laughing, still shouting: "'Kaise Bane' dead. Ha. Ha. Today 'Kaise Bane' going to get some thunder. Jah say so." The student nodded his head, observing that the stress furrows of frustration had already disappeared from George's face. Rajiv made a fresh cup of coffee and returned to his books. It was his first year at the university, and there was much work to cover.

Shortly afterwards, he engaged himself in concentration, and then, like an unwanted intruder, Bob Marley and the Wailers thundered into his room with "No woman no cry. . ." George was fiddling with his volume, testing its full impact. A moment of silence, and then another of Marley's records. Rajiv was listening to Jamaican politics and civil misery. But this attentiveness was accompanied by the bass drums which had taken on an insane glee in pounding the tender tissues of Rajiv's brain. Rajiv stared at his books in growing frustration and anger. After a while spent pacing his house, swearing, and cussing under his breath, Rajiv decided George must be mad. He would go and talk some sense into the fellow. Then it struck him that George must be filled with hate, that his only weapon of revenge against "Kaise Bane" was Bob Marley! What to do. Where to go. Rajiv was aware of his inside fear, aware that his nerves were being riddled. He thought about his wife, Paula, who taught school at St Augustine. After three years of marriage, they were still in the middle of fulfilling their aspirations. He could not concentrate on his studies. With Bob Marley echoing on the tree tops, Rajiv stepped outside not knowing whither his feet might carry him. Three lots further along the road, was a neat board-house within the most tidy surroundings. Mr Maharaj and his wife were fond of flowers and their garden was ordered and perennially in bloom. Even their kitchen garden had order to it. Rajiv saw Maharaj reading in his gallery. The man was in his early thirties and was in training to become a pandit. Religion had not played much of a part in Rajiv's life, and the day he married Paula, he had converted to a Catholic. As such, he could not bear to hear Maharaj expatiate on his gruesome visions. Their conversations were always brief. Maharaj boasted that he was a "yogin."

"Rajiv," he heard Maharaj shout his name and realized he was glad to speak to somebody. Before he entered the neat gallery, Maharaj was babbling: "Last week I turn full pandit, you hear? Starting from this Saturday, I keeping yagna for seven days." Rajiv was groaning within as Maharaj added: "I inviting you and Paula to come. Teacher and university people good and respectable. You all fit to attend yagna." "Maharaj–" Rajiv noted the hint of offense at his omission of a title. "Pandit Maharaj," he added, "we are happy to accept your invitation. We will attend your yagna." "Very good," Maharaj smiled serenely.

Bob Marley was still loud and the bass drums were irritating. "Doesn't the noise disturb you, Pandit Maharaj?"

"Noise? What noise?" the pandit replied smugly. "Listen to me, Rajiv. When you follow yoga, nothing could disturb you. You hear only what you want to hear." Rajiv was a long way from reaching a position where his mind was in control over matter. He couldn't see how it was possible not to hear George's music. He wanted to say so, but Maharaj was speaking again: "You see that room behind you? It is a holy room. It is where I pray and practise yoga. Though I still a yogin nothing could bother me. No noise. Nothing. When you know yoga, you live without fear." It appeared that I-man George had bought all of Marley's records. Maharaj wasn't hearing but Rajiv couldn't help his battered ears. "We will come to your yagna, Pandit Maharaj," Rajiv said again, excusing himself.

He followed the street, gazing at the rapidly changing environment. The mud and board houses were being demolished one by one and replaced by concrete bungalows. The wealth from oil was reaching out to everyone, and Abdul Village was no exception. Two hundred yards or so later, and with Bob Marley quite inaudible, Rajiv entered the snackette. The drinkers were few, and he sat alone toying with a beer, biding time, and cooling his temper. Finally, Rajiv returned to his home to find that all was silent. He appreciated the relief. In the evening, when his wife arrived from school, Rajiv complained to her. Later, as soon as I-man George returned from the whe-whe yard, he began to play his new found joy. Paula, a dougla, was young, merely twenty years old, and Rajiv, peeved once again by the loud noise, was simply appalled to see his wife dancing to the reggae music. "Is this some kind of a joke to you?" said he. Paula stopped her dancing and glared at him. "If you can't beat them, join them," she replied, before retreating to the kitchen. They were not used to quarrelling. That night when Paula attempted to mark some of her pupils' papers she found the noise quite disturbing and began to share her husband's frustration.

And so, Rajiv would study while the village slept. Gradually, as the days went by, George played his music less often. One morning, when Rajiv wondered aloud to Pandit Maharaj if Rastaman had killed "Kaise Bane," the pandit explained: "You ever hear the saying, 'Come see never see?'"

"Come see never see" had a bit of a chain reaction, and Sybia was now playing Indian records. However much Rajiv tried to bear up, he cussed all through the loud songs, cursed the people who spun the records. And then, with great joy he thanked the good Lord for the few hours of silence and forgave his neighbours.

"It couldn't be worse," he would still complain to Paula. But he was learning to survive between the hours of noise and silence.

Christmas arrived and a few more record players were added to the neighbourhood. That holiday, while Mr Sudace played bhajans and Sunardai "Kaise Bane," Dick blasted the village with calypso. Victoria meanwhile loved country-and-western. But I-man George outdid them all and sought to superimpose what he called his culture over all others. After a full hour of frustration and another spent in cussing, Rajiv mumbled to his wife: "I-man suffering from echolalia."

"Echolalia?"

"Yes, he has difficulties in identifying pronouns. He thinks I am he, and he is me, and so on."

Paula laughed. "The holiday will soon end, and the villagers must work."

"Yes," Rajiv mixed a rum and coke. "In the meantime I am nothing but a cripple. A cripple filled with hate."

"We could leave Abdul Village, you know," Paula pointed out.

"We could?" returned Rajiv. Both knew they hadn't the means to move house. And Rajiv was loath to leave the village of his birth. He was friends with the trees, the river, the environment. The thought, however, remained as a future alternative.

Early in the new year, in a moment of glad relief, Rajiv reflected on some past reading: God created the world, then He created the stars and the heavenly planets to make divine music for His pleasure. So it was thought. Rajiv reflected again on his earlier years in the village, when music was made by the chirping of birds, the single voice of a housewife at work or in leisure. Fowls, animals and insects provided sounds then, and Nature, in the form of wind, rain and sunshine gave life to everything. All things come to an end, Rajiv consoled himself. He wasn't satisfied with the progress he'd made at his studies, and he urged himself to do more work. From time to time, he would have brief conversations with Pandit Maharaj. Folks from far and near brought their problems to the pandit, and he did earn a sense of respect from the Hindu community. His recent yagna was well attended.

This early morning, Rajiv was distracted by loud voices coming from opposite the pandit's residence. From his gallery, he saw several men already engaged in cutting down trees and clearing the land. Pandit Maharaj, he saw, was beckoning to him from his backyard. Strolling over, Rajiv inquired: "We going to have a new neighbour?"

The pandit had more information. "I cannot say who own the property that side; but they going to build a church there." The Pandit's slight shudder did not escape Rajiv's eyes. He asked "What kind of church?"

"A church. What you expect?" he returned. "Abdul Village done upset; it done spoil."

"But you have yoga to defend you." Rajiv couldn't help his words.

"Yoga is the most powerful thing in the world," the pandit agreed. Then he smirked, adding, "But is not the only thing in life. People have to live too."

Feeling rather smug, Rajiv left Pandit Maharaj. Perhaps, he thought, the coming of the church would lend a sense of religious respect to the residents of Abdul Village. Perhaps, he hoped, it might even have a balancing effect on the loud noises. As the days followed, each household was accosted by the pastor and his delegation. One half of the villagers were incorporated and began turning out to help in the building of the new church. Pandit Maharaj damned the few of his devotees who subjected themselves to the new order, whereas Mr Abdul's family, who resisted it, suddenly realized how great was the religion of Islam. Rajiv and Paula welcomed the fatted pastor and his members. They confessed to being Catholics but promised to attend. The pastor did say, then, that the pope in Rome was the true devil. But Rajiv was happy to see I-man George take off his music set to receive the pastor and his delegation. Here was respect granted without being asked for or earned! The man from Galilee was as powerful as ever.

Some four months later, in the middle of the midsummer vacation, the church officially announced its opening. The concrete structure appeared awkward. Four square unpainted walls with glass windows to the front, and a wooden door to one side amounted to a nightmare. If anything was missing, the Sabbath congregation, dressed and adorned as if for a wedding, completed the bad dream. Two thirds of the church people came from outside the village, and these were endowed with large voices. They sang hymns, and shouted amens and hallelujahs to the pastor's booming sermons. Rajiv was now appalled to hear fundamentalist interpretations of the Bible. He was aware that the music boxes were all silent, but at one o'clock the church dispersed and Bob Marley promptly filled the interim. Four o'clock evening, the church was back again, singing and sermonizing until the eight o'clock hour. All day, Rajiv had stared in frustration at his books. He waited for an end to the noise, but they congregated shaking hands amidst loud and forced laughter, and Abdul Village did not become free until ten o'clock. Rajiv spent the rest of the night in the study.

"Constant dripping would wear away a stone," Dickens had explained. Early the following day, church members were nailing pews and swinging cutlasses amidst shouting gossip and peals of raucous laughter. Rajiv's rest was broken, and even Paula's customary Sunday siesta had come to an end. This church showed itself to be active every day.

If Rajiv had felt that its presence might have a balancing effect on the loud record players, he was sadly mistaken, for the pastor now installed his own mike with which he drowned out the village music. It was not possible for Rajiv to keep to his schedule of study. If he was able to study some nights, during the day his rest was rudely disturbed and he was unable to regain his sleep.

"I want a record player," Rajiv finally said to his wife. "A loud-playing record player." Paula laughed and replied: "So, you've decided to join the villagers? Is that your answer?"

"It is the only answer. You fight fire with fire, hate with hate, noise with noise," Rajiv returned. "Besides, it was you who once recommended that I join them if I can't win them." It was not what she'd meant, but Paula would not protest. Rajiv was twenty-four years old, and she'd observed how the village noises had whittled down his nerves; his physique was thinner, and he had become pale, with blue veins puffing outward from his limbs. Paula would buy the record player. She too was disgusted at the church's attitude. Money was their goal, she'd long observed. It was not merely the loud and sterile sermons which affected her; as a teacher Paula was appalled at the licentious behaviour of several young couples: an attitude which the fatted pastor appeared not only to condone, but to encourage. It was Saturday, and she would buy the player this very morning. "Rajiv," she said, "what records should I buy?"

Rajiv contemplated the air for a long while. He laughed wryly in his mind to think he was an Indian but detested Indian songs. I-man had a monopoly on Bob Marley and Dick on calypso.

"Look for Tom Jones," he began, "and Englebert Humperdinck. You might find Johnny Matthis, Stevie Wonder, Aretha Franklin or Gladys Knight. Country-and-western is fine music." The pastor was shouting his sermon, and Paula said: "I will add Shadow and Arrow." Paula left for the city, and Rajiv, assaulted by the noise, strolled to the snackette. He spent the hours drinking rum and gossiping with the villagers. They were not as appalled as him. Still, they resented the alien church which had divided their village. Those who had converted had made themselves exclusive. There was much hate in the snackette and in the village as a whole. The evening had come, and Rajiv was half drunk when he saw his wife returning in a taxi. He left the snackette with a bottle of Vat 19 rum. As he neared his home, the mike coming from the church blasted his ears louder and louder. Rajiv thought it an obscenity, and he entered his house as if driven by rage and hate. He inspected the instrument of noise briefly, seeing that Paula already had Arrow set to play. "Wait," Rajiv said, gesturing with his hand. The pastor completed his sermon, and called on his flock to join him in singing a hymn. "Not yet," cautioned Rajiv again. He moved to mix a rum and coke.

They were singing the second hymn. Rajiv was so inured to the church, he knew their next item would be a silent prayer. The moment of silence arrived, and he was shocked to note the absolute silence in the entire village. He turned the switch and moved the volume upward. Arrow sang nothing. But the bass was exciting and loud enough to shake his galvanized roof. Rajiv was now stricken by his conscience, but he was doing what he felt he had to do. "This ought to teach the noise makers some respect for others," he shouted to Paula. His wife was dancing and enjoying the music. Rajiv felt that the village had violated his right to exist as a decent human being; they'd given him the licence to fight hate with hate. His stricken conscience, soothed with several drinks of Vat 19, gave way to his appreciation of Tom Jones and others.

The church retaliated in kind. The pastor employed all his volume so that his own voice was lost, and he was forced to readjust. They continued, seemingly undaunted until eight in the night. Rajiv was listening now to Englebert Humperdinck when I-man George appeared at his door-step. He came with Bob Marley.

"Ay, Rajiv," said he, "I and I hearing you loud, man. I want you to play this record."

"You having a Vat, George?"

"I and I not afraid of that," George grinned. Rajiv accommodated Marley on his player, while they drank and shouted and even read lips to understand their conversations. "Kaise Bane" was dead. Long live "Kaise Bane." I-man admitted he was free from racial prejudice, that he held no dislike toward foreigners. He was simply a West Indian who believed in Jah, and that Bob Marley was the reincarnation of the great Shepherd.

The church congregation had disappeared as they now drank in the gallery. The night was at last silent. Even the insects and the frogs appeared to be numbed by the day's din. "So you giving them church people some thunder, eh?" spoke George.

"I only giving them some of their own medicine. It is no longer possible for me to study, or to live. I have no peace of mind."

"All the people have to relieve their stress is their music, Rajiv. You can't stop that."

Rajiv had read those words in the newspaper, and he'd wondered where they'd really come from. He wasn't about to argue, or to point out that it was Sunardai's playing of "Kaise Bane" that drove George to Bob Marley. He felt a temporary and a kind of perverse satisfaction that he was able to retaliate with his own noise-making. The moment belonged to him. Just before George took his leave, Rajiv said: "I-man knows the golden rule: Do unto others as you would have others do unto you."

Mr Maharaj, pandit and yogin of Abdul Village was no longer on speaking terms with Rajiv and his wife. The pandit was holding a ten-day yagna, and he'd hired a mike to assist him in his long prayer. The church was affronted and the pastor voiced his anger at the obscene worshippers of idols and mud. The pastor's mike ended at eight o'clock; the pandit's continued until ten in the night. Calypso, reggae, oriental and occidental music overlapped and filled any remaining gaps of silence. Rajiv was fast becoming an alcoholic, and Paula the complaining wife. Mrs Abdul was ancient and ailing. Sybia spun records all day long with the intention of keeping out the other noises;

and the ailing mother complained and cried. Sybia was damning and cursing the Hindu yagna and the church all the while. Just as she shouted: "This is Caca Village!" her mother passed away.

Amidst the din of yagna and the church, the Abdul family held a single night of wake and buried their mother the next day. Rajiv, drinking alone in the snackette, was in deep thought. Not even death could move the villagers to share a moment of grief at Mrs. Abdul's passing. At his home, Rajiv attempted to reflect on the old lady in her earlier years, and to share a prayer with God for her passing. The noise proved an abomination and had crippled any ability to feel and, therefore, to think. It had for a long time crippled thought and his books had gathered dust. Paula and he quarreled daily now. Rajiv saw how his life was being led by noise, and was at a loss to do anything about it. This was a Sabbath morning. Paula was at school giving extra lessons, and he'd left the house wide open, with Arrow's bass pounding out its testimony against the church.

The pastor had seen this act in another light. "The house of Satan is before you," he'd made his flock to understand. "God will prevail!"

"Amen, hallelujah, praise the Lord," they'd chorused.

Rajiv was then known as the devil of Caca Village. Early one morning in the first week of June, I-man George was about, collecting whe-whe marks. The police were creeping up at his back, and a couple of villagers were shouting out: "Run, Ras, run. Police behind yuh." George stared at the villagers quizzically. Marley had destroyed much of his decibels and he was unable to hear or heed the warnings. For his illegal activity, I-man was to spend nine months in prison.

Paula, going on twenty-one, was endowed with a mature and exciting physique. The last Saturday of the month was their wedding anniversary, and Paula was determined to celebrate the event. Her husband was once as virile as the Babylonian goat. Rajiv was at his bottle, and all Paula's attempts to lure her husband to bed were to no avail. Rajiv was hearing the pastor's loud voice in his head. When church came to an end, and all had departed, he still heard the pastor's preaching. As the year progressed, Rajiv was more and more aware that his marriage was on the rocks. He kept putting off any attempt at returning to his studies. And in his impotence, he stared at his alluring wife in jealousy. Rajiv kept the bottle at his side.

One ten o'clock morning he heard shouting next door. The pandit's wife, Shanti, was screaming. Rajiv rushed outside only to check himself abruptly. Pandit Maharaj, staring straight ahead, was walking naked along the street. Rajiv felt his own degradation. Shanti, with a blanket was running toward her husband, covering his nudity from the mocking eyes of the villagers. In a short while, Shanti took her husband away to the doctor. Some three hours later, she returned and called to Rajiv. He stepped across with his bottle to Maharaj's gallery. Shanti spoke between her tears: "Doctor send meh husband to mad house. What I going to do? Look how meh children crying for dey father, eh?"

"Maharaj will get well, not to worry," Rajiv consoled.

"You think Maharaj going to get well, Rajiv?"

"Yes, but I don't understand how he got sick."

"People done saying is bad vision he see," Shanti related. "But I know better. Maharaj was deep in yoga, when he stay just so and get mad. Is every day he complaining about the church."

"He once told me that with yoga nothing could bother him," Rajiv pointed out.

"True. But I know is that church that put obeah in meh husband to send he mad. Last night, the pastor light candle on Maharaj head, and read bad psalm to trouble meh husband." Rajiv couldn't argue and took a drink from his bottle. It wasn't yoga, or panditry, or visions, or the church, he felt. It was what had destroyed his own life.

"Why are you drinking so much, Rajiv," Shanti spoke with concern. "Long time now I looking at you drinking, and I want you to stop." Rajiv stared at the pandit's wife for a moment. A well-kept housewife about his own age. He felt the need for another drink, before he said: "Your husband is not alone, Shanti. We will talk later."

That same evening, Paula and Rajiv had their last quarrel in Caca Village. Paula was fed up and could take no more. Rajiv had thrown away his university career for the bottle, and until he was prepared to do something about his deteriorating situation, she would be found at her mother's home. Rajiv stared in helpless silence as his wife packed and walked out of his life.

The following week with the pandit's wife for company, he increased his drinking. Rajiv fell sick and spent two weeks in bed. Then he made an attempt to clean house, to put his books and himself in order. Caca Village was now silent, except for the church and some short intervals of calypso.

Rajiv was reading, and then he thought he heard a bass playing. He stopped, straining his ears to listen. The sound was very faint, but it affected his thinking. He kept straining his ears. Rajiv threw his book aside and went out to his gallery. The church was empty, staring awkwardly at him. Now it was laughing, mocking him. It was his enemy, and it laughed at him all day. And when the evening came, the congregation arrived in cars of hooting and laughter. Then for three hours, the pastor roared, blaspheming the name of the Christ. From the darkness of his bedroom, Rajiv peered through the parted curtains. They were leaving in cheers of laughter. And the night was pitch black and silent. One hour later, Shanti heard the church's glass windows being smashed. By the time she looked across, the church was blazing in flames. The next day, the devil of Caca Village had disappeared.

The Insiders

MADELINE COOPSAMMY

The bank clerk asked politely, "May I help you?"

"Yes, please. I'd like to see Mr Langford." She looked at me. Surprise first, then pity flickered in her eyes.

"I have an appointment," I added quickly. Eighteen years old, I had graduated from a hard school. I had seen those looks since I was old enough to know.

"Could I have your name please?"

"Amelia Joseph. Mr Langford . . . I mean . . . Mr Ramdass sent me. He . . . Mr Ramdass . . . made an appointment for me."

"I see," the girl replied, looking at me as though to say, Who the dickens is Mr Ramdass? "Well, I'll see if he is free. Will you have a seat please?"

From where I sat, I could see her enter the manager's office. My handkerchief was twisted into a tight rope in my palm and my skirt tightened and I hurt when I sat down. Perhaps he'll insult me. With a population of more than ninety percent of black people on the island, somehow banks like these had managed to keep the racial composition of their employees as pure as the crystal mountain streams. Occasionally, there was a slight yellowing of the waters, or a gentle muddying, with here and there a Chinese face or a spice-coloured mulatto with Negro hair, flattened and combed flat, to ensure that its owner would pass muster.

Perhaps bank managers like Mr Langford have a well-tried formula for keeping out people like me. Perhaps the office boy will throw me out. Or perhaps it may be done more subtly. I'll be ignored for two hours and then I'll have to go away. I shook myself. *Don't be ridiculous. You've been watching too many American films. This is not the southern United States. This is Santa Maria, 1958. Things are changing.*

I could not forget the ease with which the interview had been arranged. A touch of the receiver. A cool voice saying, "Mr Langford, please." And then: "Mr Langford? This is Lal G Ramdass, here, from next door, from Sterling Hardware Company. Yes, Mr Langford. Sure. Oh, business is fine . . . Yes, I hope to be at the Rotary Dinner tonight. At the Queen's Park, is it? . . . Yes, The Poinsettia Inn is always more relaxing . . . Good. Well, Mr Langford, I have a young lady here who has just graduated from the Convent of the Sisters of the Sacred Heart. She's a very bright young lady and she's looking for a job. I was wondering if you'd care to have chat with her. Perhaps you might have something to offer her . . . Yes . . . Good. Monday at nine, then?"

I had held my breath, expecting at any moment there would be an embarrassed, "Yes, I see. . .Well, that's fine. . .Yes, I quite understand your position, Mr Langford."

There had been no such reaction at this end of the line. Instead, a triumphant, self-satisfied look on the face of Lal G Ramdass, as he turned to me.

"Well, then, there it is. As easy as clapping hands, wasn't it?"

I sat tongue-tied, the effect this man always had on me. I had known him all my life. To him I was still nine years old. He persisted in believing I was brilliant, and met my attempts at conversation with warm and instant agreement and the occasional flattering contradiction. Conversation was never a two-way street with Lal G Ramdass. He talked and the world listened. That is, his family, his friends and his employees. I often felt that everyone expected too much from him, and I sometimes felt guilty that I, too, depended heavily on him to solve the world's problems. But underneath his kindness there lay the shrewd business mind and a knowledge of people that enabled him to survive and carve a niche for himself in the tough world of Santa Marian commerce. He was the first East Indian businessman in the heart of the downtown business area. He spoke beautiful English, which set him apart from most of us who spoke our own brand of English, with our own unique accentuation. It was rumoured that he had taken elocution lessons. No one would ever have guessed that he had only an elementary school education. I told myself that I should not worry about his helping me too much, for after all wasn't he my godfather? In Santa Maria, the term "godfather" opened doors and gave privileges to the godfathered and unpleasant responsibilities to the godfathers. Through the lean years after my father's death, he had done his best to keep us from starving. We never called him "Uncle". It was always "Mr Ramdass," or in private, "Lal Gandhi." For he had assumed the name of the great Indian leader, probably hoping that something of its glory would rub off on him. Lal G Ramdass, like most third-generation East Indians in the polyglot Caribbean community that was Santa Maria, strove hard to retain his fast-breaking link with Mother India.

And now Lal G Ramdass had got me into this position and I wanted to run. The girl said something to the manager. He looked out. He saw me. He looked down quickly at his desk. He shrugged his shoulders. The girl came back. As she lifted the latch of the door to let me through, once again I saw the flash of pity across her face. *I don't want your damned pity. I'm superior to you. But you don't really know that, do you? You are neither black nor white. A "red-skin" nobody is all you are*. For this was the epithet that non-white Santa Marian people had coined to describe people like her.

The few steps to the manager's office seemed eternal. If he patronizes me, I'll tell him that he's nothing but an English empire builder who should go home where he belongs.

"Miss Joseph?" He waved vaguely in the direction of a chair opposite his own. "Sit down, please."

I sat down gingerly on the edge of the chair.

He leaned back in his chair and surveyed me speculatively. He interlocked his fingers and placed the tips of his forefingers on the edge of his nose. He wore a light-coloured business suit and he was an ordinary middle-aged white man, but to me he represented the worlds I could not enter. He stood for money, success, power, elegant houses in Hibiscus Park, acres of neatly tended grounds and the yet un-set sun of the British empire. I still aspired to his world, and in my heart I was sure that I deserved it. I was bright, I was young, I was not unattractive, and I was fearless. I could belong in his bank, for I felt I was as good as the other clerks. I had had the benefit of a convent education, a privilege not given to many non-whites in the 1950s. Our family was a respectable one. My father had been in business, and had it not been for his untimely death and the unscrupulousness of business managers, I would not have had to sit here at the feet of Algernon Langford, asking for a job in his bank. From the loose morals and social structures that existed in those lush Caribbean islands, our family was exempt. There were no common-law relationships in our family. Though the descendants of East Indian immigrants, we did not sell vegetables in the market place, or sweep the streets or plant cane. We could not then, be classified as coolies, the name that Santa Maria gave to East Indian peasants and labourers who tilled the land or worked at menial tasks, living in mud huts and storing their money in the earth under their beds.

Algernon Langford carelessly flipped through my credentials, which I had carefully presented to him on entering the room.

"You have your 'A' levels, I see?"

"Yes sir," I whispered eagerly, "in English, Geography and Spanish."

"Really?" He raised an eyebrow. Instead of feeling proud of my achievements, I felt embarrassed. I caught a glimpse of his eyes as he lowered them again and his look was cold and noncommittal. His eyes, his whole bearing, conveyed an attitude of dismissal. They said plainly: How dare Lal Ramdass subject me to this? What is Sterling

Hardware worth anyway? But I won't give him the chance to say I never granted the interview.

"Well, Miss Joseph." Algernon Langford's fingers reverted to the position they had held before, carefully interlocked over his nose as he relaxed in his comfortably upholstered swivel chair. "Do you think that you would like to make a career of banking?"

I don't give two hoots for banking. All I know is that this is a bright, shiny bank and I'll be the first of my kind to get in. All my friends will be consumed with envy and people will whisper: She works at the Commercial bank. I wonder if he asked that question to Nanette LaSalle, the French Creole girl I used to sit next to in class, whom I had noticed cashing outside? Nanette LaSalle had not even completed high school. My 'A' levels gave me entrance to university. What would he do, I wonder, if I said to him: No, I don't want to work in your bank. I'm sure it would be quite boring. I really want to be a journalist or radio announcer, or write novels, or go to university. But you see, I need a job first before I can even think of university and going away to England or the US or Canada, and anyway, I was sent here by Lal Ramdass and when Lal Ramdass is determined to be kind, you do what he says and ask no questions.

So I answered faintly, "Yes, sir." The monosyllables would be much more effective than an effusive dishonesty I could not bring myself to fake. The heady, instant success that working at the bank would give me could not be compared with the deepest longings of my soul. Who in my neighbourhood would respect me for working at the *Daily Telegram*? And what would the male-dominated paper offer me but the Women's Page or the Social News? What did I know of recipes and fashions and cocktail parties and the Country Club? Non-whites were not allowed there, though to read the Flamingo column in the *Daily Telegram* anyone would think that the whole of Santa Maria caroused happily there every weekend. But most of all, Lal G Ramdass did not know anyone at the *Daily Telegram*. Being a businessman, he knew Algernon Langford, who was aware of his assets and banked his money.

"Well, Miss Joseph." Mr Langford must have decided that this was taking up too much of his precious morning, so he suddenly leaned forward and said, "We'll let you know if anything comes up, of course. Though right now I can't say that I have anything to offer you."

Liar. Gloria Mckinnon was leaving to become an air hostess, a job even more prestigious than any at the bank. I'd heard that from the Sunday morning gossip on the church steps, the time and place for the gathering of the clan, all the recently graduated daughters of the Convent of the Sacred Heart. It was the time for hearing who had got jobs in the downtown businesses owned by the white French Creole and English aristocracy of the island. It was the time to face the sick feeling in the pit of my stomach when I realized that they were all getting jobs, and I wasn't. Everyone else had gone into their worlds, ones far removed from mine, now only two months since graduation. They had more influential godfathers than mine it would seem, or perhaps many, while I had only Lal G Ramdass.

I rose. I had read enough to know that the interview was now at an end.

"Thank you, sir," I said humbly, for in spite of the brave façade that I had constructed around me as I came into the office, I felt the same way I had felt on my first day at the convent, an awed little Indian girl who by some fluke was among the daughters of the wealthiest and most powerful people on the island. Over the years my pride in belonging to that revered institution had made me forget that I was in it, but not really of it. Now it was brought home to me what I really was. *You're only a little coolie girl,* as Santa Marians would say. *You have a brown complexion and long straight black hair, and though you're proud of your ancestry, in this town you'd be better off if you had some trace of white blood in your veins. If you were Chinese Negro you might have got the job, but being a coolie—and in the eyes of these people that's all you are—you can't make it. Your only contact is a godfather who is coolie too, so you can't make it.*

I walked out of the office, feeling his scorn burning at my back. I hoped desperately that the red-skin girl would not be there. Perhaps the Negro office boy would have to raise the latch of the door for me. But she was there and I had to face the humiliation of meeting her and I sensed she knew that I had failed. I could not even look into her eyes for I knew that the surprise and pity would now have changed to cool triumph.

Common Entrance

RAJNIE RAMLAKHAN

"Munna!"

"Yes Papa."

"Pick up yuh book right now! Ent you have to write Common Entrance jus now."

"Yes Papa." Munna reluctantly put away the Biggles she was reading and picked up her school bag. God, how she hated homework. Munna was attending Spring Village Hindu School which was just opposite her home. But Papa was forever on her case to do her homework.

"Man, I fed up with this chile yes," he grumbled. "She have to write exam soon, but you ever see her studying?" he asked Maya, the elder sister. But Maya buried her head in her math book and pretended to be concentrating deeply. Papa turned to his eldest child, Tej, but he was also busy with some textbook.

"Look at how you two does pick up yuh books every evening and do yuh work. I don't have to stick behind you all the time. Ent that is why all yuh win College Exhibition and going to good schools?" he asked of no one in particular. Papa carried on and on, not waiting for or expecting any answers. Tej and Maya knew the routine well. Every evening, shouting and screaming at Munna to study. Why didn't he leave her alone? If she wanted to fail, that was her business. She would pay the consequences.

Exactly the same thoughts were going through Munna's head. Why didn't Papa leave her alone to do the things she loved? Reading Biggles and Agatha Christie figured high on the list. But Papa was not impressed. Only reading textbooks impressed him. In fact, one day he caught Munna reading a comic book and boy, did he explode.

"Reading that trash!" he screamed. "You think reading comic book go put you anywhere? Those things does only corrupt children's minds. I don't ever want to see them in this house again," he warned.

And so comic books were banned along with other diminishing pleasures. But Munna could not see what the big deal was about Common Entrance. The work seemed simple enough. She had no difficulty in understanding or remembering it at all. She always did well in her homework and tests. And she usually finished her work quickly.

So why couldn't she fly a kite or pitch marbles with the boys? Munna enjoyed nothing better than a ramble by herself through the only savannah in Spring Village, chasing frogs and catching butterflies. Setting laglee to catch birds was a pleasure unsurpassed. Papa seemed to understand when she described her outings to him. He really did not seem to mind at all. But then some neighbour or relative would get to him.

"Lalman how you bringing up that chile. Whole day she playing like a tomboy. Is not so to bring up girls." Or, "Lalman, you ent think Munna should be studying her books for the Common Entrance? Look at how Kamla and Sudesh and Nanan studying hard. You think she could ever pass if she continue that way?" Or, "Lalman, why don't you keep Munna in the house and teach she some house work. Girls must learn to wash and sweep and cook. This playing marbles and cricket with boys whole day is not good behaviour for girls, man." And so the nagging would begin again.

Two weeks before the all important examination, which was being held for the first time, Papa suggested that Munna and Maya go to their Nani for the weekend in Pasea. Oh, what joy, thought Munna. She would be able to do the things she liked. As soon as they arrived,

Maya headed for the bedroom with some textbook. That girl was always studying and doing well in school. Papa was so proud of her and was always boasting about her to his friends. If only I could be more like her, Munna thought.

Munna, on the other hand, rushed outside to join the game of cricket that was in progress. The boys reluctantly let her join, for she was not an easy person to get out once she started batting. And Munna was in rip-roaring form that evening.

"Munna," shouted Nani. "Gyul come inside right now and pick up your book. Look at how hard Naresh studying."

Naresh was Munna's uncle but they were the same age. Her Nani and Mama were pregnant at the same time. Naresh was repeating the exam, having failed the first time. He really wanted to do well and studied hard all the time. Munna did not write the exam the first time because of her late entry into school. So what should have been a pleasant weekend turned out to be miserable. Munna spent the entire time staring blankly at some textbooks. She always did this when she was forced to study. But it seemed to make everyone happy. So why not?

The day of the examination came. Munna finished the work early. There was nothing to it. She knew most of the answers. When she got up to leave the room, she noticed most of the children concentrating deeply on the papers. She hesitated to leave. Only when three other pupils got up did she leave the room. What a relief! Now she was sure she could pursue her happy exploits in peace. But no. The talk went around. Munna could never pass that exam. It was so hard that she could not do it. So she left the room. And Papa went around with a thunderous expression on his face.

Then someone told him that a private school was holding their entrance exam soon and he should send Munna to write it. At least she would get the chance to attend high school and not waste her life away. Papa agreed. So Munna registered to write the exam for the private school and the studying started all over again. Luckily, she had mastered the art of pretending to study whilst her mind was roaming the open savannah or flying the blue skies with Biggles, her favourite hero.

The day before the exam results for the Common Entrance came out, the head master assembled the pupils together to read the results. He announced rather sadly that out of the thirty pupils sent up only five passed the exam. Not an unusual thing in those days of few secondary schools. He read the list. Four boys had passed and Sudesh, Naven and Naresh were not amongst them. Only one girl had passed the exam for the prestigious girls' high school next door that Maya had passed two years before. Her name was Munna.

Janjhat: Bhola Ram and the 'Going Away' Plan

NARMALA SHEWCHARAN

Me name Bhola Ram, rass. Not Totaram or Lallaram or stupidy Bill. Is not today me born. But is ah bad t'ing when you gat to please woman. Some people barn fuh beat dem and some people barn fuh please dem. Now all me life ah try to live like in de Geeta and de Ramine. You think dat woulda satisfy she. But ever since Dularie sissie and buddy gone America, and de nayhbour son down de road marry abroad, Lilwantie picknie all gone away and even Jaissie ah try to get somebady to marry to take she away even though she so old.

Dularie nah gat resting. Fust, she get it into she head dat is too late fuh she and me (t'ank de lard), so she try to marry off de big gyal. Deh all arrange it in America. You all know wha' become of dat? I tell you. Me shoulda sharpen me cutlass a little more dat day. Nah fuh de ducks Dularie cook as if she gat duck farm, but fuh dat no-good rascal, de one wha pretend to come fram America. Ah woulda sharpen de cutlass pon he backside if ah de catch he in time.

Anyway now she gat a new scheme up she ass and is involve she involving me again. I going to tell you all about it, but dat is she calling. She going to some Jandi and she want me to dress praperly because de people come fram abroad. Me gat a good mind to wear me backdam pants, but when Dularie start pon you even the cotton wool in you ears get weary. She bin specially to Gargetown to buy a silk kurta. One hundred US fuh it. Ah think she get rabbed. But you can't tell Dulaire anyt'ing. Dat is she shouting now.

"Man, you nah intend to come in fuh dress. Like you plan fuh turn up at the people place late." Me gat cows fuh mind, rice to plant and she studying people Jandi. "Look Jaissie coming up de road ahready. Is time we start hurrying."

De woman ahready gat me in the silk kurta. You woulda think me come from abroad too. Jaissie join us. I remembah Jaissie long ago. Was even talk of me marrying she, but she twist up she nose at de family, den she went and marry de pandit son and look wha' happen to he. Dularie never did like she, because she t'ink Jaissie is fat and anyway Jaissie looking fuh outside man, so she stop worrying about she and now deh de best of friends. Breeze cyan pass between dem.

Is like de whole of outside come to de Jandi. A whole heap a cars park up pon de dam and people dress up so much is like deh win de lottery. De pandit is a man fram outside too. Everytime he finish he Sanscrit, yah talk bout "the people in New York." I t'inking dis going to get Dularie more wild. Is not'ing going to stop she now. She hunch me in me side everytime somet'ing connect, but I ain't gat time fuh dat. Ah come here to a Jandi. But now otha people mekking noise now so you can't hear wha de pandit sehing. People t'ink deh have lil money, deh buy God. So he stop de Jandi. Is a fight going on pun de road. Dem lil cacarass boys wha' nah know how to wash deh behind, smoking dope and fighting over woman. Deh nah frighten nobady. Except Pujarie. Pujarie. Hah. I gon tell you 'bout him. But now de Pujarie in between dem telling dem to have manners and respect and some of dem high and deh want to argue but deh looking scared and remembering de last time somebody argue with Pujarie wha' happen to he.

Dat was de time when Nimric and he family move here to take deh inheritance. Now in dis place people nah have racial. Everybady ah live peaceful. Ruth, dat was Nimric auntie, she used to get along wid everybady. She go to people Jandi and people go to she Christian work. She was de midwife here. Everybody treat she like deh own.

She get a big funeral. She nah had children so the house went to de nephew. He come here wid he town style looking to pick story and play wrong and strong. De first man he pick a story wid was Manbodh. Now everybady know dat long ago, Manbodh nah tek raaspass easy. He is de first man wid de cutlass. But Manbodh papers coming thru' soon at de embassy and he nah want not'ing to hambug dat. So Nimric t'ink he get away wid it, so he t'rowing he weight around, puff up like a turkey cock, picking pon otha people. But den he want fuh go play like pon Pulmattie, Paro sixteen-year-old daughta, an' Paro ah Pujarie sister.

I know Pujarie better as Babsie, when he didn't go around raising jumbie, and when we was all small boys togetha, grazing de cows and trying to mek bushrum easy in de backdam when nobady around. In dem times he was a different kinda person. He nah coulda even fight praperly. Me remembah how he sid down and cry like a gyal one time in de rice fields when Zappo beat he up. But dese days Pujarie mekking up fuh dat. He disappeared fuh couple days one time and when he come back, he tell everybady how he bin underwater, getting up he spiritual powers. Now he talking wid de Devis, de Dutch people and people t'ink he ah de biggest jumbie man round here. Except dat you nah suppose to call him dat. Because Pujarie on God side, except as far as Nimric concerned. De man was he worst nightmare. Dis is wha' happen. Pujarie send a message around, telling Nimric to keep far from he family. De man wha' bring de message try to mek Nimric understand.

"Listen," he tell Nimric, "dis man gat powerful t'ings wid he. He wake up all kinda dead. You know dah man wah deh seh bury in Gargetown, only nah he in the coffin. Pujarie gat hold of he ever since, when he body fall out de plane on de way fuh preserve he to stay just like how he dead forever. And dat not all–" But Nimric nah listen.

"He can fool allyuh coolie," Nimric seh. But de man still ah try.

"Listen," he almost ah beg Nimric because he bin good friends wid Ruth and he nah want see no harm come to she family. "Listen," he seh, "dat not all. He do Kali puja. You nah want to mess wid dis man." But Nimric just ah laugh and when Pulmattie pass by he house again, he kissing he mout' at she and trying to pull at she sleeve.

Well Pujarie nah botha wid no moe messengers dis time, except fuh de dead fowlcock wha' deh by Nimric gate next marning, blood all over de place. Nimric pick up de fowlcock, cussing all de time. But you could see he look funny. People seh was he own self he do wrong to hold the dead fowl cock and dat he bring it all pon heself. First, de gyal he live home wid tek in wid stomach pain. She go ah de hospital, but it nahwuk so den she gone to a lady deh call motha in de next village, an' de lady tell she to pack she bags and run. Could be she coulda just seh dat because de live home woman had all dese marks pon she back where Nimric practice pon she. But dat was de last time Nimric see she.

He still nah worried and still ah try to play bad. But den the mini bus he driving give up e' ghost. E' just refuse to start. No matter how much Nimric and de one man he had wukking wid he and de people he beg from de roadside try to push and tug not one t'ing coulda move it. Deh open up de bus and spend a whole week 'pon it. He lucky he nah get he dead den fram de steel dat run in he foot when he de crawling out fram under de bus. As fuh de bus, it still lying by de mechanic shop whe' deh push it because Nimric nah gat money to re-pair it. Look is round de corner from de Jandi house. If you strain you neck you can see it. Dat old dusty, bruk-up van pon de dam.

Anyway, dat was just de beginning of de luck fuh Nimric. Every-body sehhing he done dead ahready. But he still try to play de fool even if he hopping on de foot wha' get bore. He gat a job as a conduc-tor. But dat nah last. Some lady from town run he wid an umbrella for troubling she daughta. He nah lose he job fuh dat because dat is wha' all dem conductors does do. Is Nimric heself decide to hide because he frighten de umbrella woman and anotha' lady who was waiting at de bus terminal fuh he, sehhing she want fuh talk 'bout money fuh she child. So he stay home waiting fuh de bad luck to pass. Only he is a man wha' can't sit still, so he gat fuh go exercise in deh backyard, walking round barefoot and fergetting de cut in he foot because it nah hurt no more. Dat is when de bone fram de fowlcock run in he foot.

Now is ah funny t'ing. Nimric fling dat fowlcock on de junk heap pon de dam and when he mash it in he backyard he t'ink is de Pujarie wuk again. But was de people who live near de junk heap. Deh nah want not'ing to do wid Nimric and he fowlcock. You all know a fowlcock bone nah dat sharp but if you coulda hear Nimric holla you woulda t'ink is ten woman in de labour room. Anyway dat was de end fuh him. De place gat a sign fuh sale, but nobady nah come to buy. Is dat old house near de main road. De one wid de cabwebs. Now I hear he in Suriname trying to get dem Jukka people to help tek off de obeah.

"You nah come eat, Bhola."

Is Dularie come back from sharing de parsad. Dularie help mek de parsad, so she gat to share. Dularie always gat to be in the middle of every t'ing. Sometimes I t'ink if de pandit nah watch out, she would tek over de wuk. Me ah wan strong Hindu man. Nah get me wrong. But ah like a peaceful life. And now wid dis stupidness she gat in she head 'bout America–look dat is Jago coming fuh to talk wid me. She nah gon like dat. Jago bin America and come back. He nah like de place. But people seh is because he can go and come anytime he please dat he gat so much style. If he de had to buy visa, woulda be a different tune. Ah t'ink de embassy people really stupid nah fuh give everybady visa. Because people nah really want to live in America. Deh just want to go and come. Like Dularie. She seh she want to go live in America. But mark me words. Once she get visa, she gon be in and out of dere like she gat sting a nettles.

Jago gat on a silk kurta like me, but de clath a shine more.

"Sarju ah do good wuk. Everybady talk good 'bout him in New York," he seh to me as he sid down pon de bench. Sarju was the pandit.

"So you going back soon, Jago boy?" He shaking he head. "I not like de cold. De place different. Is only nice fuh old people if you want to live fuh free. But if you gat money is better over here." Jago got plenty money. I tell he how Dularie gat it in she head to go live in America.

"An admire Dularie, she gat plenty strengt'. Any'ting she mek up she mind fuh do, she gon get thru' wid." Dis is nah wha' Dularie t'ink ah listening to. I could see she swell-face from far, but when she meet she smiling at Jago and asking he 'bout all de family back in New York, even de ones wha' barn over dere dat she nevah meet, like she ah all of dem personal friend. But she nah really want me sitting, talking wid Jago.

She pull me over to where Jaissie and Babsie, the one wha' call heself de Pujarie now sitting. Deh been cooking up t'ings. I can smell it fram far. When Dularie put she mind to it, she can get people fuh do anyt'ing fuh she. But I hear dem embassy people nah easy to move. De Pujarie might have to go underwater again to get more powers. De Pujarie stretch he lip wide, showing all he thirty-two.

"Bhola Ram," he seh. A couple ah people look 'round and den deh look away. Deh nah want to know wha' going on.

"De Pujarie ah come to lunch Saturday. He gon bring some friends wid him," dis ah wha' Dularie tell me. Jaissie jump in, "I gon come and help you cook, Dularie. I can go to town anotha day." De Pujarie smiling at she. He always de gat he eye pon Jaissie. Jaissie get turn down at de embassy ah couple a time. Ah nah t'ink Dularie worry 'bout she getting in de way. Maybe de Pujarie planning fuh help all two of them. Ah wish deh would keep me out of it. Saturday ah was going to dig up de tomatee bed and ah de plan to keep an eye on Blackie. She not milking good. Dularie looking at me funny. Ah seh to de Pujarie, "Ah gon see you Saturday den." De Pujarie gone to talk wid some otha people who gat troubles. Since de man wha' dead now, de one wha' tell everybady to eat rice flour, carry de country to de dawgs, everybady gat troubles.

Dularie seh she gon tell me later wha' going on. Now she want to talk wid some of de people wha come in fram America. Is two big ladies. Deh come and sit next to she. Jaissie gone off. Ah could see she talking to the de pandit, but he gat a wife, so she outa luck dere. De two ladies wear real fancy sari, and deh hand and deh neck weigh down wid gold. Deh mekking a fuss over Dularie. She mekking friends wid dem, talking 'bout Richmond Hill and how everybady moving outa de area because it getting bad. One a de lady shaking she head. "Is so," she seh, "we moving to Long Island soon. Is a better place fuh family."

"Dat is where we gon go when the visa come thru.' Is what you t'ink, Bhola," she hunching me again.

"Ah nah mind where ah go," I seh. Just so long as me cows wid me, ah wanted to tell she. But me know dat would cause she fuh tek off pon me. De lady dem looking at me and smiling now. Me wid me nose mash up fram dat time when ah de fall off de tractor and bend it up pon de big stump dat was sticking out de field.

"You lucky," deh tell Dularie. Dularie smile so much you t'ink she jaw gon get lock off. But she nah intend dem to leave 'till she mek full use of she luck. By de time allbody get up, Dularie had arranged to stay wid dem fuh couple weeks when she reach ah New Yark. Ah have to go pelt down some mangoes from de tree because she pramise to give dem achar fuh dem to take back. She talking 'bout de full-ripe mangoes on de otha tree, too, but ah t'ink dat get saved. Ah hear de people at de New Yark airport ah tek 'way all de mangoes. Nah matter how much you hide it in yuh suitcase, deh know where to find it. And you all know how dem can wrap up t'ings fine fine and push it all over de suitcase so that dem immigration people have to tumble long but deh still ah fin' it.

Anyway ah t'ink is time to leave, and ah getting up, but she seh, "Siddown and wait." She gat to go talk to Pouti. People nice to Pouti because of de bad luck she had at de embassy. But Dularie just fast wid sheself. Is not dat she want to console the gyal. She want to find out everyt'ing wha' happen. Even if she wasn't planning to go fuh she own visa she woulda still want to know. But is Pouti own motha fault because of how she treat de boy, Bara, wha' Pouti marry, trying to mek he leave she daughta' even after deh marry. Roop, the motha' she t'ink she de best t'ing in de village. Is nobady good enough fuh she daughta, unless he gat plenty money. She turn de whole dowry story upside down. Dat woman never de want he fuh a son-in-law. You shoulda hear how she used to cuss de gyal when she fasten she eyes pon Bara.

"Dis kiss-me-ass gyal nah hear. Dis kiss-me-ass gyal want to kill me. When dis kiss-me-ass gyal see me in de grave den she gon be happy. Me send she a school and she a study man. Wha' God gie me ayuh kiss-me-ass children fuh, me nah know." It was kiss-me-ass dis and kiss-me-ass dat. Even she hear Bara paper come thru' to go America, she nat satisfy because she still t'ink he good fuh not'ing and she want to harrass he to mek he fuh understand dat he really lucky she gree to the wedding. But dat Roop had anotha scheme up she ass because she only agree to de wedding to keep she daughta under control. She de hoping dat when Bara go 'way, Pouti would stop behaving like jumbie deh pon she and look 'round fuh somebody better. And Roop nah want he in de family so bad, dat she really believe he nah go look round fuh Pouti when he meet over dere. So Roop tell she new son-in-law dat he nah must go in de bedroom wid de gyal after he just marry she. But t'ings nah wuk out because two years pass and the man wha' Roop had she eye on fuh Pouti marry someone else and Pouti still ah wait pon Bara. He nah come back to de country since he wukking hard pon Liberty Avenue, trying to save money to buy house fuh when Pouti meet over.

She paper come thru and deh call she fuh interview. But you know how dem embassy people stay. Deh want fuh know people bedroom story. Dem ah ask you if you find de gyal good. And de want to know wha' colour was de underwear. And piece piece how you deh wid she. Dat is chop up story. Long ago India Babu woulda tek a cutlass and mince dem piece piece by now fuh dem kind of t'ings deh want to know 'bout a man wife and he personal business. Look when Kunti spread she underclath near de bedroom window de otha' day somebody pass and see it and go tell de man. She husband beat she. And dat was just 'bout five, six years now. But dese people deh come fuh complete Kaljug.

So when deh ask Pouti she bedroom business, is wha' you t'ink she could ah seh wid de embassy man skinning he eye pon she. She try to tell he how she motha tell dem fuh wait, but was de worst t'ing she coulda do in she life. Because de embassy people not used to dealing with trut' and deh tell she to go and appeal. Now ah hear Bara planning to come home to do everyt'ing praperly, and put de motha-in-law in she place. But deh have to wait because he buy a ticket pon Guyana nonstop. You all know wha' happen dere. Roop going round de place crying but nobady nah gat time fuh she. De otha' daughta tek home one man. She seh she nah wan' to be like Pouti, and Roop cyan open she mout' and tell she not'ing. Dat is Roop coming over here now. Ah nah want to talk to she, so ah gon move.

"You hear 'bout me gyal?" She walk fast and pull me by me kurta before ah coulda go anyplace. "You hear wha' deh do to Pouti?" De whole of de country must ah hear by now. Roop gat a rivermout'. I try to pull me kurta outa she hand. Dularie never around when you really need she. "Ah see de Pujarie was talking to ayuh."

"Is me old friend," ah tell she. Ah really looking round now fuh Dularie.

"Ah know ayuh is old friend. You t'ink he could help Pouti. If you talk to he fuh me—" Ah pull me kurta out she hand. Ah nah want to get mix up wid dis. Is bad enough wid Dularie and she nonsense.

"Goh sell a cow," I tell she.

"Is wha' you sehhing. You want buy me cow?"

"Me gat plenty cow. I just trying fuh help. Sell a cow. Send Bara money fuh de plane ticket." She let out a holla so hard, like she mumma dead. Everybady look round. Is a good t'ing ah get she han' off me kurta.

"Goh sell me cow fuh dat good-fuh-not'ing–" She de calling him good-fuh not'ing so lang she feget dat she change she tune. "Is me daughta. Ah would help she if ah can, but ah only gat two cows. Dem children fatha nah lef not'ing much when he gone to de Lard." She was always a stupidy woman, wid all she t'ink she face like de moon. Ah nah gat no time fuh dis.

"If me see de Pujarie, ah gon tell he you want to see he. You shoulda go talk to he youself. He bin round here just now."

"But he nah come to you house Saturday, Bhola?" Is wha' stupidness ah hearing? Is how everybady know bout dis so quick.

"You go talk to Dularie. She is de bass." I see Jago standing by heself and I run to stand near he to escape de woman. She nah like Jago long time now ever since she husband sell Jago piece ah de land deh have by de Plantation and he sell it back a year later fuh more money. If she wasn't so stupid in the first place she daughta would get thru' at de embassy.

I find out from Dularie later dat de people she expecting to come fuh lunch is fram de embassy. One of dem. De otha man is he friend. Early Saturday marning, me get up fuh go backdam, but she collar me by de door and tell me dat after ah milk de cow ah must come straight back and nah go dig up no tomatee bed. Me ain't able wid dis foolishness no more. But you nah could a ever argue wid Dularie. When ah meet home back, Jaissie in de kitchen grinding de dhall fuh de dhall puri and de big gyal ah peel de aloo. Dularie grinding up de massala on de sill, wid plenty garlic and onion and plenty peppa. She seh she nah gon use de blender when she gat special people coming. Blender massala nah taste de same way like de old-time massala. Deh want me fuh go sharpen de cutlass again because is duck curry, Dularie cooking again. And ah sharpening up me cutlass and t'inking is de last ah do dis. Ah was one big joke because de big gyal still nah marry yet.

But Dularie happy. You gon t'ink she in New Yark ahready. She even ah sing one song, de one fram dat movie wid Meena Kumari and Shakuntala. Is de song wha Shakuntala sing because Meena Kumari only get dem sad songs in all dem movies and she mek people cry steady. Dularie get a nice voice but de onion and pepper mek it sound like she gat somet'ing in she mout'. Is when Jaissie join in de song dat ah want to go find me cotton wool. She voice so broad, you guh t'ink she ah Sham Sham Begum sistah. Dularie de want me dress up in de kurta again, but Jaissie tell she is 'merican people. De kurta nah mean not'ing to dem, so she bring out a white shirt wha' de hang up in de wardrobe lang time now and tell me put it on.

Pujarie bring a whole set a people when he meet—de boy wha' does help he, two of de boy, family an' a lady wha' he meet pon de road dat looking fuh he to help she. I see Dularie suck she teet' when she see dem at de gate, but she smile at de Pujarie and welcome all a dem like she long lost relative.

"Is wha' happen to de people, Pujarie?" she pull he aside. She t'inking bout de duck curry and ah get upset. "Nah Bel Air Springs dem a come fram. Is a long drive. But deh gon meet soon," he tell she. But he gat some work to do fuh de lady wha' he meet pon de road. She a cry so much he feel sarry fuh she. I see Dularie twist up she face, but she tell he to go in de hall, dat nobady nah gon disturb dem dere and she find match fuh to light de camphor to start he gymnastics.

De lady hold on pon Dularie and tell she "a t'ousand t'anks," calling she sistah and sehhing she gon never feget she gratitude to Dularie fuh letting she come in de house fuh the Pujarie to help she. Not as lang as she live. Dularie still t'ink bout she duck curry but she now ah feel better bout de lady and ah tell she dem ah de same people and deh have to stick togetha. De curry still ah cook pon de fireside, but yuh cyan move Dularie namore fram de hall. She gat fuh know everyt'ing wha' a go on. She nah worry bout de hall and if deh gon mess up de place because last night she rearrange everyt'ing. She mek me move de big sofa and divide up de hall so dat all de fancy t'ing wha she gat fram America could still show fuh de big shat people wha' nah show up yet. But she leave space fuh de Pujarie in case he decide fuh call up when he meet even in front ah de embassy people.

Ah tell Dularie ah gon stay on de verandah to watch out fuh de embassy people as ah nah really want to mix up wid wha' going on. I sit in me racking chair, but ah could see wha' goin on inside. De Pujarie now sitting flat pon de white cotton sheet wha' Dularie spread on de floor. De boy wha' help he ah bring out stuff fram de bag to assist de Pujarie wid he calling up. He two family, de man and de lady gone and plant deh behind pon de sofa, sitting on de cover wa' come fram outside and wha' Dularie bring out specially for de embassy people. An deh come in de house wid deh shoe on. Dularie wouda done tell dem somet'ing if was not fuh de Pujarie.

Ah nah know not'ing bout Babsie powers but one time he tell one lady bout how she husband gon fall sick and next day de man in hospital and ah hear he tell a woman wha' come fram till a Leguan bout she childhood story whe' some man interfere wid she, wha' only she de know bout. He gat a bottle a rum by he side because when he not playing in de Kali church he does bring up different t'ings. Sometime even people wha' dead. Now he talkin in a strange voice because he start playing already and he telling de lady dat she enemy bury somet'ing in she yard and dat she have to do a wuk. I see Dularie turn and watch me an ah know she t'inking bout she front yard. I nah plan to dig up no front yard. Me gat a tomatee bed to dig. The Pujarie ah whisper whisper to de woman now. Ah nah can hear anyt'ing. I see Dularie ah crane she neck to hear and de two people wha' siddown like a jackass pon de sofa tryin hard to listen. I nevah see poeple wha' a play talk easy yet. But is just a temporary situation because afta' dat de Pujarie start shouting loudly and jumping up and spinning like he nah can control heself, and de boy wha' help he ah try hard to calm down t'ings and de two people pon de sofa look real frighten, and even Dularie pull back a little.

"Calm down, Baba, calm down," de boy ah seh all de time, but de Pujarie now pon one foot, shaking he hair all ovah de place and ah jump up and down like he gon bruk up de place. Ah see Dularie look at de floorboard and ah could almost hear she wondering if she shoulda tek dem in de downstairs room where de floor ah concrete. De Pujarie stop he dance and de boy wha' a help he seh, "Is a calmer spirit come now. Yuh know he nah can control dem always." De lady wha' de Pujarie ah help start cry, but she cry out of gladness.

"Everyt'ing you seh was true, Baba. Me nah de want tell you everyt'ing because ah shame so much."

"You nah can hide not'ing fram de Baba," de boy wha ah help seh. De wuk finish now and deh tell she to come back next week at de Pujarie house. Dularie offa de lady food, not de duck curry because she seh dat still pon de fire, but some boulanger and aloo cury she cook fuh breakfast. I see a car coming up and ah holler tell she. Dularie rush to de verandah. Is two men in de car.

"Deh come, deh come," she run back to tell de Pujarie. She run down de stairs and almost pull de people out de car. De two men wha' come out a talk like Guyanese.

"He had a crisis," one of dem seh, "he wife a get picknie and he had to go to de hospital. He pramise to come next week." I see Dularie mash she mout' pon a long suck teet'. But de two men gat good news fuh de Pujarie. Is somebady passport deh bring. It gat a visa inside. De Pujarie seh he de praying lang fuh de man wha' own de passport and he glad dat he finally get thru'. De men tell Dularie nah fuh worry. Dat now de embassy gat anotha' picknie he gat mo' expenses and he glad fuh help out people.

Deh all go in de hall. De Pujarie start shaking again and dis time he pointing at Dularie. When he open he mout' is a different voice. De voice tell she, "You goin meet pon plane but it goin to tek a long time. A lot of t'ings come cross yuh way." De Pujarie ketch back heself and he siddown now pon de sofa and sehhing how he feel hungry. But Dularie want to know is wha' he mean. De boy wha' help de Pujarie try fuh tell she dat sometime when de Pujarie ah play, he nah always know wha' goin on.

"Dat duck curry smellin nice," one of de two people wha' come fram Gargetown seh. But Dularie really vex now.

"Nah worry Dularie," de Pujarie tell she, "even if yuh luck crass, remembah you gat me me pon yuh side." I could see dat Dularie nah know wha' fuh do. If was anybady else but de Pujarie she woulda done put dem outa de house lang. De lady wha' de Pujarie help earlier get up fram de corner ah de floor whe' she bin siddown. She eat she plate clean ah de boulanger and aloo curry. She try fuh t'ank Dularie again, but Dularie nah gat time fuh she no moe. She tell de Pujarie to call up again. She want to hear more bout wha kind cross she gat. De duck curry still ah cook anyway. You could see de Pujarie looking tired, but he seh he willing fuh try and help she. But Dularie nah want everybady know she business. She call me fuh carry de guests pon de verandah, de two people fram Gargetown and de two wha' come wid de Pujarie and give dem rum and sweet drinks till she and de Pujarie done deh business.

Is a sweet-talking spirit come pon de Pujarie dis time. He tell Dularie how she ah good-looking woman. I watch de Pujarie funny fram where ah sittin. He tell she dat to get rid of de bad luck, she gat to hold a jag and feed people, but dat nah fuh worry too much because she gat a strong spirit. Dularie want to know bout de visa. When she gon get it. De Pujarie nah seh not'ing fuh a lang time, den he tell she dat he see some important news fuh she next week but it gat some bad news wid it too. Dat she must patient. Ah coulda tell he dat Dularie nah know wha' name patience.

Ah nevah see two peple could eat so much like de two men fram Gargetown. Deh eat fuh twenty people, like deh just come outa jail and all de time dem ah seh how deh nevah taste duck curry so sweet. Deh tell she deh gon have news fuh she soon and dat deh hope fuh bring de embassy man next time deh visit. I t'inking dat it nah gat plenty duck left in de duck pen, and dat if Dularie keep dis up she gon have to goh buy duck fram de man wha' a sell down de road.

All week Dularie looking out fuh de postman and a wait fuh de telephone to ring and every marning she pray one hour extra because she frighten bout de bad news wha' de Pujarie seh gon come wid de good news. Friday, de postman bring two letters, but is nah not'ing much in dem. But late dat day, a special delivery come. Is a lettah fram de embassy. Dularie grab de lettah and seh she de know de Pujarie was a great man. She feget all de talk bout de bad news. De lettah gat me name pon it. Deh callin me fuh to come and uplift me visa. Ah get a shock. Ah had to siddown fast.

"Is how deh gon send you a visa and nat send fuh me too," Dularie rowing. She announce dat she gon go wid me to tell dem bout de mistake. I try to tell she dat me nevah apply fuh a visa, dat how deh could call me fuh one. She nah listen. "De Pujarie know wha' he doing," she tell me. De van wha' bring de letter come back and blow in front de house. Deh man want de letter back.

"Is a mistake," he seh, "I deliver de lettah to de wrong Bhola Ram." Dularie nah wan give de lettah back.

"Everybady know dat only one Bhola Ram live around here."

De man tell she de lettah address to Bhola See Ram. Is true. Me start fuh breathe back normal again. I know Dularie woulda mek me go on de plane if me de get de visa. All me could see was me cow lef behind and me in some cold place buying milk in bottle. Dularie nah tek lang to recover. She t'ink everyt'ing was a test, to test she fait'. She know dat she have to go and do de jag like de Pujarie seh, dat everyt'ing gon be okay and she gon meet on de plane. Me pick up me backdam hat. Dularie so happy planning de jag wha' gon help get rid of she bad luck dat she nah even notice Bhola Ram tiptoeing out de house. I goin to milk de cow. Too much janjhat around.

Blame

HARISCHANDRA KHEMRAJ

My name is Haridas. Not Harry Das or even Hari Das. They're all pronounced about the same but I know I'm Haridas. It means God's servant—whatever that means. On my birth certificate the column headed with the words "Name of the Father" is filled in with the words "Not stated". That means I am a bastard—whatever that means. My mother deserves no blame for this.

Nor does she deserve blame for what I'm about to do. She'll get it nonetheless—probably most from herself—and the guilt and remorse on top of all else might finally be too much even for her. She had been knocked down many times before and somehow managed to get up and carry on. The poisonous dart I'll leave behind is to make sure that when she falls this time it would be without hope or desire to get up. Die quickly, Ma.

In a sense you died when that home-made concoction exploded so many years ago. But how could you know? You didn't even know there had been an explosion until young Jai-Jai came rushing in excitedly with the news.

Young Jai-Jai, whose black-and-white picture, faded now and frayed around the edges, you keep wrapped in plastic and memories in the bruised grip under your bed. Young Jai-Jai, a huge wave pasted over his forehead with what—Brilliantine? Camera-shy eyes and a squeezed grin do not altogether disguise the look of someone quite pleased with himself. Twenty years old and healthy; just married to a beautiful girl; a dowry of two hundred and fifty-one dollars in solid cash—come on, world, I'm ready to take you on! Young Jai-Jai—your husband, Ma, though not quite.

You've had men after him, but you still love that boy, don't you? There had not been time enough between you for habit and use to mould him into settled forms in your mind and you are free to create and recreate him however suits your fancy. And yet, to me, with whom he spent no time at all, he is a stiff, doll-like figure, which yields to pressure but quickly snaps back to its original shape. He has never been in my mind a friendly or hostile rival for your affections, and I've never been able to maintain for long any conception of him as someone to love or hate, esteem or despise, emulate or reject. I do not feel any voids in me which he might have filled. To me he is young Jai-Jai, and except as a passing object of pity, he would have been of little interest to me but for his marriage to you.

It was an arranged marriage, but Mother told me it was also a love match. Jai-Jai had been courting her on the sly for almost two months before Goolbadan the barber came into the act. When she doesn't say it's all karma, Mother usually says it came about because her brother Premnauth was struck down with polio and she had to leave school to help out at home while her parents were out working on the farm.

"Inside! Inside! Anybody home?"

It was just after midday on a Tuesday. Savitri could always place the day precisely. Easter vacation had ended and her other brothers had started back to school the previous day, leaving her once again alone with Premnauth. She had rocked and crooned him to sleep in the hammock just minutes before, and now some idiot had to come bawling in the street outside. She did not answer. She rocked the hammock easily again. The idiot would go away.

"Inside! Inside! Anybody home?"

There he was again! She knew it was a "he" from the voice. A strange voice. It didn't sound menacing, and at the time the voice of an unseen stranger didn't automatically raise alarms in her. But she was getting damn vexed.

"Inside! Ins–"

"What you want?" She had stepped outside and closed the door quietly behind her. The voice had sounded young, and if its owner was young enough for her to be rude to, she intended to be rude. He was, and she hoped she sounded so.

The stranger didn't seem to notice. He walked to the yard gate and, putting a hand on the small hoop keeping the gate closed, said again, quietly this time and looking straight at her, "Anybody home?"

Savitri knew why he was asking the question this time. It wasn't considered proper for a young woman to allow a man into her yard, let alone her house, if there was no one else around. But she didn't like how he had phrased the question. Why hadn't he said "Anybody else"? What was she—a something, not a somebody? Or did he consider her too young to be a person in her own right? She, who in just another five months would be fifteen and who everyone said was big for her age. Keeping her features stern, she pulled in her breath a bit—not all the way—while running her hands swiftly, but as though purposelessly, down her hips. Aha! Impressive, isn't it? You wouldn't get a second look though. That was just to show you that although I might not be quite a woman yet, I'm almost there. I'm not to be ignored, least of all by someone as young-looking as you. Why, you can't be more than eighteen yourself, Mister Wave-hair.

"My brother is in the house." She knew she shouldn't have said that. It was a way of telling him he could enter the yard if he wished. But poor, sick Premnauth could not be considered a suitable person for the purposes of propriety. And why had she spoken with such grammatical precision? She hardly ever spoke like that at home.

She wasn't trying to impress the fellow, was she? He didn't have on a tie and therefore couldn't be someone important. Also, his plain cotton shirt and khaki pants suggested he wasn't from a rich family. And if confirmation were needed, you couldn't get better than those Cebo shoes he had on. Her brothers wore that same brand to school. It was strong and cheap but hell to break in, and hardly anyone with money would put up with that painful process when Coste Ilos and Clarks were available.

As to his looks, nothing spectacular, maybe even a bit below par. His limbs were big but they seemed underworked, soft, and surely could not be depended on to tote bags of paddy—or lift a girl, no, a young woman, on his shoulders and make her yell and laugh and beg to be put down. And those pointed ears couldn't do anyone good in the looks department, nor could that nose puffed out like a gul-gula with holes.

She had to admit she liked his thick black hair though, and especially that big wave in front, which could sink a balahoo, as the girls liked to say. Most of the young men these days were wearing hair so short it stuck out like day-old grass. She had always liked waves. She had a vague memory of her father with a lovely wave in front, which she used to play with when he lifted her squealing, high in the air, and then settled her astride his neck. But her father didn't wear waves anymore. He was fast getting bald and paid scant attention to the scattered bits of gray left on his head.

"Down, Ricey! Down, No-name!" she quieted the dogs. They had been growling ever since the stranger approached the gate, and when he lifted the hoop and seemed about to push the gate open, they jumped out from under a guava tree and, barking furiously, were charging forward with seemingly murderous intent. The hoop was dropped back in place and Mister Wave receded with a startled leap, as though bounced back by an invisible wall.

Savitri snickered but quickly assumed a serious face again. Little did he know that Ricey and No-name were much bark, little bite, and that a single authoritative shout would send them scurrying off to bluff and blow from a safe distance. It might be fun to go up to the gate as though to let him in and then suddenly yank it open, say "hootsim" to the dogs and watch him trying to negotiate bumps and holes at full speed, with Ricey and No-name baying at his Cebos. That would teach him to talk properly to girls who were almost fifteen and big for their age besides.

But it was just a thought. Strangers were not treated like that in Matori. And looking more carefully now at the one about thirty feet away, she couldn't help but feel a bit sorry for him. His shirt was dark with sweat and his shoes powdery with dust. He must have been walking a long way in the hot sun and had to be tired and thirsty. He now looked too pitiful to have set out to be offensive to her.

He seemed to become aware he was under scrutiny and of a sudden began glancing around him and up and down the street. Was he thinking of leaving? Savitri found she didn't want him to. It wasn't that she was attracted to him, or any silliness like that, she told herself. It was simply she couldn't let him go away with a bad impression of her. "Wait!" she gestured with a raised palm and smiled. He looked startled again but he didn't leap. He leaned forward as though apprehensively. She dispatched Ricey and No-name to their shed at the back of the yard. "Back! Run! Back!" The dogs ran out of sight behind the house. Had they woken up Premnauth with their barking? She listened for sounds within but none reached her.

She had told the stranger to wait and thought the polite thing to do now was to go open the gate herself. Her feet were bare and as soon as she stepped off the jute-bag mat outside the door, her soles protested at the sudden heat from the boards leading to the gate. After two or three steps she could no longer walk slowly, with dignity. She had to move at a half-trot.

That's what Mother always says—she had to move at a half-trot—but at times I see her dashing forward with abandon, black sheeny hair streaming in the wind. I cannot see the expression on her face, but I see the hair changing into a hard gray of worry and pain. I could urge her to slow down, turn back, keep away, but I can only look on helplessly as her hand reaches for the hoop. But then again, if it were possible for me to warn her away, I might never be born and might therefore not be around now to look on with fear and trembling. Am I to accept then that it had to be so for me to be—and to be what I am? And if I can't? But what's the use. I needs must rip open the fabric of time and I don't know how to. I look and there's a fabric.

I look again and there's none. It's like being trapped in a magic mist which is and is not. You'll have to answer some hard questions from me, God!

Counting the encounter that Tuesday, Savitri and Jai-Jai—for it was he—met exactly fifteen times before they got married. Tuesdays and Thursdays for eight weeks straight, barring one when he was down with a severe flu, and once on Sunday when he and his escorts came to see her. If I'm to believe Mother, Savitri and Jai-Jai never kissed during that strange courtship, never held hands—although their fingers did touch occasionally—and never looked soulfully into each other's eyes. Seems a bit of a stretch to me, but I'll give her the benefit of the doubt for the moment. Mother says they maintained all the conventions save one, but still felt deliciously wicked and, Savitri at least, somewhat guilty at times.

She had promised herself to tell all—suitably packaged of course—on the evening of the first meeting. She would treat the whole matter as a big joke, pouring ridicule on the stranger and making herself out to be a very reluctant hostess forced into the role by her mother's constant reminders never to turn away people in need. He looked ready to drop—typical town softie, ha ha—and that was why she had let him come in and eat his lunch in the shade of the empty sheep stall. Isn't that what you would have done, Ma? Maybe even invited him into the house. I didn't do that, of course. Wouldn't dream of it!

Shortly after dinner her father went outside to lock up the chickens and ducks against marauding opossums and she decided to get it over with quickly. "Hear this joke that happen this midday just after–" But Sugrim unceremoniously cut her off. Joke? That reminded him of a really good one about the Math master Sir Benjamin, and Savitri should give him a chance to tell it first.

She was used to this—Big Brother having his way. She didn't always allow it these days, but right now she didn't feel like fighting, especially since she wasn't at all sure how her story would be received. She half-listened to Sugrim for a minute but he seemed a long way from his punch line, and she decided against waiting for it. Someone might remember she had been about to say something and she suddenly didn't feel like saying it anymore. "The wares! I better go wash them up before it get too dark." She hustled outside to a small shed with a washstand, where dirty dishes and pots had been placed a few minutes earlier by Teemal and Raju.

She spent at least ten minutes longer at the shed than was necessary and when she returned inside and sent Anand and Bharat to bring in the now clean utensils, evening routine had set in and no one brought up the joke she had been about to share. And even though she was having second thoughts about telling all, more so now that her father was back indoors, she still felt miffed. Well, she wasn't going to bring it up again. No one had wanted to listen, no one cared enough, it didn't matter. And right then she made up her mind to let in Mr Jaiprakash Jaimangal of the wavy black hair if he came by the following Thursday as he had hinted he would. Blame it on Sugrim!

But Sugrim or no Sugrim, Jai-Jai of the wavy hair might never have returned to the farmhouse had it not been for soon-to-be fifteen Savitri , who was big for her age. He was attracted by the size of her breasts and wanted to nestle his head between them. At least that's what Mother claims he told her on their very first night together one week after their marriage. But I find it hard to believe Jai-Jai said anything like that. There is a slick suavity to it that just does not fit in with the image I have of him. The Jai-Jai I conceive of is much too awkward to pass on sexy compliments to his virginal bride. Did Mother make it up then? If so, why? And come to think of it, when exactly did she tell me this? I'm unable to pinpoint a time or place and besides, it's not the kind of thing a mother would tell her son. Maybe I dreamed it all up. Whatever its source, it constitutes a reality as valid—or invalid–as any other making up my world. I have nestled on that ample bosom myself and found it a comfortable place to be, and maybe, despite my disclaimers, I do consider Jai-Jai a rival for your affections, Ma, and don't like the thought of his deriving similar comfort from you. I won't pursue the point. No comfort in it. I do know Mother told me Jai-Jai was back two days after their first meeting and Savitri was outside to let him in almost before he was through with the first "Inside!"

He was just as sweaty this time round, but less tired looking. His big wave seemed to surge higher and it was easy to tell his Cebos had been given a brisk wipe shortly before his arrival in front of the gate. Funny, but his gul-gula nose and pointed ears didn't look so bad now—and who said looks were that important anyway? Dilip Kumar for one wasn't handsome, and look what a big star he was!

Mai, Mai, Mai

SASENARINE PERSAUD

Kesa is gone. Two months: not a letter, not a card, not even a call; a "Gita, I've arrived —will be back for Lakshmi's wedding . . ." or "De sun is great for my arthritis," or even "The pain still here, hope the heat helps in a couple-a-months . . ." Trick? I say, he's gone for a holiday when anyone asks. But you know . . . and whom can I talk to except you.

I think of all sorts of things now—like Ma and Pa. They separated since after the war; forty-how-many years till she died and she didn't take another man. She was a strong, self-willed and stubborn woman. But for all her ways you had to admire Ma. She still loved Pa. Why they left? She never said, never talked about it and we were scared of her, always too scared of her to ask. I myself a grandmother, meeting her that last time—the year before she died, still couldn't dare put such a question to her. You never could question Ma. She would give you that look and the questions died on your lips. I suppose she got it from Nani, her mother. Nobody could question Nani, not even Ma! For years all Pa said was that the separation was because of Nani. Nani was a fireass, a fireass until the day she died! If a bird disturbed her sleep she was ready to do battle with the bird, if the dog barked too hard, he had better make sure he was out of range of Nani's long walking stick. Nani had that laathi for as long as I can remember and she didn't need it as a walking aid until well after Kesa and I got married.

It was one of Nana's sticks. I never knew Nana. He died long before I was born. Ma herself remembered little of him, except that he was very tall and thin and was a very good stick-fighter, and men were afraid of him, even black men. Ma said that he killed some sardar in India with his stick and escaped the authorities in indenture across the kala pani. He was an excellent swimmer, but he died in a flood when his boat capsized in the Mahaicony, rain falling nonstop for a week. When he died Nani took one of his sticks wherever she went. Ma felt that Nani had learned some stick-fighting from Nana, and everyone believed this so nobody bothered her. She was young when Nana died, thirty I think, but she too had never taken another man. Why? Could I dare ask Nani, why? Betwa, one of Nani's friends, a woman about Nani's age, had ventured to ask one day.

"Eh-eh Betwa yuh mih mai or wan investigative reporta? What dherraass yuh wan' know! Yuh mih mai eh gyaal Betwa?" Nani's quick and caustic response was not without humour and musical rhythm. She could have been singing. All the old people talked in that musical rhythm and you could listen to it forever, when they conversed about anything; the government, elections, crops, animals, prices, people—but these changed. What never changed were the activities centered around pujas, parabs and the mandir, and about karma and fate. They would say, "a dhe karma, dhe karma" or simply "Karma! What happened had to happen"—but until Jonestown, I never thought much about the cycle of sameness. They were printing that picture–Jim Jones's empty chair surrounded by all those dead swollen bodies and the huge sign hanging from the ceiling with: THOSE WHO DO NOT REMEMBER THE PAST ARE CONDEMNED TO REPEAT IT all over the papers. All the radio announcers were repeating it at the end of the news updates. Then, I remembered Satya who was two years older than me, and I remembered Ma and Nani. Satya was only one of our sisters who had dared defy Ma and Nani, and everybody else when she cared to.

Satya's husband, an only son, was from a wealthy rice-planting and rice-milling family on Leguan in Essequibo river. Two weeks after the wedding he hit her for "answering back" his mother. Satya wrote a letter to Ma. Ma called me to read the letter for her. The very next Sunday Ma sent Kesa and Bhunoya to Leguan. Kesa was hot-headed and passionate but Bhunoya was easy-going and a good mediator. Bhunoya was the most likable of all my brothers-in-law and perhaps because he was the first I liked him most; I could do no wrong for him—your father was a special man. Even Nani agreed with Ma that he was the best son-in-law. And he was such a masterful singer of bhajans and the filmi songs, so charming, so kind he would give away his last dollar!

When Kesa and Bhunoya came back from Leguan with Shiv, we were all surprised as they did not leave with Shiv. Kesa was smiling.

Turning to Bhunoya, Kesa said, "Leh Sandeep tell al'yuh wha happen." They had arrived early in the morning at Satya's to find the place in an uproar. Shiv had just ripped a paling stave off the fence in pursuit of Satya's husband, Baiju, whom he had already hit once or twice. Kesa hurriedly placed himself in front of Baiju while Bhunoya talked to Shiv and led him away to a neighbour's yard just as Baiju's father appeared with a shotgun.

Shiv was shouting from the next yard, "Yuh think I afraid a dhat blasted gun—Baiju, yuh touch mih sister again, a beat yuh ass like a snake." Bhunoya coaxed the shotgun from Baiju's father; when he opened it, it was empty! By the time they left at the end of the day, there was an understanding, all would be well.

But Satya had insisted, "No mother-in-law, nobady order mih about like some lil chil—nat even mih mother!" On the trip to Leguan, Shiv caught the same ferries across the Demerara and Essequibo rivers as Kesa and Bhunoya, but hid from them, and he was first out the ferry and into a taxi to Satya's. Shiv was about fourteen at the time and angry with the world, with Nani and with Pa . . .

Ma was pregnant with Shiv when she and Pa separated so Shiv never knew Pa, and the hate he had for Pa for forty years, he got from Nani. Nani never had a good word for Pa, always bad mouthing him. But there was a deeper reason for Shiv's dislike of Pa and of Nani.

Nani said that Pa had claimed that Shiv was not his son. For years nobody had questioned this—not even Ma, not until Nani died anyway—and then nobody was able to find anybody else who heard Pa say so. No even Ma. Did Nani make it up? And why? Shiv was the splitting image of Pa . . . In those early years of the separation, before settling down with his other family, when Pa visited, Nani was conspicuously absent and Shiv avoided him, would not answer his questions or entreaties. Pa would shake his head and leave. It hurt him . . .

For years after the "Leguan licking," Shiv and Baiju avoided each other. In a sort of isolation in the Essequibo river, Satya and Baiju lived absorbed in their children, the coconuts, the cattle, the rice, the ricemill, while I was taken up with the children and Kesa. And when Rupa died, and especially before Bhunoya married back, I was taken up with looking out for Rupa's three children. I had promised myself when your mother died I would look out for the three of you. There were the visits but Satya was still far away.

Then bam! Jonestown and Jim Jones quoting somebody else about forgetting history and being condemned to repeat it! Two years before, after twenty years and four children, Satya left Baiju. The divorce went through just months before Jonestown. Baiju had never hit her after that first time but there were rumours of other women. Satya finally caught him. She was firm: she didn't want him back, and she didn't want another man. There were her children, and there was God! Only the Almighty one could trust, depend on, call on without fail! I was skeptical at first but Satya's mind was made up. It was like seeing Ma and Nani all over again. She went to the Brahma Kumaris and fell in love with their yoga and meditation. Nothing else was good for her, none of the old pujas, not even some of the foods. We drifted apart. For me there were the children and Kesa, and moving to Canada. Yet somehow I thought Satya would change her mind. Nani and Ma were of a different time; a time I didn't want for the children or any of you; a time I was determined to correct for myself. There is so much to read here and learn. And your uncle Kesa always grumbling why in my old age I becoming scholar . . .!

"Dha good—yuh can rread and wrrite and do rricthmetic—but why dhem gyaal dhis a guh all ova dhe place? Theatre, theatre!" Nani scolded and fretted when I went to the theatre with Shiv or Ma, or with Bhunoya and Rupa before she got pregnant. Nani questioned every movement of the house and yard. Her eyesight was failing but not her sense of perception, or her sharp tongue. I had seen Kesa and he had seen me. Once before going to the theatre, Bhunoya had taken his car to the Esso gas station to put air in the wheels. Rupa and I were in the car and Kesa, a mechanic who worked in the gas station gargage, came out to help Bhunoya and Shiv. When Bhunoya and Rupa went to buy gas, weekends, they would come to take me for a ride. Nani knew. Real fireass that woman!

"Marrrid time marrrid time marrrid time," she sang one day as I came home. "Gyaal yuh know what dhem tassa drrum seh. Ee'seh 'Marrrid a wan good thing, marrrid a wan good thing, trrouble deh behin' am dham dham . . .'" She tapped her stick to the music, tapped her feet from the hammock, swayed her head to the last two syllables and laughed. Ma found out about Kesa, met his aunt with whom he was staying in town and then went into the Mahaica creek to find his mother.

I only went up to sixth standard in school and then that didn't matter. I had looked forward to marriage, it looked so good. There was Rupa and Bhunoya—he with his flash and charm—your father could make anything look good. A real gem your father! Rupa was happy. And there were the Hindi movies always ending up with marriage, but the life after? Now? Now in another month Lakshmi completes her exams and graduates from the University of Toronto. I wished Ma was alive for this, and Pa—only four months now, almost exactly a year after Ma died. Isn't it uncanny?

Ma was seventy-nine—weak eyesight but unfailing voice, strong arms and legs. Shiv said she walked to every place nearby, the mandir, the market, the theatre—O she loved her theatre, the Hindi movies . . . Three weeks, three weeks before the visa arrived in the mail Ma had a heart attack. At least Satya had finally made peace with her. Six months before, Satya and Ma made up. Satya had blamed Ma for Bihari's death. Bihari, the eldest, had to drop Ma to work on his cycle, pick her up in the afternoon, take her wherever she wanted, and every Friday he gave his pay envelope to Ma—even just after he got married. Ma banked his money for him, gave him money when he wanted and quarreled with him for spending too much on clothes, cigarettes, and later on drink. But you know how he got the smoking and drinking from her! Poor Bihari, he was "The Man" after Pa left! But why he put up with Ma, even when he married? We knew that with marriage it would come to an end. But how! He rode into a car one Friday evening, coming out of a rum shop. Some bystanders said it was an accident, said he was too drunk to realize that he was riding in the wrong direction, some said he was pretending to be drunk, that it was not accident. Only he knows . . . Satya said Ma couldn't let go of Bihari. I always felt he could have said no—it was in his hands. Ma couldn't be other than she was. She had to be strong and tough and bring us up, and Bihari could only be what he was—weak! What was could only be what was! Divorced and on her own with her children, Satya finally understood Ma, or learned compassion from her meditation and yoga.

Kesa didn't want me to go back when Ma died. "Yuh just came back from holiday. And she dead already!" But I went anyway. I cried all the way—except in Trinidad! That place hard, unfriendly. Ten hours waiting for a connection at Piarco, not a place to rest your head, nobody even offering a cup of tea, and Trinidad airline clerks rude, rude! But after the cremation, with Ma just gone, Shiv reluctantly agreed with us that it was time to make peace with Pa who was sick and could not attend the funeral. I wanted him to do it before I returned to Toronto. Sometimes, you know that there will be no next time. When Pa heard Shiv had come, he came out on the road to meet Shiv. He had not walked out to the roads in months.

Shiv was still angry. "Why you say I was not your son?" he asked as soon as we sat down in the verandah.

"Son, I never said so. Look at you, look at me. If there is any child who is my child, it is you. Who said so?" Pa's voice was strong, perhaps with outrage too, his English precise. Pa had retired as Assistant Registrar in the High Court. They said his English and knowledge of law was as good as any of the London trained lawyers, his handwriting better than any in the country.

"Nani," I answered after the silence.

"Your Nani! That woman! Ruined your mother, all of you, me . . . I still love your mother, I always loved her . . ."

Shiv cut him off, "So why you left her?"

"A long story. Your Nani was an illiterate woman. Sure she knew Hindi but she couldn't read it, or write it. And she felt your mother didn't need to know too . . . I came home one day with some film star cards. The Hindi film star cards had just come out for the first time but were not available here, and a lawyer just back from India brought me a pack. Your Nani found them in my shirt pocket and took them to your mother. She told your mother I was seeing other women and had their pictures in my pocket. There was a huge commotion. Your mother believed her. They literally threw me out. Your Nani wanted to use her stick on me. What could I do? I went back to explain to your mother when your Nani was out, to explain to her what the cards were. Your Nani hid them—so I couldn't even get a pandit, someone they trusted, to read the cards and explain to them. And who knew about the cards then? It was four years before the first set of cards were imported in this country—you grew up with them. A marriage down the line for film-starcards and illiteracy! That is why I have always insisted your mother send all of you to school . . ."

"But why didn't you get somebody to explain? Why didn't you make up back after the cards became popular and Ma knew?" Shiv asked hotly.

"Well, life moves on. I was alone living in this house—well the old one—your Nani wanted us to divorce and your mother wouldn't see me. Your stepmother use to come and clean and cook for me. Two years. She became pregnant. I still wanted your mother back. I used to come, Rupa would remember—she was the oldest—to see all of you, and your mother agreed to make up, but not your Nani. Well I didn't care about your Nani, but your mother insisted she had to take care of her mother! She was a stubborn woman, your mother. How could I live in the same house with your Nani. She never liked me and she would cause trouble again. Well, I was stubborn too. I had my own house. Why should I live in your Nani's house? We were young and that was how it happened. Who is to blame? And then your step-mother got pregnant again. I also had a responsibility to her and to your other brothers. I finally married her—and she is a good woman. She has never, as I know, treated any of you badly. You know the rest." Pa was right. Auntie Rita was always good to me whenever I visited him—and after all these years, she has never been rude or unpleasant. Much younger than Pa, and still such a beautiful woman . . .

"Pa, why did you never tell us these things years ago?" I pleaded, crying inside.

"Nobody asked—and it was no good. I was remarried, had another family and I could never make your mother look bad. Things happen . . . son I'm glad you've come—I don't want to go with any secrets, any unfinished business. Another thing, I'll tell you. I have another son in England for a white woman. A lawyer, the same time the separation happened, she was here doing research for the Foreign Office. She wanted me to go and live in England with her. I had still hoped for your mother. Her name is Cynthia Waithe. Your brother's name is Jaipaul. Jaipaul Waithe. I lost track. He also studied law . . . Rita," he turned to the house and shouted, "Rita . . ."

"Coming Goo." She came with the drinks. "A cook some roti, a'yuh gat fuh eat before yuh go. Anybady wan tea?"

"Some water please, Auntie Rita," Satya said.

"Rita, bring mih Ramayan—and the Mahabharat too. So Gita, you learnt to read Hindi too eh?"

"Yes Pa. And I've improved my English these last couple of years. The facilities in Canada are good."

"I'm proud of you. And your daughter in university? She knows any Hindi?"

"Nah Pa, but Dalip—Rupa's son, you remember him? He knows. He is like you, Pa. He is going to India next year. I will go too. He is always telling me to write—record all these things. He wants to know about your father, what year he came from India . . ."

"Goo," Auntie Rita came back with the two bulky books wrapped in red cotton.

"Thanks. Too old to read now. Eyes hurt. Gita these are yours, and Dalip's. Yes, I remember him, he used to sit in my lap while I read these books. I used to sing the chowpais to him. Seems yesterday. There are dates in those books. But write down these. My father and mother came to British Guiana in 1902. They were married in India. I was born here in 1904. But your chacha was born in India. They sailed from Calcutta. They were indentured to Peter's Hall estate. This land was the first land they bought after their indenture. Pa's name was Suepaul and he died in 1945 after the war. Ma was Eliacha and she died in 1955. Let me tell you what I remember of Pa. I don't remember which village in India but I know it was in UP—somewhere between Kanpur and Lucknow. Pa was a big man. Handsome, long hair which he tied at the back, and he had sideburns. He was very muscular—a sardar on Peter's Hall estate. And people respected him. I remember the time when he beat up a big black man. Well, the black man was the tallest man on the estate and a bully. He used to terrorize the Indians. Pa planned for him. Pa was strong; he could lift a bag of salt with his teeth. He got a bag of sand and suspended it from he roof in our cowpen. Every night he would spar and punch that bag, and butt. He was superb in butting, and that was his secret weapon. Your chacha and I would watch him every night. Well Friday afternoon at estate pay office, this bad man bullying people again. Pa walked right up to him and pushed him. He rushed Pa swinging. Pa ducked and butt, ducked and butt, one, two three four times. Quick succession. Blood dripping from bad man mouth, teeth in his hand—dazed and on the ground. When he collected himself, he said, 'Coolie man yuh good!' and he shook Pa's hand. They lifted Pa on their shoulders, walked him round the village and brought him home. Tell that to your children and grandchildren . . .

"You, Shiv, I heard about you too. You learnt karate, afraid of no man eh—you are your aja self! . . . And yes, tell them too how he led the march from Peter's Hall to town to see the governor. Thirteen dead, sixteen wounded when the militia opened fire at Ruimveldt . . . Pa was shot in the arm. The same year me and your Ma got married—1924. We got married the year before and had to wait another year and do another ceremony. For the bhariat we used tram cars, and a car—Pa's car—my first motor car. It was an afternoon wedding—beautiful . . ."

When we said goodbye I knew I would never see Pa alive again, but Satya said she had gone back—and Shiv. When Ma died, Kesa had mixed comments. Four months ago when Pa died, Kesa cried. Home all day himself with pain no doctor could cure, Kesa must have been thinking of death too, his arthritis, pressure, sugar . . .

"Dhis nat country for humans! This cold no good for people," Kesa repeated over and over.

"Well Daddy, go to California, spend some time with Rai. It's hot there too and sunny . . ." I have never called Kesa by his name out of respect.

"Why you want mih burden mih son. He gat his wife and kids, you forget. Only place is Guyana. We still have our house there. I'll be a burden to nobody there."

"But Lakshmi wedding soon. Wait till after de wedding . . ." I could not persuade him.

"Yuh hear what she say. She and Anil plan their own wedding. And she only want a small Hindu wedding, just close family. The friends and distant relatives for the big reception. I not going to die in dhis cold!" he responded.

I cursed as I haven't in years, give him good. I shouldn't have, but I couldn't help it. Why he wanted to go? And why am I so afraid? History? Satya doesn't care for history; we make our own history, she always said! Thirty years. When Kesa arrived in Georgetown he called Leela: daughter not wife. And the next day he called Lakshmi. I picked up the extension.

"Excellent weather!" Green green green, flowers, sun, fruits on trees, birds singing. Music. We at your chacha now. Huge celebration. Even your grandmother dancing! And the pain going already, almost gone. This is a country to live in. That cold will kill me. Anyway, I will be back for your wedding, don't worry baby," he still calls her baby, "did you pay my taxes for me, and my bills—need more money? Alright, take care . . ."

"Daddy, you don't want to talk to Mommy?" She asked, insisted. Ah but a daughter feels for a mother. Why I loved Ma, and Ma loved Nani, despite all!

"O alright!"

"Mommy, Daddy on the line—please pick up the phone."

"Okay." I uncovered the mouthpiece. "Daddy? How you feeling?"

"Pain, lots a pain still. Too much pain but it going, it is that blasted cold."

"And your mother?"

"Improving—but gat to go." Click!

Just like that! Thirty years. History. Sun. Ma, Pa—the separation, the pain, ah the pain. And whose side? I trick you, you trick me? Who trick who? Leela has her own kids and husband, and her life to live. And Lakshmi is taken up with her classes and the wedding. Maybe Kesa right. This is a lonely place! Nobody to talk to, nobody but you? God bless you child, God bless you son!

Going to Guyana

CYRIL DABYDEEN

Why I wanted miracles to happen as I boarded the Guyana Airways jet at the Miami International Airport in steamy, swirling heat, I didn't know. A sense of parody or pantomime mixed with a vague feeling of loyalty to a mud-brown, alluvium-and-silt-clogged land kept me sitting up straight as the plane jolted and accelerated along the driveway, then finally took off.

I'd been living in Canada much too long, and now I felt compelled to return. Chris (short for Krishna) everyone called me, a name too familiar, devoid of resonance; and I'd put off returning until now, wrestling with an awkward but prolonged alienation, in the county, as.with women, in infatuation or love. Don't get me wrong, I kept on socializing. "You could get any girl you want," said French Canadian Nicole, my current date. "Just put on a navy blue blazer, and smile." But Nicole also hinted that I sometimes made her depressed because of an unexpected absentmindedness. Why wasn't I given to dancing all night, as she wanted? Once I caught her studying my shoes, and she said she could tell a lot about a man by his footwear. She could? Allusion to penile prowess? I told her I'd often walked barefoot for long hours as a child on my way to school in a foreign land, the dreary tropical heat bearing down on me, which I could never forget. Ah, I wasn't going to deny my origin.

Now in midair, floating in space with all worlds turning, anxiety rising because of what was ahead, or what not to expect. A tallish, slender-looking stewardess in mauve, charcoal-hued suit, kept walking gracefully along the aisle, as I looked at her; and I kept thinking of having travelled often in Canada, criss-crossing a vast land because of my work on behalf of the Canadian government, which was how I'd met Nicole. I'd immediately liked her ease, a touch of Mohawk in her too, casually mentioned when we were together one night, as she'd muttered that I didn't look "Asian."

The plane humming, and I kept looking outside into the vagueness of clouds, oddly longing for ancestry.

"So why are you going back there after all these years?" the lanky hostess in mauve asked to me in a surprising moment.

I shrugged.

Clouds moving miragelike, with passengers getting up, forming a constant stream along the aisle where an odd assortment of baggage, parcels, material was stuffed in every corner of the plane it seemed: in every jot of space between their legs, the sides. A growing listlessness and yet frenzy in me amidst the plane's drone, with everyone wanting to get there quickly, it seemed.

Strangely now I felt no strong obligation to return, the plane seeming at a standstill, as if somewhere amongst thick trees, forests, my mind in a lull. Then she came again, the lanky hostess. Who was she? I tried to pigeon-hole her by race, origin, the more aloof she looked and the higher we climbed . . . and drew closer to the tropics. Fragments of time and place: canefields, trade wind wafting. The other stewardesses walked by, but it was Arabella—the lanky one—I kept looking at even during the sudden turbulence: the plane pitching, the passengers restless. A Chinese man, surprisingly tall, stretched out his arms windmill-fashion unwittingly hitting out. An African, an immediate victim, grimaced.

A scuffle in midair, with rebukes, name-calling, of a distinct racial cast.

"Is wha' happen to you, man?" cried a midair combatant. "You not see you hittin me?"

A screeching response from the other, "Man, you talkin' like you still back there?"

Snickers, then laughter as the parody was acted out among the passengers. Arabella pursed her lips, and everyone expected her to mediate. "Let them fight," she calmly said.

The African sucked his teeth with a sharply hissing noise. The Chinese yelled a further rebuke, his eyes a full glare. An obay mulatto woman who'd boarded the plane from New York City let out her own flurry of words. Laughter echoed down her section of the aisle, mainly from an older man whose jaws moved up and down like a strange contraption. "You all lookout wid this Guyana plane," he said. "Someone goin' to take it over in midair cause the government not able to pay the rent. Guyana now blasted bankrupt!"

Arabella yawned, appearing as if she'd been through this before, then murmured: "No one's going to take over this plane." Her fixed sultriness reigned. "The Captain tell you to say that, girl?" came a retort from another passenger.

"No Captain goin' tell her to say that," someone else hissed. "Women not stupid nowadays."

Arabella kept up a determinedly aloof air.

"How d'you know?" snapped another.

After a short silence, someone said we'd soon be flying over Havana, which caused a screech: "We're no longer communists cause socialism's done for." Only Arabella didn't seem amused. Captain's voice on the intercom came to indicate our flying time, like destiny itself.

Arabella again passed by the aisle and looked at me intently, as someone else added: "A plane can withstand all kinds o' pressure, even if it's a blasted Cuban communist plane."

"Yes," came a quick answer. Then collective laughter followed, echoing everywhere.

The entire six-hour flight was now becoming an eternity, as I kept conjuring up an ocean, green grass, all of the "tropical paradise" I was returning to: a place close to Venezuela; and thoughts of Georgetown, the capital, being lashed by tidal waves despite the seawall, mangrove and courida . . . threatening the entire coastland. My father's own backlands imprinted in me: he still there, hoary headed, herons picking at his thin-bodied cattle on muddy coastal ground in the Canje district. Scooping up cow's urine from a fissure in the ground to salve his thirst in the wilderness of the place.

One passenger, then another, got up as if searching for an exit. A voice close to me said: "Maybe we'll never land there." My tongue's own clacking sensation, dry-mouthed. Then a louder voice called: "Guyana not so green anymore."

"God, you don't have to bad-talk we country. We born there," came a high-spirited rejoinder. Arabella seemed not so aloof anymore, now that we were closer to "home."

The trade wind whirling against coconut trees leaning like tall old men against zinc-roofed houses. Night's onslaught of rain causing all to sway and bend, the thunder-crack of an entire forest overwhelming now in the plane's sudden dive and inevitable crash. A cry escaped my lips: I'd been sleeping and was having a nightmare.

The man next to me nudged me fully awake. Further images, the black-watered creek in the Canje with dog fish or perai. Clusters of water hyacinths, algae, amidst flowers bursting out in effulgent sunlight everywhere.

"Tired?" came a voice, Arabella bringing me back to the present, hips barely pressing against my shoulder. "Maybe you're not so eager to return." A rasp in her voice, discomfiture. Banana leaves, the creek's shimmering haze; and she smiled, and maybe to her time did not matter anymore.

"Things have changed," she said.

"Are you telling me?"

Syllables rounded out, the dialect of silence echoing nostalgia's powerful grip on me . . . as we drew closer to Guyana with further tremors and impulses of home. Arabella quivering, I sensed. "Have you ever thought of leaving yourself?" I asked.

"Never." Her lips tightened.

"Why not?"

She became quietly wistful. "I come and go all the time. You and your kind, also come an' go." Her hips wilfully swayed, carrying all of the aisle with her.

I rubbed my eyes. A few passengers rousing from their own short naps made instant catcalls, hissing at her. Did they? The captain's voice again, announcing that before long we'd be in Guyana. A ritual excitement in the cabin. The next moment I was the captain himself, steering this large insect of a plane, losing altitude. Someone laughed in anticipation, then the captain's monotone voice once more: "I'm afraid, ladies and gentlemen, we can't land there just yet."

"Why not?" cried a hundred voices all at once.

The captain's professional drone: "There are no lights at the Guyana airport."

"No lights?" a tight gasp, hiss.

"Electricity breakdown, you see," said too matter-of-factly.

I looked out in the mirage and aura of hinterland, jungle looming up, thinking of Timehri Airport and primitive paintings reminiscent of aboriginal wall art. The captain apologizing—the plane would now go to the neighbouring airport, in Surinam.

Someone started hiccoughing. Arabella—as if she expected this—wagged a finger at him. Outside, the darkness, rock paintings: figures of ancient Caribs, Arawaks darting about in impenetrably bunched forest. The hiccoughing got louder. Night's unwelcoming: the plane turning around, throbbing. . .going away from Timehri.

I rubbed my eyes the changing light: reality. . .Canada, North America, all far away as if in a different time, a different planet or galaxy.

Four o'clock in the morning: our weird fate to be here at this time, as the mood changed from dull excitement to listlessness, then desperation. Sounds from another scuffle: now an East Indian, very thin, pointing a finger and saying: "It's your kind, you are to blame. The politicians of you race—that's why we're here." Words charged with an overwhelming sense of exile, or outraged ethnicity: this amidst more vegetation in a genuine chiaroscuro world, then darkness, intermittent light. The obay woman shrieking an accusation about corrupt politics in the Third World. Another, less loud: "All I'm concerned about is getting home safely. I fear for my safety in this Godforsaken place. I fear every blasted thing now: snake, tarantula, scorpion. God, I want to get back to America!"

Another, behind me, cried, "Is we bad luck to arrive here"—as if thrust into a hollow vortex of rage. "God," the wrinkled East Indian man's turn, again, "my family would be waiting for me at the airport all night long. I last saw them ten years ago. Now I am here, in another country. What for?" He burst out laughing crazily, adding, "Next time I'm travelling Air Canada."

"Not Pan Am?" someone jeered from the opposite end of the plane.

When suddenly the ground heaved, I saw Arabella coming out of the captain's cabin, her hair slightly tousled. Maybe now she'd tell us if indeed there was a blackout at Timehri: so strange in this age of universal electrification; or if there was a coup taking place in Guyana.

Coup?

Guns firing, staccato coughs of bullets; cinematic image after image, recurring, rearranging. Arabella defying my suspicions because she really knew, and the captain also knew. The motley group of passengers, dumbfounded, also knew, but me. The East Indian man wailed, "I shoulda never been born in such a place as—"

But another rejoined, "Where you want to be born then, in England?"

"Na America" came a sharp-tongued reply.

Why not Canada? I turned, intent on looking at the last speaker. But Arabella again drew closer, face florid, perhaps now defying me to ask about Guyana. My quick recollection or consciousness: history, a place still known as paradise or a long-lost El Dorado as I'd often told French-Canadian Nicole; and Sir Walter Raleigh gallantly throwing his coat across a ditch for the Queen to step out on. . . followed by a vision of the dreaded Tower of London.

Arabella laughed as someone else hissed: "Yes, is America we'll end up in anyway."

"Not Canada—where everyone's immigrating to nowadays?"

"It too damn cold there," drummed another.

"Too far from the blasted equator?"

We quickly landed in the steamy, sultry Surinam heat where soldiers conspicuously milled about in heavy-booted fashion.

Arabella standing next to a determined chocolaty-looking First Officer, the tallest man I ever saw, with voices hissing all around, haranguing about America, Canada. Next came a ghettoblaster's celebration or invasion, reggae sounds amid Dutch gibberish.

Arabella, as I watched her, again muttered to the pilot who was leaning closer to her, as if about to start nibbling her ear, all in the familiarity of further colloquialism. Someone else, one of the combatants—the Chinese—hovering in the darkness let out: "We could collectively change things around here. Bring in big investment from Hong Kong, Japan, all of Southeast Asia."

"It'd be exploitation whichever way you think about it," a bespectacled woman—an intellectual or zealot—answered.

"Look at America, it built on exploitation," the Chinese man retorted.

"The exploitation of blacks!" the obay one caterwauled.

The first officer now tried speaking to the passengers one by one, exhorting them to be patient: the frailty, predictability all around, resolutely muttering that before long we'd arrive at our destination. And he yet again blamed the ubiquitous blackout.

Laughter.

Arabella's breast rose, and so different she appeared now, troubled-looking. Amidst the ghettoblaster's loud peal, like derangement, with Bob Marley's "Burning Spear," she again drew closer to me in perplexing light and darkness at this hour. "You know," she said, "I'd once thought of emigrating. But I hate filling out all those damn forms. Those awful questions they ask, they want to know everything about you."

She had been leaving all the time, for places in Arabia, the Far East, all she had read about and imagined.

"I wanted to leave Guyana badly. But then I always think about Albouystown, that alley where I came from."

I listened with growing fascination and curiosity; she was becoming increasingly nostalgic. "My family's still there." The intensity on her face, eyes quivering. Why then did I imagine her a model in Paris, London, New York: a professional photographer on Fifth Avenue taking shots of her at different angles, all her natural flair?

"I could never really leave," she grated.

But we were ready to leave Surinam now, finally heading home for Guyana.

Timehri, our rushing up to it in the cabin's excitement as everyone got jolted into full consciousness. Soon there would be the loud greetings of relatives, friends. Arabella's head tilted back, she laughed. The trade wind and the ghettoblaster's reggae still in my ears, the line to the customs officials quickly becoming a crowd, a scrimmage, with more soldiers milling about. One thin, gangly youth let out, "Is where all-you come from?"

"America, where else?" came a strident reply.

Another grunted his impatience because he couldn't find his suitcase, blaming the inept customs staff, then sneered, "Gosh, they're yet to become efficient here."

Someone else added, "You'd think you're back in the dark ages," and strangely guffawed.

Arabella beckoned to me: she knew a way through customs, and the fastest taxi to Georgetown. Soon we were hurtling along on a tortuous road—leaving me breathless and yet staring at her lovely face as she shrieked with laughter. "Where are we going next?" the driver asked, the humid air reeking of burnt tire, with houses on stilts crashing down on us on all sides. Came Arabella's instinctive answer: "Albouystown." Not Jonestown?

Lips quivering, as if with religious tremor. The taxi veering, screeching to a halt next to a busy alleyway. Arabella said, "I want to show them I have a friend come from America." She meant me.

"Show them?"

"Yes." She smiled.

"I am from Canada."

But she was already encouraging that I take good note that there were no large houses here, as we stepped gingerly on mud-caked ground. She confidently led me through a maze of small huts and houses amidst ancient smells of paraffin, salted cod, rotten potatoes. What would French Canadian Nicole now think of my being here? A dozen heads peeping out at once, gleeful children's faces; Arabella waving to them, their contrasting expressions, teeth jutting out whitely against black lips. The eyes almost incandescent, asking: Who is he?

An older woman with a basket of fruit on her head—colourful mango, papaw, pineapple, banana—sauntered by, pointing, asking who I was, or wasn't. Arabella's eyes flickered as we stood before a corrugated-looking hovel.

Sinewy, webbed faces, arms, dozens of them, were now all around Arabella, as if she'd been away for years. Faces, mouths, the old and young alike, all welcoming her. "I bring home a friend, Ma," she said to the oldest woman around.

I inhaled more of the mixture of iodine, cough syrup, stale food, old clothes, overripe banana. Other zinc-topped houses around, in a sudden shimmering brilliance everywhere.

Arabella said, "He come from America, but I can show him we're all the same," and emitted a throaty laugh as she glanced fully at me. "Look at he good," she added.

Eyes searching me in unabashed curiosity, then they started laughing. Nicole, do you hear? Do I still look "Asian"? Arabella: "See, America's made no change in him all these years."

Hands pawing me, all of Guyana pressing closer to me. An old man, small-headed, looked at me in a grandfatherly way, and other old women and men, webby hands, rheumy eyed, bending forward to look closely at me. Arabella started calling out their names one by one, as a child close to me chanted: "America-America," pink tongue sticking out. The old woman droning like a bee, her words yet audible: "So you're really from 'merica?"

"It mek no difference," someone else cackled.

Arabella took my hand, and it dawned on me that in North America maybe nothing was ever real. But here, in this Albouystown alley with all the faces still looking at me, would they ask me about skyscrapers, cars, videos, TV's, fridges, computers, washing machines? Bare gums, chapped lips, still asking.

Arabella's face sculpted with intensity, as another muttered about Africa: there where Arabella might have been a princess. Ah, her actually being on the cover of *Vogue*. I imagined a photographer's indulgence or extravagance.

I was hungry, and before long on the table was put salted cod reeking in coconut oil. Tomatoes, plantains, cassava, other vegetables such as okra. They watched as I ate, quickly; a fleck of oil dripping from a side of Arabella's mouth, a pink tomato skin clinging to her lower lip.

I wiped my lips.

The children tittering.

I sucked at a bone next, holding it between my teeth.

"Eat good," the old woman urged.

"Maybe you will never go back to 'merica," another muttered. Arabella, I kept imagining, in a specially made diaphanous gown or evening dress, Manhattan's best, stunningly displayed on her. The designers, journalists, purchasers, buyers, admiring her elegance. Was she truly a long-lost African princess?

Outside, rain started pouring, water kicking up from the ground; Arabella reassuring me that soon the sun would be out again, always the sense of changing tropical weather.

She quivered next, "You must leave here, though."

Lightning flashed, as Arabella laughed, inquiring about ice and snow in the same breath.

My temperate self, I reminded her, muttering about readjustment, while imagining beech pine, spruce, as much as I was among taller trees in the greenhearted forest not far from us.

Impulsively I said, "Why not come with me to Canada?"

"Too cold there."

"I've survived."

"Don't tempt me." Still long gowned, diaphanous, I imagined her to be. "I belong here."

"There too."

She laughed.

"You know it." Why I said that, I didn't know; yet I detected her quickening heartbeat. Further tremors of day and night as the rain stopped. My further imagining: as we walked hand in hand she still the center of attention and being interviewed on radio, TV All of America, Europe, Africa, Asia: watch her good.

"No," she repeated, she wanted none of that, bracing herself against my invitation, new impulses.

The relatives encouraging her, urging: "Arabella, go with him. Have no fear."

Now I started fighting to come to grips with myself; with my ties of place, and my father not far away in the Canje, close to where thick vegetation floated down the narrow, sinuous creek. A bloated dead cow moving along with a brightly yellow kiskadee or heron perched on its back. A rich molasses smell in the air not far from a large cane factory. Next, a silk cotton tree swishing, long-memoried: associated with Dutch lore.

. . .Travelling farther down the Canje—Arabella and I—going to a place called Magdalenenburg where the first slave rebellion had occurred. More thick vegetation, roots of strange trees on continually buttressed soil. A mandrake sky overhead, then becoming dark, blackened. A howler monkey's strange bark, presaging more torrential rain.

Arabella clung to me. "We must leave now at once." She breathed harder.

Her relatives grinning as if they knew something about her I didn't. Who really was Arabella? Nicole also asking; all of Canada, America, asking. My father now greeting us, and also asking. The place called Magdalenenburg, and the early slaves also asking. Did they recognize her? Did they? A really lost West African princess as she was?

We started meeting again the other passengers from the plane at this unpredictable time on the coastland; their recognizing Arabella, never me. And it wasn't her fault that the country was like this, they said. "We should never have come back here," the obay woman hurled.

To Arabella I whispered, "I will remain here with you."

"Will you?"

Then we heard: "A coup has just taken place. The new government's decided to ban all flights out of the country."

This repeated in a singsong fashion on the radio, without malice or hate, only with a surprising nonchalance or indifference.

Arabella shrugged. And immediately I imagined the two midair combatants, the plane wobbling, with Arabella still close to me. Water swirling, leviathans crashing or tumbling in my sleep maybe. Once more soldiers moving about because we were indeed in a state of siege.

Instinctively I looked up, seeing another plane high above. Who did it belong to?

Arabella also looking up. Some of the other passengers with us pointing at it. Air Canada? Were they coming to help me escape from the real danger they figured I was in because of the coup?

Ah, Nicole, she'd engineered it, hadn't she? She who (as she'd told me) was sometimes friendly with a high-ranking cabinet minister in Ottawa—maybe the Minister of Defence. And I was a Canadian government official, didn't you know? All possibilities about rescuing me because of the growing turmoil all around.

Arabella put a hand to her eyes, squinting. Slave drums beating, the silk cotton tree swishing funereally. My feet firmly planted on hard ground.

The others around Arabella, moving closer to her.

Nicole laughing, I suddenly heard, then muttering, "We heard about it—the coup." She did? Nicole admonishing me next: "See, I told you to wear a dark blazer and smile a lot"—her unfailing sense of humour. Did I still look "Asian"?

And Arabella, I kept looking around for her in the excitement because of the widening coup, she standing next to the old woman, her mother. They were both waving to me.

I also started waving and yet nodding to my hoary-headed father.

"Goodbye," I cried to him, one final time.

The intense heat of the tropics everywhere—. And Arabella was still looking at me from *Vogue*, or some other Paris or New York magazine. The obay one sitting next to me on the plane now, getting a ride back to New York, she said, adding with irony: "Young man, you belong with them; not up here where there are no combatants."

"None whatsoever," she added after a while.

In her laughter I heard Arabella's voice, and instinctively waved to them below, one more time, not believing it was my final parting: my disappearing act. Arabella waving back from below, with her entire family, it seemed. Waves beating in memory and consciousness, like the self disappearing across climates, against an assault, gunfire indeed in the strangest of acts.

Nicole instinctively moved closer to me; and then quietly started talking about being in love akin to being in a wilderness: she who wanted affection, not just passion, she said, in the breathtaking space of our going to a new place called home.

Buckee

ROOPLALL MONAR

O Jesus Lord, if only you could strike this Rita with fire and brimstone? Get rid of she for good, Buckee wished again, throwing her fleshy hands in the air, pacing desperately in the downstairs flat that heated midday.

You don't see how she want to kill me Lord Jesus? She's pure malice and hatred, Buckee pleaded fearfully, breathing heavily as she took the armless chair by the open window overlooking the street.

You mean to tell me Rita blind like bat. She didn't hear what I did for Patrick, eh? I take he out the gutter when he wife dump he off for a next man. Is me Buckee who make he a man again. Yes, Patrick was drinking, getting drunk, falling down in all them drains . . . Buckee reminded herself, lips trembling, head turning heavy. Tru-tru, me have to see this obeah man. He have to do away with this bad-minded Rita—

Yes, it was Patrick who told her to leave her job a week before he migrated to New York.

"Yuh kill yuhself enough. And look what yuh do for me," Patrick said gratefully in bed the night before he left, cuddling her affectionately. He knew he owed his life to her. And as soon as he began working he would be sending a monthly allowance for her. She must not ask no one for anything, neither must she try to get a man friend, he cried in a tone mixed with concern and threat while dogs barked outside and cats sprang atop fences.

"Heh, man is tonic? You is the only one. Tink me want to knock-about the place? Me name call with this man, that man? What the Lord Jesus would say?" Buckee assured him, stroking his hands lovingly as tears streamed down her roundish face. She vowed to live a life of abstinence, attend church regularly, do charitable work in the village whenever she was called upon. Such tasks would ensure she maintained her chastity, she pointed out.

And as promised, as soon as he got settled, handling his own money, had a place of his own, he would return, marry her, file in papers, he reminded her at the airport the Friday night after he checked in.

"Yuh're crying. What happen?" Patrick asked in the bench, resting his hairy hands on her shoulder as he waited to go on board.

"Is just that . . . is just that when man go America, Canada he take up with another woman. He fuget the woman back-home," Buckee stammered, shifting in the bench. A mixture of perfumes floated in an air of shuffling feet, innumerable voices.

She felt so lonely now, deserted. How would she make out without him? Who can tell, suppose he take up with another woman. He can't live with his sister for too long, Buckee told herself, wracked with uncertainties, watching Patrick thoughtfully. May the Lord guide him in the right way, she hoped, weeping inside.

And she wept more after Patrick left. She couldn't sleep too. A kind of delirium swamped her during that week. She tossed and turned in bed sensing his presence as her eyes closed. She complained about the heat, the thieves, the biting headaches. At last, when she did manage to have an hour sleep she dreamt of the good times she spent with him.

She saw how she rescued him from the streets after his wife left him for another man. The delicious dinners they cooked together—macaroni, baked chicken, fries, fry rice. . .smiling and petting in the kitchen, nostrils filled with a mixture of spices.

"He's not your kind, your class, Mummy," Buckee's daughter snapped vehemently one Sunday morning in the flat, telling her mother to let him go.

Buckee had just taken up with Patrick. So far, she had not found anything unbecoming in him. "You blind to see the decency in the man?"

"Decency! Heh! You mean the shame you brought upon yourself. A non-working scum. You know what people are saying?" Her daughter cried one evening, flinging her fingers in confusion. "If he were a good man you think his wife would have ditched him? Tell me?" she added, looking so devastated in the chair as gentle wind wafted through the open window.

"He's loving. He's caring. Your father never use to give me love, attention. He uses to treat me like dirt. Yes, he uses to spend more time with friends, other women in Lombard street—"

"But you could have changed him, Mum. Many wives do that," the daughter said severely one dewy morning, pointing by the doorway, dressed for work.

She recalled the many heated quarrels between her parents—the slaps, the cuffs, the curses, each accusing the other of being stone-hearted, neglectful. But still, with dogged determination, they could have mended their differences, the daughter thought as she waited for a bus on the road.

"Me didn't know how me fall for you, woman," Buckee's husband used to say, looking so guilty. He blamed his eyes, which drew him to her youthful body.

"We never 'gree on nothing. You worst than one dunce–" he exploded in the kitchen one day, pointing accusingly. He felt like strangling her.

"Is the same dunce you was killing yourself for," Buckee sneered one night in the bedroom, trying to examine her own feelings. Indeed she was hurt, humiliated, the husband accusing her of everything that went wrong in the house.

More than once he deemed her a rotten slut, squaring angrily, thinking whether to cuff her or not. "Is why you don't dead, eh?"

She tried many times to change him, telling him the purpose of morality, love, happiness. She spoke with the pastor, his uncle, his boss, all the while enduring her suffering stoically. She prayed too, but he was still the same man, hardened and insensitive.

Hopeless and utterly frustrated, Buckee began complaining of ill health. It became worse whenever she heard the man was drinking in Sammy's rumshop by the roadside. Yes, another heated quarrel when he came home, stomping, assaulting the furniture, ridiculing her within earshot of the neighbours.

Fearing for her sanity and unable any longer to stem his insults, his outrageous behaviour, she went by her mother, bursting in tears. Months later, she secured a downstairs flat in Grove village, working as a nursing assistant in the Hospital. Her daughter, totally disoriented—blaming her parents for her dilemma—moved in with her grandmother.

She visited her mother occasionally, trying in her own way to console her. She advised that she prayed regularly. "The Lord never forsake those in need. Open your arms to him—"

"Daddy is in the interior with a gold-mining company," the girl said one bright Sunday morning taking coffee from the teapot atop the stove. She wished her parents could reconcile. If they only knew what she was going through.

Two years later, it became obvious her mother couldn't live alone. She needs someone to talk to, express her innermost feelings, the daughter surmised one evening, vowing to do her best to make her happy.

She bought gifts, delicacies, arranged outings, dinners, but somehow, to her chagrin, she knew she couldn't fill the void in her mother's life. . .the distraction that swamped her. Only a man could do that—

But to her own perplexity, her instincts repelled Patrick. She saw him as crude, outlandish. There was no tenderness in him, she stressed during her visits, persuading her mother to let him go. "Just wait. A decent man will enter your life."

"Patrick is gentle, caring," Buckee reminded her, explaining in detail, however, the differences between her father and Patrick. "Your father was a bully. You know what it is to live in fear?"

Deeming her a stubborn, persistent woman unable to see further than her nose, the daughter decided to keep out. She feared a confrontation with her mother, hoping time would jolt her into reality. Then she would see her mistake. Yes, see that Patrick is not the right man for her—

"He's kind. He's loving. When me fall sick he cleaning me, cooking, mash me skin, bathe me," Buckee would tell the women proudly in the grocery shop by the roadside, traffic heavy, dust curling.

"And dat is what count," the women would say strongly comparing the behaviour of the other men—those who whipped their wives, driving them out the house, hardly giving them any money. Others who kept "sweet woman," ill-treating their wives all the while. And what about those who refused to work?

"Is tru girl Buckee, when yuh get one angel don't make him slip thru yuh finger—"

Indeed Patrick was an angel, Buckee concluded on the fifth night, cocks crowing outside, dogs barking in the street. She had just awakened, sweating, heart beating uneasily. She dreamt some mishap had stricken Patrick in New York. She saw blood dripping down his head as though he was battered but she couldn't locate the place or the person who did it. She knew it was a bad dream with many forebodings. After switching on the lights, and drying herself, she took her Bible atop the bed head, knelt on the floor aside the bed and began praying fervently.

She pleaded that danger, in its many forms, must not strike him. He should get a job quickly, settle in, plan his future. . . she begged that Lord Jesus should always be around him. In return, she promised to attend church regularly, do the Lord's work, spread his teachings.

And it seemed as though her prayer was answered. Patrick found a job in a warehouse in Brooklyn. "The pay is not enough. Six dollars an hour. I am looking for a basement to live. I love you," he said in a letter, promising to send money, to call when he got his own phone.

After reading the letter four times, Buckee felt she could walk in the skies. Her face brightened each day as the morning rose in the front yard. It was then, aware of her promise to the Lord, that she began advising the women how to cope with their respective problems, or what to do whenever their alcoholic husbands turned violent. "Have faith in the Lord, my girl, and things will change."

Yes, you misjudge him. It doesn't matter he's not literate. He's gentle, loving, kind, Buckee told her daughter one Sunday midday, looking radiant in the kitchen. Patrick had begun sending money for her, promising to come down and marry her. "I need you here," he wrote, insisting strongly that she care for herself.

But Buckee had already begun doing that, knowing that one day she would be living in New York. She changed her hairstyle, bought new dresses, skin creams, looking at herself often in the bedroom mirror satisfied at last how the dresses fitted. New York, New York! she whispered softly in bed oblivious of the neighbours' quarrels outside, the drift of traffic, barking dogs.

And in her fancy, she saw herself in New York walking aside Patrick stupefied and bewildered by the skyscrapers, intertwined roadways, the posh cars, the busy intersections. In her dreams, she saw herself eating exotic food in MacDonald's and Wendy's, smacking her lips deliciously. Her mouth still dribbled when she woke up, the aroma of delicacies flooding her nostrils.

And in a craze to appease her cravings, she prepared delicious meals, taking her time with the Lowmein, Chowmein, singing, seeing herself in New York. At times, she couldn't help feeling the presence of Patrick in the flat murmuring her name softly.

Then, thinking her imagination was playing tricks with her, she retired to bed, sobbing, whispering his name lovingly. And each time she was besieged with such memories she woke up with a lost appetite amidst the crowing of cocks. Her craving for Patrick grew stronger. When would he return to marry her? Sponsor her?

Sometimes she wondered whether she was getting mad or maybe swamped by a mysterious fever.

"Girl, de food, de dress, de climate gon make yuh look young," the women would tell her in the roadside shop, looking a bit envious as they sorted out their items on the counter.

"Is only lucky people could go there!" they exclaimed, wishing they were that fortunate.

But she must not allow her fancies to drown her. No, no, Buckee said firmly one day as she cleaned the flat. She was thinking what to cook for dinner, what to wear for the evening service. But in the nights, as usual, a kind of self-torture awaited her. Her fancies kept returning. In the morning she woke up with terrible headaches.

Heh!—is just imagination, she would say, lathering her head with Limacol while she made tea. No doubt about it, Patrick would indeed return to marry her.

Then one night—occupied fully with the flooding in the village—she dreamt that Patrick was embroiled in some kind of fracas with his blood-relatives. She tried to examine the dream, dissecting each part, but alas, she was unable to arrive at a point that would have quelled her misgiving. Swamped with fear now she moved lifelessly in the flat that day, pondering all the while on the outcome. A day or two after, her fears increased. Patrick wrote, saying he would cut down her allowance money. His sister, Patrick said in the letter, was urging him to reconcile with his estranged wife. The woman lived alone in Chicago. It will be good for the kids, the sister claimed, advising Patrick, however, with no malice whatsoever, not to return home, not to marry Buckee. If he wanted, he could still maintain the friendship but he must not commit himself to her. Somehow she, Buckee, would find a job, a next man . . .

Buckee was shattered. It took her two days to digest everything Patrick wrote, reminding her not to worry. He would fight them to the last. He still loved her and would send money occasionally. At least, he still stand on his promise, Buckee whispered consolingly in the kitchen, unable to eat or sleep. She was filled with rage whenever she reflected on Patrick's sister Rita. If only something bad could strike her? She wants to boss Patrick's life. Is just because she sponsor him? Buckee kept repeating to herself, raving, lips frothing. She saw her life crumbling like roach-infested walls falling apart—the words "New York" whirling in her head like water in a whirlpool.

She knew her health was going. She must see a doctor. And the following Monday morning as she dressed to go in the city, Rita's telegram arrived.

"Leave Patrick alone. He is making up with his wife. It will be for your own benefit—Rita."

Unable to stand the shock, Buckee sank lifelessly in the settee. Fighting with her own emotions, she burst into sobs bewailing her misfortune. An hour later, she dried her tears, arranged her clothes then flew over, quick-footed, to Molly across the road, telegram in hand.

"Is betta me drop dead, Molly. Drop dead—" Buckee wailed breathlessly in Molly's couch, handing her the telegram.

"O God, is what cross come ova yuh life? Like yuh gon neva go New York?" Molly uttered unbelievably by the Singer sewing machine, eyes widened, studying the telegram.

"Is what yuh gon do?" Molly asked, eyes narrowing piteously, fanning herself with her hands. The heat was strong outside but traffic still roared in the road. She knew Buckee loved Patrick and had counted to live with him in New York, bidding her time in the meanwhile until—

Molly knew there was nothing she could do except to console and advise Buckee. She too had experienced such brain-wracking agony after her husband left her for a dougla woman in the city. She often wished something dreadful would strike her husband or the woman, "dat low-class slut . . ."

Breathing slowly now, eyes reddened, pinkish dress dishevelled, Buckee looked at Molly as she struggled with herself. Aware of the weight growing heavier in her head, she saw New York like dry leaves crushed in her palms. Indeed, she was humiliated, insulted. It seemed as though Rita was trying to strangle her, murder her. How can she allow Rita to get away with this callous act?

"Is ingratitude, Molly. Ingratitude. Rita know I take out Patrick from the gutter when everybody give him up. I clean he, feed he, teach he manners. You know everything, Molly. . .everything—"

"Yes gal Buckee," Molly replied softly, her sympathy reaching out to Buckee. She too thought at one time Buckee was being too considerate to Patrick. Yes, she didn't care if Patrick worked or not. But it seemed Buckee knew what she wanted. At last, Patrick became a changed man. He got a job, went to church, and cut-off from drinks, spent more time with her. Rita was happy when she heard, thanking Buckee wholeheartedly in her mails.

"Lord fatha," Buckee shouted hysterically, senselessly clutching her head with her hands, pacing. "Yes Lord, why don't you strike Rita. She is in my way. Look the sacrifice I make. I neglect my own daughter, my own sister for Patrick. Is this the thanks? Tell me Molly?"

"Gal Buckee, nobody can see in the future though yuh making plans but still—" Molly said thoughtfully, trying to console Buckee. "Life is so topsy-turvy. . .yes."

"Me have to get Rita outa the way. She's the block in me life. But truly speaking Molly, me just want get in New York legal. Patrick could go along he way after. Yes! me telling you but Rita is the block. And me plan to sponsor me daughter. O God Molly, Rita destroying me life. Tru-tru, me have to see one crack obeah man for she. Kill the ungrateful bitch. Did Patrick wife ever know how he come back a man. . .what me do fo he ?"

Far from Family

RAYWAT DEONANDAN

Sometimes Feroze would clutch the sides of his head and think about twisting off his own neck, like he saw once in a strikingly vivid Hong Kong martial arts film. It wasn't a prepubescent deathwish, or an expression of Hemingway-style machismo unlikely for a ten-year-old, but simply an act of boredom.

He was convinced that regular daily neck twists, vigorous of course, would eventually allow him to look backwards, 180 degrees, like an owl.

"The boy will break he neck!" Uncle Mustafah would exclaim to his wife. "Look at that damn-silly boy. He go twist off he own head, then he mumma will take *me* to task!"

At such times, Auntie Farah would suck her teeth and sputter at Mustafah without even looking up. "Quiet, na! The boy's not able to break his own bloody neck. Not unless you help him. Then his mumma will tar your backside for sure."

This particular summer afternoon, however, Feroze quickly became bored of self-decapitation and decided that he would teach himself to fly. He dashed down the thin hall of Uncle and Auntie's suburban bungalow, leaping at every fifth step. With each leap, he soared higher. It was only a matter of time and practice, he told himself, before he would be able to sail across the sky alongside the birds.

"Well, na, look at that boy!" Uncle Mustafah dropped his newspaper. ''Ten damn-silly years old, and he think he able to fly. That boy's not good in he head!"

"Then maybe you shoulda let him twist it off," Auntie Farah said. Not once during the exchange did she look up from her magazine. In her keen mind's eye, the events within her own household were played out with Stratfordian vividness; she had no need of actually seeing her husband and nephew.

"Feroze!" Uncle Mustafah barked. "What if you hit you head, eh? What will you mumma say to me then?"

"Okay, Uncle," Feroze said. "I'll go downstairs."

"Hmmph," Uncle Mustafah said, disarmed by the boy's unexpected obedience. "Just don't try flyin' in the basement," he said more softly. ''Damn-silly boy."

Feroze was more than willing to abandon his aerodynamic experiments for the moment. The austere basement, usually a forbidden place in which to play, promised greater stimulation.

There were no basements back in Trinidad, Daddy had said once. Back home, he had said, the sea would rise too often during the year, and anybody damn-silly enough to dig a basement would see his whole house float away! He said that most of the houses were propped up on stilts, which had seemed to Feroze to be a very entertaining prospect.

His cheeks brightened at the prospect of frolicsome play. Imagine the kind of diving and fishing one could do from one's own front door! The image tickled him for days, until he had overheard his parents recollecting a long-time story of when Millie, an elderly neighbour, had been washed away to sea during one of the floods.

Since then, the reveries about stilted houses had remained quietly in repose, hidden somewhere in the archives of his brain. He was reluctant to let those houses go completely, regardless of their odious connection to drowned old ladies. They were one of the last images given to him by his daddy before a slippery road and faulty brakes had left him and his mumma alone.

The resilience of youth shielded him then, as he descended the bungalow stairs. Death, anger, sickness, and loneliness are all quick darts whose pain is to be endured an instant, but whose effects are felt long afterwards; there were more immediate matters to consider. Such is the strength of childhood, that all mortal distractions could themselves be diverted by simply inventing adventure. And so an epic Arthurian quest was begun, as heroic young Feroze crawled expectantly towards Uncle Mustafah's secret dust-ridden chest.

The thing had lain there for as long as Feroze could remember. He knew that Uncle and Auntie had brought it from Trinidad, and that Granddaddy had brought it there from India before. Feroze had never been allowed to see what was inside, and had never asked. Though sometimes at night, when he was supposed to be asleep, he had heard Mumma and Uncle and Auntie rummaging through it, laughing and sometimes crying.

In the chest lay power. A strange kind of power, not like Merlin's wand or Rama's bow or Suleyman's sword. The chest was evil, he was sure, because it preferred to lie in the dusty shadows of Uncle's basement, where the odours of incense had settled and the colours of worthless Caribbean paintings had faded and caked upon the floor.

Instruments of white magic would certainly glisten in the darkness like the crescent moon against the black cloak of night. They would give a ping when touched, flourish when wielded, and blazon with thunder and fire when invoked.

He was fascinated by the chest and by its influence. This old black leather box, from a dirty and forgotten country, exuded subtle and evil magic which had aroused his family's sentiments.

Anything that indirect, he reasoned, was hopelessly cowardly. And anything embodying such cowardice, Daddy had once implied, was no good to anybody.

Venomously, the chest hissed through its imagined reptilian aura and poisoned air. In the lightless nether region of the basement, Feroze fought the tidal wave of terror that constricted his throat and taunted him in a way that only imaginative children understand; he was compelled to continue, but the very thing that made his quest bewitching terrorized his ten-year-old heart.

But he pushed mindless terror from his thoughts, as Daddy had once insisted when the power had gone out one night. "The *jumbies* are like bad dogs," he had said. "They can smell it when you're afraid. So *act* brave, and you will *be* brave."

He flung the lid of the chest open. Inside were not the decaying bones of prehistoric dragons, nor the silken capes of some undead sorcerer; only photographs, littered about inside the chest like autumn leaves on the front lawn.

Some were recent, from the last ten years. Feroze could tell, because he recognized himself in these few, his gawking brown child's eyes beaming back at the camera like a ghost from his past, peering back at him through the lens in a twisted, knowing grin.

The rest were ancient and precious, all originally black and white, some coloured by hand like photos in the old National Geographics in Uncle and Auntie's dining room. Many were of his dead daddy, a face almost forgotten now that years had filled the emptiness he had left behind. Feroze lingered upon these awhile, but found no comfort in them. The man they portrayed sometimes semiclothed, often adrift upon a fishing raft, or drinking rum on the porch of a stilted house, was a stranger to him and brought him no closer to the lost philosophy that was his father.

But many of the other photos, most of these torn and taped back together as if someone had pretended to discard them, were of a man Feroze had never seen before. The Indian man was tall and skinny, good looking the way scrawny rock 'n' roll stars were supposed to be good looking. His black hair was oiled in every picture and pleated flat against his scalp. One photo that caught Feroze's eye was of this man, bedecked only in a lungi and a scheming smile, adorning a Trinidadian beach with a pretty mulatto girl on each arm.

In every picture, the stranger beamed, brighter than the tropical sun that fed his warmth. His features were similar to those of Feroze's father in youth, though darker and leaner. And behind those smiling eyes floated a distracted brooding entity, poised precariously between play and design.

On the back of the beach photo was an inscription: *Raj and his friends*, April 16, 1968

Feroze could not have recognized the handwriting, that of a poorly educated Caribbean Creole-speaker, taking great pains to demonstrate penmanship skills inherited from the British system. But he had once heard someone allude to such a thing: an echoing voice cursing "impositions" and "imperialists incursions"; possibly the voice of his daddy or one of his countless forgotten uncles.

He did recognize the gummy india ink, typical of all his parents' documents; and the big flourishing R's, his mother's trademark.

But who was Raj? Most Indian men from Trinidad looked pretty much the same, since they were all supposedly descended from common stock. That's what Daddy had said: they all came over on the same few ships from India back when the English were looking for cheap labour.

"Feroze?" came a hesitant call from upstairs. "What you doing?"

"Nothing, Uncle!" Feroze called back, slamming shut the lid of the chest. He had neglected to put away the photo of Raj, so it lay conspicuously by his knee as Mustafah cautiously made his way downstairs.

Surprisingly, Uncle was not angry. But on his face were etched the lines of grandfatherly concern that usually caused adventure and jollity to flee from Feroze's heart. "You see him, na? You Uncle Raj." Mustafah sat cross-legged on the floor next to Feroze.

"Uncle," Feroze said. "Who is Raj?"

"You daddy's brother, boy. Bad news, that Raj, bad news."

Uncle Mustafah creased his lips and nodded solemnly, contemplating past pain.

"How come?"

"Break you daddy's heart, na. If he mumma been alive, he woulda break she heart, too."

Feroze gazed at Raj's visage, entranced by its genial facade. The distant eyes sprang forth from the photo, traversing oceans of water and time, to seize his nephew's imagination. Had this beaming man been evil? But evil men don't smile so openly; everybody knew that. What had he done?

"Fightin' and wildin' in the street, that boy," Mustafah said. "Just like you daddy." He laughed, the lines in his forehead smoothing over, his waxen face flushed with the aura of memory.

"Did Raj kill somebody?" Feroze asked.

"Na. He na kill nobody." Mustafah thought for a second, the magical aura gone now, replaced with a hue of vexation and analytical recall. "Far as m' know, he na kill nobody."

There was never a time when Feroze had not known Mustafah to be a shabby old man, full of anger at the young, of yearning for the old, and of resentment of the middle aged and successful. Especially when his words were of death and killing, the ripples beneath his eyes seemed to deepen, and his eyeballs receded further into his skull, as if he aged another twenty years each time he pondered a death.

Mustafah was silent now, almost oblivious to Feroze's presence. He was far away. This was more sadness to settle like dirty snow upon his family's house, to push down on the foundations, chilling their bones and drying their air.

What had Raj done?

"He na do nothin', boy," Mustafah said suddenly, his hard skin cracked with a forced smile. "Nothin' that you got fo' know about." He rose quickly and hobbled up the stairs as briskly as he could. The old stairs creaked as if they were going to break. But they always made that noise and yet were as strong as the day they were first built.

Feroze immediately dove back into the chest. Perhaps within its guarded interior he could find a clue to Raj's mysterious life.

Pushing through its priceless booty was like cowboy archaeology. Feroze was Indiana Jones of the old photographs. Two hands were folded in inverted prayer, forced down through the pile, then pushed outward to sift through the disturbed reservoir of Kodak paper.

An edge brushed by his left thumb, pressing hard against his soft brown flesh, sawing across the microscopic valleys and mountains that formed his fingerprints. A line of blood slipped along the fissure, mingling with the silver nitrates in the chest, enhancing the treasure a thousandfold.

His eyebrows creased in pain, then relaxed as the sharpness relented. The mixing continued, and drops of his blood beaded upon several glossy surfaces like tears on the freshly waxed kitchen floor. His fingers seized upon a new surface, rough and old, yellow and fragile. He gingerly lifted it from the assortment, careful not to let his trickling blood be spread upon it.

It was a birth certificate, handwritten and quite ancient. Raj Kumar Bengir, born June 13, 1951, Port of Spain, Trinidad & Tobago. Mother: Alya Bengir, housewife. Father: Lal Bengir, general labourer.

He put the birth certificate aside and placed his cut finger inside his mouth.

Salt! Like the dry desert sands of northwestern India, like the brine waters that washed the beaches of Trinidad. The taste of blood was strange to his tongue, though familiar to an elusive part of him.

He forged on through Solomon's mines, the sacred stockpile of family recollection. In it, he found four faded Caribbean passports; tickets of release, further magic items that had transported his family across oceans and continents.

But that was all. There was no more.

Raj was a criminal, it was clear. A thief and a murderer, like all those loud swaggering Trinidadian men.

Through squinted eyes, the scene is blurred, and Feroze flies amongst the birds. He soars upon the wings of a child's paper airplane, borne over vast stretches of water and half a continent: a voyage much shortened by the space warp of imagination. Beneath him, an abscess on a calm blue face, rests a quizzical pointed island upon which a swarming body of ants sways with undulations.

Feroze sees the one ant who is unlike the others. It is alone and devious, locked into a circuitous hunt.

A black Indian panther on his turf, Raj stalks the pristine beaches, consuming rum and women like sickly and slow Asian deer. Muscled and directed, a machine of single intent, his body is bathed in its own salted sweat and the sweet liberated blood of others.

A blight upon the throbbing island, his predatory machinations are a deafening light in whose shadows the panther hunts with nose and eye. Feroze smells his musk, his salty breath, and tastes the playful hunger within him.

And what has happened to him?

Like all natural criminals, he is smuggled away to a far place. Maybe England. Maybe India.

The panther stalks anew in a richer land.

Feroze placed the things back into the chest. Driven to silence, he swooned as the stillness of the solitary basement submerged him. One last item was held back, though, cached in his pants' pocket, perhaps unconsciously.

He pushed the chest to its original resting spot, careful to leave everything the way he had found it. There was no Holy Grail here, no Solomon's Mines. Still he would leave no trace of his passing.

He went back upstairs to find Uncle and Auntie slouching about, reading magazines. He sneaked up behind Mustafah and flung his arms about the old man's shoulders.

He smells the talc upon the wrinkled neck.

"Uncle," he whispers into Mustafah's ears. "Where is Raj?"

"He deh in England, boy." And Feroze smiles contentedly, knowing he has interpreted his vision correctly.

The gears of time still creak backwards in old Mustafah's head, though, conscious of tragedies and lies, responsibilities and the ties of blood. He is hardened by the deaths of family members: brothers by marriage and race. One is lost in a car accident while his wife and son wait at home. The other, tormented by a shrinking beach and the brevity of youth, drinks Paraquat and has his innards melted away by the herbicide. Such is the fate of an unthinking desperate panther.

Feroze's eyes glisten with the absorption of a false revelation. His black cat roams England still, flailing terror across the countryside, scratching paths to caches of buried demonic treasure.

In Feroze's back pocket rests the true prize, the egg from the treasure chest's nest: his father's passport. Detailed within the creased and blurry black and white photo are the lines of fatherly concern that marked his face until his end. But in the narrow grooves that emanate from the sides of the eyes, like rays of sunlight, Feroze sees the twinkle of ambition that had possessed his father, and had drawn him and his brood to a new home far from the islands, far from family.

American Dad, 1969

MARINA BUDHOS

There was a time when I believed my father to be the only man in Queens, New York, who could not properly hold a garden hose. He failed me in other ways too—with garden spades, lawnmowers and barbecues—all industrious fatherly talents that flourished up and down the courtyards of Windsor Parks, the garden apartment community we lived in.

I'll say this for my father: he was a terrific toilet scrubber.He had seized on this chore when my mother began to get disgusted with a husband who only had the energy to teach high school and come home to nap and eat, and complained that he didn't do enough in the house. We don't do that back down there! he growled back at her—down there being the Caribbean. But come Sunday morning now, my father disappeared into the bathroom and from behind the door came great, slopping noises. When he finally emerged two hours later, the toilet was polished to gem-like brilliance.

The problem was, toilets were private and all I cared about at the age of eleven were public things—like soaping the car or attending PTA meetings—acts my father seemed to willfully deprive me of, all because of something called his "foreignness." I honestly didn't know what this foreignness was. It was like an aura of words and perception, invisible to me. Maybe if I could see it, I'd be a less disagreeable daughter. I'd escape those bitter freefalls of disappointment each time he failed me, like when he didn't know a slang word or could not cut my birthday cake into beautiful slices, for all my friends to see.

The spring of fifth grade, having won the spelling bee and having received an A-plus for English, I was especially furious about my father's refusal to use the word "mail." It was my job to fetch our mail from the slot and bring it to him in his bedroom where he sorted out bills. Without fail, he always called out to me, "Come, Jamila, come! Bring me those mails!"

"Mail!" I corrected, walking up the carpeted stairs. "Say *mail*! No *s*!"

My father would peer from behind his thick glasses in confusion. "All right then," he shrugged. "Mail."

Which only infuriated me more. Why couldn't my father get mad! What a terrible burden to be the child of a foreigner whose grammar needed to be corrected.

My shame over my father was aggravated even more by my best friend, Elizabeth Heller. Elizabeth was blessed with a father who did everything my father could not; he sat on the community board, marched for civil rights, held peace parties for the Vietnam War and dressed up as Santa for our Windsor Parks Christmas party, even though the Hellers were Jewish.

And so it was to Sol we went when things got bad at school over the war.

What happened was this:the week before, the sixth-grade girls staged a protest. They marched into Thursday assembly, black bands around their arms, and refused to sing "The Star Spangled Banner." Our teacher, Mrs Amster—nicknamed the Hamster—who led our assemblies, was so furious, the minute she brought us back to our class she unfurled the map of the world, letting it snap against the blackboard. In a quivering voice, she whispered, "Now I'm going to tell you why we have to fight this important war." She grabbed a pointer and showed us North Vietnam "It starts here." The pointer began to twitch, inching down the brown horn of Indochina, into the blue, open space of the Pacific."And if we don't stop communism, you know where it will spread next?"

The entire class, wide-eyed with fright, chorused, "No, where?"

"I'll tell you where!" With a flourish of her arm, she slammed the pointer into the map. "There!"

We all stared, aghast, at where the pointer rested:Australia! New Zealand!

Even I was a little terrified, though the next Thursday assembly, Elizabeth and I joined the sixth-graders and refused to sing "The Star Spangled Banner." The Hamster blushed, fixed her gaze on us, and scolded, "If you dare act like those older brats back there, I'll make sure this is put on your permanent record!"

I giggled; Elizabeth turned pale. In fact, I'd only gone along with the protest because I hated Thursday assemblies: the required white shirts and blue or red skirts; the high-ceilinged, chilly auditorium where we stared at the Hamster's upper arms jiggling in the air as she led us in dreary, patriotic songs. Most of all, Elizabeth and I wanted to be like the sixth-grade crowd, the cool girls with straight hair that brushed the soft, bleached bottoms of their Levis; the girls who made something as noisy and unpleasant as standing up against the war seem so natural, like tossing back a cool drink.

Saturday afternoon, when we told Sol about the Hamster and "The Star Spangled Banner," he was sitting at their patio table, gluing together one of his sculptures. I always found Sol's sculptures incredibly ugly, like the rest of the Hellers' apartment, which was supposed to be very modern and American, something right out of *Life* magazine. To me, each piece of furniture looked lonely and gawky in the big, empty rooms.

"You're absolutely within your rights about not singing, girls," Sol told us. "It's a Fifth Amendment issue. Under the letter of the law, strictly speaking, no one can prevent your freedom of expression."

"So Mrs Amster can't make us sing?" Elizabeth asked.

"You betcha, girls." He winked and wiped his hands on a rag. "Sounds like your teacher needs a little lesson in constitutional rights."

My face began to tingle and I felt a renewed sense of outrage quicken through my veins. With my own parents the message was always much more narrow and self-serving: Go to school, don't make trouble, don't stick out, and don't open that smarty-talk mouth of yours. I savoured the delicious prospect of another fight with the Hamster, bolstered by terrifically reasoned Sol Heller by my side.

"I'll tell you what kids. If Mrs Amster gives you a hard time, I'll represent you to the principle myself. How's that sound?" He stood, bits of wood flaking off his sweatshirt.

"Oh Dad!" Elizabeth threw her arms around her father and buried her face in his stomach.

"And what about a little Carvel for you protesters, hmm?"

I stood there, not sure whether to accept. My mother, with her stream of ready bitterness, always told me Sol Heller was a phony; he didn't know the first thing about what real people struggled with. But I too wanted to throw my arms around Sol's stomach and weep for the sense of belonging and outrage he confirmed in me.

A few evenings later, Mrs Heller called up our house and asked if Elizabeth could stay for dinner since she and Sol were delayed at a fundraiser and then had to stop off for late-night cocktails before heading back to Windsor Parks. My mother, who'd just come home from her new secretarial job, held the receiver with one hand and sent her high heel spinning through the dinning room. A skinny run showed up the length of her calf. "Of course," she drawled. "I know what a busy life you lead, Marge."

Dinner was pretty bad. My mother was furious because my father forgot to take out the pork chops for defrosting. We jabbed at our tough, wrinkled meat, not able to say much. Elizabeth stayed very polite. Elizabeth was always polite, never raising her voice, never saying a bad thing about my family, though my mother was always making nasty remarks about hers—"I'm surprised your mother only buys you those plain white pants," she'd said to her tonight. "You need something a little brighter." Elizabeth's quietness seemed a part of that discreet sense of belonging, of right and wrong, that had always eluded me.

After a while, my mother lifted her tired face and glared at my father. "My God, Reginald. Look at you, shoving your food in your mouth like that! Can't you eat like a civilized human being? This is America! We eat with a fork and knife here!"

"What's the matter with you," my father grumbled. He mashed his napkin into a crumpled ball, as he always did, rice kernels clinging to his greasy fingers.

I kept my gaze on Elizabeth. Her face was lowered and she grasped the sides of her plate, as if holding on for balance.

"This is horrible," my mother went on. "I work so hard and then I couldn't even get a bus. I don't go to any parties. I don't go anywhere. I come home and have to watch you eat." The back of her chair slammed up against the server, silverware rattling inside. "I can't stand it."

My father made an annoyed grunt. "So don't stand it." As if to spite my mother, he shoved an outrageously large forkful of rice and meat into his mouth. A trickle of kernels dribbled down his chin.

For a second, I watched the hard angles of my mother's elbows fly sideways. I wondered if this was going to be one of those awful moments in our house when she seemed to break into a thousand pieces and the room grew dark. I shut my eyes, filling myself with numbness.

But no, her voice had dipped down into reasonable tones. She was normal again. We were a normal family. "Jamila, you clear the table," she told me. "I've got better things to do." Then she left the room.

After the three of us cleared the table and loaded the dishwasher in silence, we sat out on the porch. It was an early spring night, but already the sky took on that dirty-pink summer tinge. Beyond the trees, the cars parked in the parallel slots sighed and ticked with heat long after their owners had walked away. It was that time of year when people hosed down their small gardens and brought out folding chairs in the Windsor Parks courtyards and wore last year's cotton outfits, their faces hopeful, though a light wind brushed goosebumps on their arms. It was as if everyone was doing a stage rehearsal for identical activities in the summer, when the women's hair would frizz, and we could hear the tinkle of ice cubes across the oval of grass, like small, musical chimes. It seemed so clear, so simple, and ordinary, yet it was this very ordinariness that seemed just out of reach for my family.

"Your mother's off in a bad mood again," my father commented after a while.

"Yup." I began kicking at Elizabeth's chair legs.

"I don't know, Jamila. I can never get it right. What I gone and done wrong now?"

I did not answer at first. A part of me was thrilled that he'd consulted me. Another part was mortified that he'd asked in front of Elizabeth.

"You could do more in the house," I tried.

"How can that be?" he cried. "A man earns his dollar. A man wasn't raised to fuss in a kitchen."

I cast a look at Elizabeth, who kept pulling her sweater over her hands.

"You could go to Parents Night," I suggested.

My father fell silent. I'd picked an old sore between my parents. How many times did my mother complain that my father, a math teacher for Godssakes, never once helped out with my homework. He didn't even know who his own daughter's teachers were. It was as if, in front of our frightened faces, shimmered a terrifying headline:

SECOND-GENERATION DAUGHTER OF WEST INDIAN IMMIGRANT CANNOT DO LONG DIVISION. WINDS UP AS CHECK-OUT CASHIER AT WALBAUM'S.

I was about to reach over and pat my father on the knee, reassure him that it was okay, he didn't have to show up at Parents' Night since it would probably embarrass us both, when my mother called from the window.

"Reginald, have the Hellers come home yet? It's getting very late. Did they even leave a phone number?"

She stood by the parted curtain in an aquamarine terry cloth robe, wearing a clay mask that showed the deep clefts of her cheek, her downturned mouth, like an exaggerated melancholy clownface.

"I don't know," my father mumbled.

"They could call at least."

My father said nothing.

"Tell them when they arrive that we have things to do too." But she didn't move from the window.

"Reginald?"

My father never answered. We all stared into the night, Elizabeth too. After a while, two headlight wands swung across the trees as a low, blue car pulled to a stop. Classical music bubbled into the air; a door opened, a disk of light crowning the bald head of Sol Heller. "So how's our two leaders?" He called out through the dark.

Marge Heller came stumbling out of her side of the car; as she wove toward us, I noticed she wore a skirt made of silvery material; a pair of silver high heels dangling from one hand. She looked to me like a woman astronaut arrived on a new planet, not anyone I would ever know. Now, she wobbled to a stop, grass bent around her ankles. From the window, my mother raised a hand—half hello, half an angry salute, her face a strange, sullen stone colour. "Oh, hello," Marge giggled. "Why is everyone so gloomy?"

After that evening, I vowed to initiate my father into the finer points of being an American Dad. First off, there was his wardrobe. My father hated suits, ties, and shoes. When he came home from work, he skimmed off his shirt, his socks and shoes, then paraded around the house in a pair of flimsy boxer shorts. Sometimes he didn't even pull down the blinds.

I began to bug him. Each time he came from school, I'd already laid out a pair of newly pressed slacks, a polo shirt and dry-cleaned cardigan. "Put them on," I told him, in my most adult voice.

"But I don't like this sorta thing!" he protested.

I waggled a pair of loafers I had specially polished. "And these are for around the house."

He put the outfit on, though he told me the loafers pinched his toe corns and the cardigans made him sweat. He trudged miserably around the house, fumbling for his pen or wallet.

There still remained his hair: great, loopy curls greased with Brylcream, pompadour, fifties calypso style. I threw out the tubes. I threw out a lot of other things as well. I swept his bureau top clean of all the pennies he had collected, along with the crushed, greasy wrappers from the Jamaican meat patties he would buy after school. My afternoons were spent neatly arranging his math books and student exams, hopelessly scattered around the living room. And I corrected his grammar: to the word "mails" were now added "shrimps" and "torch" (for flashlight), "gone" instead of "went," "there" instead of "dere."

My father began to fray with irritation. His brow would fork into angry lines as he asked, "Why you have to be so high-strung, Jamila? You turning crazy like the rest of this country!"

Then I began to turn it on myself. I had always struggled to keep my bedroom in any real order. The room succumbed to an almost tidal madness: dresses and blouses twisted into one another, pennies rolled, crayons broke, socks became mysteriously unmatched. I began to rage at my own disorderliness, all of which seemed the fault of some other way of living I didn't want to know.

Something new was starting to come over me: an awareness that the world was actually split into several orders. There were the neighbours in the courtyard, who worked hard in the city all day and took the IND subway and Union Turnpike bus home, arriving wilted in their suits and polyester dresses to catch the last fragrance from the oak trees, a faint smell of exhaust lingering in the air. They cared about getting a good deal on linens during the January white sale, keeping the tough boys from nearby neighborhoods away from their cars and daughters. Above lay the Hellers, a sea layer touched with an almost godly phosphorescence, where people rode in a moonlight of parties and important meetings; where gestures mattered and words rang smooth and clear. And far below, in the muddy bottoms, swam my father, who ate with his hands and didn't give a hoot about what other people thought or whether his boxer shorts showed a tear. I found myself giddy, sick with swimming between them all.

I began to turn mischievous, full of darker, random rebellions. In my notebooks, I scribbled odd cartoons of the Hamster's flabby arms. At Thursday assembly, I flipped up the pleated bottoms of other girls' skirts to show their underwear, made them shriek with surprise. Elizabeth would watch me, chewing a hangnail. I knew she was afraid of me, and whenever I sensed she might disappear into that quiet region of politeness, I grabbed her by the wrist and dug my fingernails in until the blood showed and she let out a quiet, painful cry.

At Parents Night my father wore his best tweed jacket with suede elbow patches. Even though he should have been comfortable in school corridors, he was sweating heavily, feet clomping as he stumbled into my classroom like a prisoner released into a courtyard of other convicts.

"You must be Jamila's father!" The Hamster sat perched on the corner of her desk. Today she wore a magenta tweed suit, a sprig of plastic berries pinned to her collar. A tiny brass-painted American flag was fastened near the buttonhole of the other collar.

"Hello, hello!" my father bellowed, heading for the chair she offered. Then he halted. He wasn't sure what to do first: sit down or shake her hand. Instead he started to bellow again while he stood about a foot away. "What do you think of my daughter as a student? She doing all right? She a good girl?"

Since the Hamster didn't respond at first, he decided to shake hands and sit at the same time, yanking her arm as he dropped with a grunt into his chair, raincoat bulging on his lap. A quiet, anxious trickle began leaking down my spine.

The Hamster's hands were folded in her lap; one plump calf swung back and forth. On her face spread that familiar sickening smile I hated. "As you are probably aware, Jamila is a very bright girl. Very bright. On the Iowa Standardized Reading Tests she scored a nine-plus, which means she reads well above her own grade level. And she's doing good in math. She masters the new math concepts with great ease."

A more dazzling show of relief could not have bloomed on the face of a father who's just learned his terminally sick kid was cured. Thick streams of sweat trickled from his hair roots. "I'm so glad!" he mumbled and jumped from his chair.

The Hamster held up a palm, plastic berries jiggling. "But there's another issue I wish to discuss with you, Mr Lukhoo." The Hamster's eyes took on a misty, sentimental gleam. I never knew exactly the meaning behind this expression, but I understood it was calculated to make me feel guilty.

"Mr Lukhoo," she went on, "If you don't mind my asking, are you an American citizen?"

My father made a motion to straighten in his chair, but he was too big for the narrow seat. His lower lip pulled tight against his teeth. "I'm a teacher. I'm a math teacher, like you. Almost ten years now. Board of Education, Andrew Jackson High—"

"Then you especially understand our duty as educators to convey a sense of citizenship and responsibility to our students."

I knew my father had only heard one word: citizenship. I had a sudden urge to reach a hand out and cover his frightened eyes with my palm. Instead I watched in silence as he began to squirm and shuffle his feet. The tips of his curly black hair were wet. "What you getting at?"

"I'm talking about Jamila's refusal to sing 'The Star Spangled Banner.'"

"She what?" His swung to me.

"It's really quite terrible," she went on. "To think of our poor young men risking their *lives* overseas. Saving *us*. And your daughter and a few others who will go unmentioned, acting with such *disrespect*. It's a shame, Mr Lukhoo. A terrible shame."

My hands were jammed into a tight, sweaty ball in my skirt. I couldn't look at my father.

"What's the matter with you, Jamila?" my father cried. "Why you not listen to your teacher?"

"Because."

"But you can't be going about with ideas of your own!"

I didn't answer. I imagined myself sitting at the Heller's patio table, calmly collecting Sol's clean and righteous words. The sensation was very pleasant, as if my mind was a slender bottle, filling up with lovely bright pebbles.

"The thing about Jamila is she's very intelligent, very quick," Mrs Amster remarked. "But sometimes she turns a bit aggressive. She gets these ideas in her head. They're often, well, not very reasoned, if you get my drift."

My father sat in a crushed heap in his seat. He could not even look at me.

I don't know what happened next but I remember jumping up and waving my arms in the air. Sounds clattered out of my throat, harsh with anger. "Elizabeth's father says I have a right!" I shrieked. "Sol Heller says it's in the Constitution! I can go to the principal!"

"See what I mean?"

The two of them stared at me. The laughter of parents shot like fireworks behind the door.

Then I burst into tears. My speech seemed as stupid as my father's. He opened and shut his mouth, as if he could not breathe. Shame came pouring through me, black and dirty, burying those beautiful words of a moment before. I was ashamed for everything and at myself for having embarrassed my father. And then I was ashamed all over again for doing the very thing I'd always faulted my father for. I'd let strangers see inside.

On the drive back, my father kept getting lost, so we looped round and round the Grand Central Parkway. "See what you done!" he complained. "You got me so upset, I can't even drive proper!"

I said nothing. Why was it that whenever my father was upset with me, his anger became hopelessly mixed up with his own confusion in this country? Another terrible headline seemed to flash across the windshield: WEST INDIAN FATHER DRIVES CAR THROUGH HIGHWAY BARRIER. SAYS HE WAS IN DESPAIR OVER PARENTS NIGHT.

As we were getting out of the car, I took one look at the cluttered seat, messy with textbooks, pens stuck into the cracks, and complained, "Daddy, when are you going to get this cleaned already?"

This time, he didn't scoop up his things but made a nasty, sucking noise with his teeth and slammed the door shut. "Why you have to pick on me?" he yelled.

"And why can't you do things right?" I yelled back.

"I earn my wage! I send you to school! It's you who don't do things right! I didn't come to this country to hear this from my own daughter! What kinda daughter are you, criticizing your father all the time?"

We stared at one another. My father's chest rose up and down. His black eyes flickered once at me, then at his shoes. He made that sucking noise again. I hated him at that moment.

The next thing I knew he was stalking away from our house.

"Where are you going?" I called.

"You see," he said.

"Daddy, please!"

"You see what your old man got to say about this!"

"Forget it already!"

He had reached the Hellers' apartment and banged on their knocker. We stood there for what seemed like forever. Do something, I thought. But I could think of nothing short of turning on my heel and fleeing.

When the door swung open, the Hellers' maid stood on the threshold, wiping her hands in a towel. For the first time I saw that my father looked a bit like her, with her heavy, dark features, a scowl across her eyebrows. She didn't say a word as we were ushered inside, then disappeared on rubber-soled shoes.

Sol came into the room, looking like a genial TV Dad as he held out a hand. "Hello Reginald. Why don't you sit down?"

He sat on a canvas chair, diagonally across from my father, who slouched on the couch. Elizabeth and I clambered onto a lounge chair strung with bristly cords. It felt as if we'd have to shout to hear one another.

"You want to tell me what happened?"

In short, anguished bursts, my father began his sorry tale of Parents Night, and his terrible disobedient daughter. Before he got very far, though, Sol held up a palm and said, "I'm very glad you've given me an opportunity to discuss this matter. Elizabeth's mother and I are also very concerned."

A relieved smile showed on my father's face.

"It appears this teacher is a real right-winger," Sol went on.

The smile faded. "But my daughter—"

"I can assure you, Reginald, I've already started some actions."

My father let out a few feeble remarks, chewing out phrases like "hard-work-and-what's-it-all-got-me-but-a-sassy-mouth-girl," but Sol didn't seem to hear. He kept dropping other kinds of words about "district rulings" and "petitions," and "parental pressure."

"Yeah, time I put a little pressure on this headstrong gal," my father agreed.

Sol kept going, while my father slumped in the flat cushions of the couch. He had not removed his coat and I noticed faded stains around his zipper. He crossed a leg, showing a tiny, ragged hole in his shoe. I began to have trouble following Sol's voice. I could not help feeling that Sol was not really talking to my father. His lips moved, but his body remained angled away from him. The sight was heartbreaking to me. I was used to hating my father, loving Sol.

Soon I stopped listening and stared at everyone's hands. I noticed my father's hand, especially. It was limp and curved, on its side. I thought about all my father had been forced to do with this hand, learn to use a fork and knife the American way, use paper napkins, scrub a toilet. It occurred to me how far a hand can travel; how it can tell the truth and lie as well. Then I noticed Sol's fingers making vague motions in front of his face and Elizabeth's hand tucked under her thighs.

Finally, my father rose from his chair. He stood in the middle of the room, patiently waiting for Sol to finish. Eventually, Sol trailed off, embarrassed. My father's brow was knit into a thoughtful scowl. He did not look angry, but tired, as if pulling from some deeper part of himself. He spoke in a clear and simple way, the voice he used when explaining an algebra problem to a particularly slow student. "Let me explain something, Sol," he said. "I come to this country seventeen years ago and this beautiful place take me into its arms. You know at my school they take me and treat me like a son? I proud to sing that song. And my daughter, she got to be proud too."

Sol wiped his hands on his trousers. "That's all very well and good but there's a more important issue at stake here—"

"She got to sing."

A silence opened between them, bright and round as a bottle. Into it flowed all the words I knew Sol thought about my father; how he was simple and wasn't the kind of man you could invite to a dinner party or ask onto a volunteer board. He wasn't someone you could introduce by saying, "Meet my friend Reginald. He's from the West Indies and he's also this terrific civil rights lawyer." Or, "He's a famous actor and he can sing calypso." My father was simply himself, a math teacher with a hole in his shoe. Sol's eyes glittered. My own eyes hurt from seeing so hard into so many things.

Outside, the air was cold. My father's face no longer wore the ashamed expression he'd been carrying around for the past few weeks. He began to walk back to our apartment, without saying a word to me. It was early evening and the sun was setting, lighting up his arms, his legs. His black hair blew in the breeze. Then I saw it: a rim of sadness, of foreignness I wanted to dive inside. I began to run, hard, flinging my arms tight around his waist, hearing his startled laugh as I pulled that luminous difference deep inside myself.

The next Thursday morning, I did as I was told. I struggled into my scratchy, navy wool skirt and my white shirt with the cardboard collar that made my neck sweat. And thick white stockings with a chain of red roses latched up the sides. In the bathroom, I let my mother clip barrettes into my hair and fold a cotton hankie with THURSDAY embroidered in one corner. "Smooth your brow," she told me, "Why do you have to look so worried, like your father?"

At assembly, I sat next to Elizabeth. She was dressed in an orange popsicle-coloured shirt and her white hip huggers, like any ordinary day. "It's too bad your Dad said all that," she whispered, nodding toward my skirt.

My hands cramped in my lap and I turned away. I had never sweated so hard.

The sixth-graders trooped in last in dungarees washed to a snowy softness, sweaters with just the right amount of droop—the kind of outfits my mother wouldn't let me wear. "Ragamuffins," she called them.

They stood in a row with slight, knowing smiles on their lips and winked at Elizabeth, who smiled back. All week long, there had been phone calls, meetings, even a new mimeographed leaflet that smelled of fresh ink. Sol Heller had already been to the principal. Sol Heller was planning to take PS 117 and the Hamster and anyone else who got in his way to court.

The singing began. It was raggedy and uneven, from too few voices. I stared at the sixth grader's faces. They looked to me as if they were full of excellent thoughts, about bombs and massacres and Vietnam and babies. They were thinking of how good they were and even the bad singing which surrounded them seemed part of this same world where right and wrong, singing and not singing, were beautifully clear.

"You did a nice job, " the Hamster told us at the end of the ceremonies. She glared at the rear rows. "Considering."

Then we all thronged into the yard for recess, like coloured sand pouring on to concrete. First-graders, fourth-graders, and last of all, the sixth-grade girls who coolly slid off their arm bands. The air exploded with shouts, blue ties twisted off, girls scratching at their uncomfortable dresses. I watched while the sixth-grade girls surged around Elizabeth. They touched her shoulders, her elbows, her head, as if she was already elusive. Her brown hair shone like silk in the sun.

After that, Elizabeth didn't come around much. The Hellers began to take her with them to their parties, so I stayed alone more often. My own house broke into silent, painful cells. My father slept too many hours a day; my mother began taking night courses at Queens College. I stopped badgering him and he soon slid into his old ways, forgetting to take out the garbage, the living room cluttered with his papers. And my mother stayed in the kitchen downstairs, elbows jabbing the air. We were an odd family, always fighting, not sure who we were meant to be.

My mischief turned inward, and I became shyer, more watchful. I did strange things, unacceptable things. I befriended boys who didn't live in Windsor Parks. Not the nice kind; boys who lit fire crackers in bottles or twisted off car ornaments. With my mother's Polaroid camera, I began spying, taking pictures of the Hellers' parties or when Elizabeth played with other friends in the backyard. Sometimes I mailed the photos to Elizabeth's new friends and wrote on the back, STAY AWAY FROM MY WINDOW.

By junior high, I became the sort of person who collected details about other people's lives. In school I kept a notebook on every other kid and all my teachers. I wrote things like, "Mrs Schuldenfrei wears false eyelashes and probably weighs about one hundred forty pounds.

I know for a fact that she is dating two men and she is thirty-one and unmarried." About Johanna James, a girl from Barbados, I wrote, "She is too tall for her own good and shouldn't wear high heels. I have noticed three different boys, really men with raincoats and cars, pick her up after school. She is beautiful but not so smart. Even though she was voted seventh-grade Vice President, I don't think she'll ever go to college."

I would go through each kid in the class, and jot down every bit of information I could think of. After I read back my notes, I felt myself float up above the identical garden apartment roofs, belonging nowhere, on my way somewhere. I spent a lot of hours walking up and down the Windsor Park streets, lonely, unhappy, aware of myself in ways I hadn't noticed before: my funny, pigeon-toed walk, just like my father's. My stare, trying to see into things which were ugly, never said. And there was also my habit of scrunching my face into a frown, as if permanently annoyed at a world that had cheated me of something I could not yet name.

The Job Interview

CHRISTINE SINGH

Kris sprang up directly at a ninety-degree angle to his sleepy disheveled bed when the alarm clock, set for ten, rang out its morning cheer. Wide awake, as if he hadn't just spent the last nine and a half hours wrapped cozily in his sheets, Kris began his morning rituals. As he brushed his ivory teeth and washed his smooth brown face, he pondered what he would soon become in a few hours' time. "I'll no longer be that skinny, geeky boy with glasses and wispy black hair. I'll be the tall, dark, rich bloke that all the magazine covers say the birds are looking for." He would soon be a real adult with a summer internship job at IBM of all places.

Kris's mother interrupted his daydreaming as she tossed his sparkling white just-ironed dress shirt on his head.

—Yuh gwine be late.

—Mum, the interview's not till 'alf one. 'ow can I possibly be late? It's ten in the morning!

—Is far fe get dere.

At first his mother's West Indian-spiced speech had embarrassed Kris; then it had annoyed him; but now he either didn't notice it or he simply smiled indulgently. He realized that unlike his father she didn't get out of the house much, except maybe to shop. Their Trinidadian friends and relatives were her only real outside contacts.

—You worry too much Mum. Look at me. Cool as a cucumber.

Kris stood fully upright, his sleek brown hands proudly peeked out of his starched shirt and his limber legs stood eagerly inside jade-green trouser legs. His polished brown shoes completed the rather majestic sight as they hugged his bony calloused feet which were pocketed tightly in dazzling new dress socks.

—See Mum. All ready. What d' I tell you?

His confidence lit up his dark room.

—Yuh an' yu' fader—nutting bother yuh. Yuh so cawnfident. Rememba wha me say—Mek sure betta dan cocksure!

He wanted to say "Belt up Mum," but his lips stayed shut.

—Yeh, yeh Mum.

He hated when she got all sappy, which usually happened when his father wasn't there. He was back in Trinidad visiting his sick mother. Kris much preferred his mother's generally obnoxious and rather crude manner, for he knew how to answer back. A quick "Yeh Mum, whatever you say," or more often "Mum, you're fifty years old! You're Trinidadian! Bloody hell. I'm young; I'm English!" To which she would retort with mock contempt "Eh, eh, how come yuh is English? Ah tell yuh already—yuh is Trinidadian jus' like me!" It was the same refrain every time. Until he ended it. "Give over Mum, will you? Remember when Cousin Vikram came to visit last summer? He couldn't even understand me. Ask him if I'm Trinidadian!" As usual, she hadn't heard a word he said. She had traipsed off to the kitchen and returned with a cup and saucer.

—Done de talking, yuh hear. I mek some tea—here tek it.

—I'm meeting Tim down at the pub. I'll get a something to eat there.

—In a pub? Boy how—

—Don't worry, Mum.

He cut her off, replying to the question she was going to ask.

—Tim just got a summer job at IBM in Finsbury Park. I just want to see how he's doing.

—You an' dat pub. Don' mek yuhself late now. And don' play, man. Be respectful.

She scattered advice all the way down the stairs and out the front door as Kris grabbed his bag and confidently glided down Camberwell Road. His father and he argued incessantly about this pub, and the rowdy football friends he drank with. "I'm eighteen, Dad. I can drink if I want," or "It's not like you don't drink, Dad." Kris had many comebacks to his father's reproaches, but his father only had one—"Your kind don't play football, boy."

When Kris was nine years old, his school football team made the South London championships. They lost 1-4 in the final but those eleven boys on the team were revered as heroes for the rest of the year. Consequently, that summer, Kris directed all his energy into kicking, spiking, and goal-tending. He and his best friend Tim spent long, cloudy afternoons just mastering the moves. After tea, in the evenings, when they were completely nakkered, they would watch matches on ITV or they would rent football films from the video store and study the players' moves. Coincidentally, that was also the year Kris consciously stopped calling himself "Krishna," his given name.

Kris's father disapproved of his son's choice of sport.

—What are you doing, son? Get rid of that bloody ball. Cricket is more fun. There's a lot more to cricket than just a ball.

—Dad, it's so boring!

—Son, cricket is your heritage.

—I'm going to play football, I am. Tim says I'm really good. I'm going to be just like Gazza.

—Eh?

—Gazza. You know, Paul Gascoigne. Dad, you dunno anything.

His father would show his disapproval by sucking his teeth, and then he would storm back into the house to yell at his wife.

—Why you got that boy out there playing football?

She would slam down the knife or the spoon she was holding and march out the front door, yelling:

—Is me fault again? How come is me fault; me nah gat time fe play wid ball.

She wouldn't return until after tea. Kris always wondered where she went—the park? Sainsburys? maybe the Cock and Bull for a couple shots of whiskey? She always returned empty handed and sober.

That year, both Tim and Kris tried out for their school football team and made it. Tim's mother invited his friends over for a cake in the shape of a football and Tim ate and ate until he got sick. Later that night Kris went to bed and happily dreamed about days of fame that lay ahead. "Maybe a scout from Manchester United will be at our final, and I'll score seven goals and block so many passes that the other team will just give in. Or maybe Maradona will be in the stands and be so impressed with my play that he'll offer to coach me."

Tim played in all the practices and in most matches. He wasn't very good, couldn't pass well, or run particularly fast, but his older brother had played on the team before so he had no worries. Kris, however, played in a few practices, but in no matches. One could inevitably find him sulking on the bench.

—Coach, can I play today please?

Whatever Kris lacked, it was not persistence.

—Not today Kris, we're winning. We don't want to change things when we're winning, do we?

Just as often though, when they were losing, Coach would retort:

—Not today Kris, can't take any chances. We need our best men in there, so we can catch up.

Kris was surprisingly patient. He waited, never complained, and the football season ended with him on the bench.

Kris's parents complained to each other when Kris was out of earshot.

—De coach unfair. He too racial.

—There are laws in this country against racism. Take care I goan' get him fired, yuh hear.

But the smile on Kris's face in the mornings was enough to deflect his father's anger. Dressed in his blue football outfit and carrying the special football shoes his mum had bought him, he'd run out the door screaming:

—Bet I'll play today.

His optimism seemed bottomless, for to him the team consisted only of fourteen of his classmates and it was only a matter of time before he was part of it. His parents, on the other hand, did not see fourteen schoolboys; they saw fourteen white schoolboys.

—Awright mate.

—Awright mate.

Kris climbed up on the same wooden stool he always claimed. The Cock and Bull had been Kris' hide-away for the past year. At least five nights a week he would meet friends there, and chat about school and girls while inhaling heavily on their Rothmans and sipping pints of dark ale, pretending to gulp it down like those balding Englishmen with round bellies. Aston Villa was playing on the hanging tele. Kris's interest in football had waned.

—So it's the big day, hey?

Kris nodded slowly.

—Yeh. I'll be all right.

—You're always so cool. It's amazing, Kris. I almost botched my interview. Me palms were so sweaty and I kept tapping me feet. The whole thing was like a daze. I don' even remember what I said. But you, mate—

He had to pause a second to flip back the blond strands of hair that had fallen in his face.

—You'll be just fine.

—Thanks mate. I dunno 'ow to get there though. It's near the C&A in Oxford Street. Where the bloody hell is that? If I get lost the job's down the plughole.

—You should get out of Deptford more often. Ride the tube or—

—What?

—Something just popped into my head. I'm meeting my brother at Zaza's—the big restaurant near Marble Arch. It can't be all that far from the C&A. Why don't you come with us? Grab a bite before your interview. Don't want your stomach to be growling while you're answering questions about your GCSE results, do you mate?

—Not bloody likely.

Kris quickly emptied his beer mug. Then the two friends strolled down to the bus stop. The bus came quicker than they expected. It took them to Mile End tube station, where they caught a Central Line train going straight across Deptford, towards the centre of London.

When Kris was thirteen he moved to Deptford Secondary, the local high school, along with Tim. Tim straight away made many new friends. For Kris though, finding friends was like fighting a losing battle. "All right Joe," or "Andy," or "Chris," Kris would say, with a big polished smile on his milk-chocolate face. He'd hear an "All right" in reply, but it would be accompanied by a giggle, a stare, or sometimes even a shove against a desk.

Kris went through his first year like this. He'd return home everyday with an air of defeat; he'd been broken in battle. His mother would fix his favourite meals—doubles, pelau, or curried chicken and rice, and his father would take him to action-packed films, but food and films were not what he was looking for.

Tim was always nice to him. At first, he tried introducing his new friends to his old ones, but none of them were interested.

—Tim, he's weird! Do you see what he brings for lunch?

They'd all burst with laughter.

Tim, caught in his own battle, decided to accept his friends' rejections and then hang out with Kris on the days his other friends were busy.

—What's wrong, Kris? You always seem so down.

—I'm all right, Tim, go with Joe and Chris then. I don't care.

Tim would storm off; Kris would quietly return to his computer.

Kris started a computer diary around Christmas time of that first year. He observed a boy do it in a film he had seen.

Dec. 3 Dear Krishna (that's what he called it),

I was going to ask Paul and Andy if I could play cards with them today at lunch. They stopped playing as soon as I got there.

Dec. 6 Dear Krishna,
I overheard Cathy and Kate talking about which boys they fancied. They laughed when they got to my name.

Dec. 10 Dear Krishna,
Tim made fun of me when I told him I had a diary. I told him I had read that Prince William had a diary and he just said "You're no Prince William" and ran off.

When Kris was fourteen, his father had a brilliant idea. Just a bus ride down the road, at the Deptford Community Centre, a West Indian Club was starting up. The posters read:

ALL WEST INDIANS WELCOME
Parents, Children, and Friends!

—Dad, I don't want to go.
—Son, this would be good for you.
—But Dad . . .
His dad yanked him by the arm and delivered him to the Centre himself.
—This is my son Kris. We're Trinidadian. He's having difficulty making friends at school. I thought this might help. And teach him more about his heritage.
The short, dark, stubby Jamaican woman greeted Kris with a sweet smile and led him into a large room where a group of boys and girls were sitting in a circle.
—Go and join the circle, Kris.
—Are you staying dad?
—No. I can't wait. Can you get home all right?
—I'll manage.

The children were introducing themselves when Kris sat down.

—I'm Mark. I'm Jamaican.

—I'm Lucy. I'm Trinidadian.

—I'm Neil. I'm Jamaican.

When it came to Kris he shyly said:

—I'm Kris. I'm, well, English.

Kris wondered if he had been put in the wrong group, for everyone was black with frizzy hair. Out of the twenty odd kids, he did spot one little Indian boy, squeezed neatly between two larger Jamaican girls. After the introductions, Kris approached this boy—Harry.

—Hiya, I'm from Trinidad too.

—Yuh said yuh was English. You doan soun' like a Trini to me.

—I was born here, but my parents are from there.

—Well, I born there, an' I t'ink this group is for children from there.

Harry glared at Kris before he ran off to join a couple of other Trinidadian boys.

—Yuh want to hear that boy talk! What reason he got for comin' here?

Kris overheard Harry as he stood alone in a room full of strangers.

Tim's brother Ben was waiting when Kris and Tim arrived at midday.

—Hiya Tim. All right Kris. Nice to see you. This is my girlfriend Sara.

—Hello, nice to meet you.

Kris's silky-skinned hand enclosed her delicate one and she twitched. A polite greeting escaped her thin pink lips and a waitress came to take them to a table.

—So why you all dressed up Kris?

—He's got an interview at IBM this afternoon, like the one I had last week.

—Oh, good for you, Kris.

Ben had always been a little patronizing, ever since the boys were small. Kris would go over to play at Tim's, and Ben would hover like an over-protective father. As they grew older, Ben eased up on Tim. Once they started GCSEs, Ben told Tim that it was great having a baby brother but it would be even better just having a brother. Since then, Tim and Ben became quite close. Kris, however, maybe since he never was a brother, remained the baby.

—So, you nervous? Ben asked, as everyone perused their menus.

—Nah, not me.

—Now don't be too confident. You wouldn't want to scare them off.

Kris half-smiled and nodded as Ben patted him on the shoulder.

Tim ordered his favourite—American hamburger and french fries. He had been on an American frenzy ever since going to New York City the previous summer for his cousin Aidan's wedding. He had met George Bell by chance when walking down Fifth Avenue; he thought it was "so cool." Ben ordered Sara a baked potato special as she giggled her approval of his gentlemanly move. He then proudly ordered his own meal after a quick flirtatious wink at his girlfriend.

—An' I'll 'ave the bean dish please.

—Oh that's really spicy, Kris.

Sara looked pleased at having saved Kris from a potential disaster.

—Oh, that's all right, I like it hot.

Sara's embarrassed expression penetrated Kris's auburn frame. She didn't like looking stupid.

—Oh, I forgot, they like spicy stuff in India.

Sara tried to excuse her mistake.

—I ain't from India. My grandparents were, but my family's from Trinidad.

Sara looked confused.

—You know, Trinidad—the Caribbean.

—I know where Trinidad is. In fact my sister's friend went there a couple of years ago.

The waitress came with drinks and Tim, who had been present for too many of these conversations, grabbed his Coca-Cola and slurped it loudly through the straw. The American-style distraction wasn't enough.

—So, your parents moved to Trinidad from India?

Sara wouldn't let it go. She felt defeated. How could this Indian boy come from the Caribbean?

—My grandparents, Kris corrected her. And it's not as if they moved.

Kris was getting frustrated. He was used to explaining his existence, but he'd rather do it later, after lunch, after the interview. Ben noticed the agitation and stepped in.

—Kris's parents came to England just before he was born. And they loved it so much they decided to stay. In't that right Kris?

He slapped his "baby" on the shoulder again.

—There was more opportunity here.

Kris explained.

—Yes, England has excellent opportunities, for everyone; doesn't matter if you're born here or not, if you're an Englishman or an immigrant.

—I was born here.

Sara's quizzical look invited Kris to finish his thought.

—I was born here. I'm not an immigrant.

Tim glanced at his friend as he sucked the Coca Cola out of his multicoloured straw. Kris seemed strangely agitated. He had these discussions all the time. "Yes, my family's West Indian," "No, I was born here," "No, there are a lot of Indians in the Caribbean," "Yeah, not many people know about that side of West Indian history." He always politely answered their curiosities, went into further detail if they asked, and then continued his regular conversation, about football or cars. This, Tim determined, was different. Kris's face was glowing like a polished apple, the uncontrolled sweat rushing directly to his hands. These sweaty masses rubbed themselves together, wrestling each other for a chance to break a plate, or hit the table, or slap a face.

Ben ordered another pint. Sara tried to smooth things over.

—Look, Kris, let's just have a pleasant meal. You seem like a nice boy. Ben says you and Tim have been friends forever.

—Uh huh.

Kris designated his anger to an imaginary Sara as the waitress set the steaming plates down. "Why was this one girl getting to him?" He felt defensive, protective, loyal, patriotic.

—That looks just like your mum's.

Tim was referring to Kris's bean dish.

—I told you she was a great cook, didn' I?

—What else does she cook?

Sara was interested.

—Lots of Indian dishes —roti, curry, pelau, dahl.

—I haven't had too much Indian. I can't take the spice. Me mum made meat and potatoes when I was growing up. It's hard to get accustomed to other things.

—I reckon you ought to try it more often.

Ben said,

—You should meet Sara's parents. Her mum goes mad over anything royal. She subscribes to *Hello* and *Now* and then Sara's dad sneaks them into the loo when she's not looking to have a peak of his own. Her mum was actually hospitalized for depression when Princess Diana died.

—Ben, stop it. My parents are just a little overly patriotic. There's nothing wrong with patriotism! Is there, Kris? You love Trinidad, don't you?

—Yeh. Sure.

Kris's teeth nibbled on his spicy beans. Sara's face tightened as she put a large forkful of potato and melted cheese into her tiny mouth.

The year following the community-centre disaster, Kris finally found a group of mates. He had joined the after-school computer club, and there he met Ron, Simon, and Aaron. They were nice boys. Kris had nothing much else to do, no one else to really communicate with, and so gradually, throughout the subsequent years, his computer skills improved. He was often asked by teachers to fix a problem or to teach younger children how to use a particular programme. He enjoyed the attention and he learned to love computers.

Kris's father often tried to get his son to meet West Indian kids at the community centre or at the temple.

—Dad, I'm not like them. Can't I just go over to Ronny's? His mum's fixing tea—beans and toast.

—What kind of supper is that?

—It's a nice change from Mum's Indian cooking. Kris's mother usually interrupted these arguments.

—Ah cook what ah know. We food gat taste. Not like white people food dat gat no taste at all.

This only made Kris more angry than ever. Often it made him storm out of the house.

Kris saw Tim every once in a while.

—Hiya Kris.

—All right Tim. What are you doing?

—Nothing really.

The conversations dwindled over time, but they never passed each other without a greeting.

Kris was labeled a "computer geek" up until A levels. He didn't mind. It was just name-calling. He grew out of those teenage self-doubting years long before his body showed any signs of maturing. He spent his GCSE years either in the computer lab at school or in the computer room at Ron's house.

Family from Trinidad came to visit every once in a while. Kris was able to see recent photos of his parents' home town and hear stories from "back home." The summer after fourth year, Kris's mother was returning to Trinidad for a friend's daughter's wedding, and Kris almost went along. They couldn't find him a cheap enough flight by the time he decided he wanted to go.

By the time A levels rolled around, Kris wasn't bothered with any straying negative comments. Most of the time he didn't even hear them. Doing well on his exams was much more important. He started making more mates as people got to know him in those small A-level classes and by the end of that first year Tim and Kris found their way back to each other. Tim never apologized for his behaviour and Kris never asked him to. The past four years just became a memory.

—What do your parents do, Kris?

Sara thought a change in direction might give her an edge.

—My dad works with the Post Office; me mum's a nurse. He makes sure us Londoners get our letters and she makes sure we're healthy.

—And you're going to work with computers, are you?

—That's right. I'm going to help bring England to the forefront of computer technology.

—I see. That's a rather bold endeavour.

Kris's anger was seething again.

—What's wrong with being bold?

—Nothing, it's just that you might be disappointed.

She had that same haughty look that Ben always had when he was "being a big brother." Kris took a deep breath, remembering his interview, and how he had better stay cool.

Sara paused to wipe some butter off her mouth.

—So how did your family end up in Trinidad anyhow?

—Bloody hell, are we starting this again?

—What do you mean?

Sara's tone was fierce.

—Your country grabbed up cheap Indian labour and stuck them in their colonies. Did your precious country not teach you that in your history lessons? You should know that shouldn't you? But no, I'm sorry, you never went to the Caribbean, it was your sister's friend. Did she not tell you about us Indians? We were dragged, whipped, beaten, and killed, just so your country could get rich.

—So why don't you just go back to your beloved Trinidad?!

—All right, this is getting out of hand.

Ben finally decided to step in. Sara looked as if she were going to throw her half-eaten potato at Kris's face.

—Kris, don't be rude to my girlfriend please.

Sara eyed her rival with a victorious look.

—Me?

Kris was enraged.

—I was simply responding to her ignorant, racist comments.

Ben's cheeks puffed in and out like a red water balloon.

—Kris, I have treated you like a brother all your life and this is how you repay me?

Tim sat upright, hiding under his New York Yankee baseball cap.

—Tim?

Kris pleaded.

—Come on mate, just sit down and apologize, that'll sort it out.

Kris whipped out a ten-pound note, slammed it on the table, making Sara's fork jump out of her plate. He took a long glance at Tim and then stormed out the restaurant door. He quickly lit up a smoke, hoping for its usual calming effect, and sat down on a bench across the street.

It was half an hour until his interview; he had enough time to compose himself and still look professionally eager by getting there ten minutes early. He read through his notes about the company, had an Orangina to cool himself off, and after using the loo in the IBM lobby, he entered the lift, which would carry him up to his summer internship. The lift stopped on four separate floors, each time accepting a smiling suited man carrying typed pages and colourful diagrams. The last one who entered carried nothing in his hands; he crossed them behind his back and stood erect with his legs slightly separated. His manicured nails stared up at Kris who looked down at the wrinkled white shirt his mum had ironed that morning. Kris's thoughts interrupted his concentration and he squeaked out an "oh shit" as his bag thudded down on his foot.

—Sorry.

He knelt down to pick up his belongings and apologized nervously to the four men who surrounded him. He looked up to smile and his brown eyes greeted four bleached white faces. "If they don't see me as English, then why should I want to be like them?" His thoughts were running marathons through his head.

—It's all right, mate. A little nervous are you?

—Yeh.

Kris feigned a chuckle. The lift stopped on his floor.

—Good luck.

The empty-handed one flashed his sparkling teeth and patted Kris's shoulder.

—Cheers.

The well-meaning gesture reminded Kris of Ben.

Kris tried to shake away tangential thoughts as he carefully paced his way to the secretary's desk.

—I'm here to see Mr Cowan.

—Your name please?

—Kris Persaud.

Her painted nails perused a rather large appointment book.

—Ah yes.

Bzzzz.

—Mr Persaud is here.

—Send him in.

—Mr Cowan is just down the hall, in room number 1417.

—Thank you.

He walked slowly, almost lackadaisically. "But if I'm not English, then . . . " He knocked on the hard wooden door. A muffled "Come in" penetrated the thick wood. Kris turned the cold knob and as he entered he thought "I've never even been to Trinidad."

—Hello Mr Persaud.

—Hello Mr Cowan. Very nice to meet you. Thank you so much for giving me this opportunity.

—You're from the Eastend are you?

Kris hesitated. Mr Cowan perused the open file on his desk.

—Deptford, is it?

—Ah, yes, that's right. I do live in Deptford, and I've never lived anywhere else. But that's not where I'm from.

—Where are you from then?

Kris sighed and stared out the window at this foreign city, where he'd lived his whole life.

—Where are you from, son? It's not a difficult question.

Kris slowly turned his eyes upon Mr Cowan's and spoke softly, furtively.

—I really don't know.

Sushila's Bhakti

SHANI MOOTOO

Sushila unplugged the telephone and locked herself in her studio. A roughly torn piece of white bristol board marked "Do Not Disturb" in thick black marker was pinned to the door.

She sat with her back upright, recalling the one class of beginners' meditation yoga she had taken a few years ago at the community centre. She placed her hands palm down on her lap, and held her legs loosely together. First her cheeks relaxed, then she let fall her lower jaw. Next she let her head rest itself on the top of her spine, instead of rigidly holding it up. Layers of concrete fell of her neck, shoulders and upper arms. There was no one around to watch her stomach expand and sag. She let go of the muscles in her bum, permitting it to spread over the seat of the chair. She took a slow, leisurely breath and was surprised at how deeply she could inhale. When she exhaled her relaxation deepened, spreading over her in caterpillar-like progression.

"God. Beauty. Truth." She paused between the words, not thinking about them, but rather feeling their meaning in her chest, in her heart. From the pores of her skin.

"Absolute Truth.
Godness. Honesty. Nowness.
The Face of Godness.
Absolute Beauty,
Truth that is in me and in everything."

She raised her hands, palms opened upward, gesturing to the canvas-stretcher covered with burlap from a basmati rice bag and said, "This is my bhakti." Her grandmother would have been proud, but baffled too. She got up, and began opening the plastic bags of mendhi. They cost $3.99. Cheaper than paint, she thought, and quickly focused back on her act of bhakti.

She had learnt the word only days ago. Devotion. Love. Not of or for worldly things, but of the Pure, True, Self. Big "S." What some people call God. She couldn't bring herself to pray to an all-seeing, all-knowing, all-powerful God. And a male one too. That would have made her feel too much like a puppet, out of her own control, co-dependent. So the concept of S(s)elf —big "S," little "s"— made much more sense.

They were Brahmins, her grandmother used to repeat proudly. But back in those days when she was a child, all that meant was restrictions, expectations, big "O" Obligations. She had to be a "goodBrahmmingirl," no loose behaviour, which over the course of time and admonishments she learned to identify. And, definitely, no taking part in carnival.

The grandmother simply did not know how to or why she should follow her son, Sushila's father, when he stepped horizontally out of his caste, into the upper crust of British-influenced colonial Trinidad society. Caste = class. "Brahmin" lost its religious meaning for all but the grandmother, who dug her feet in deeper to teach her grandchildren the Hindi alphabet and to read to them from the Bhagavad Gita. Eventually they became utterly confused, when even she, submitting to national cultural chaos, would tuck them into bed, clasp their hands in front of their chests and have them repeat after her a prayer from a little book given to her by a stranger who had come to the house to invite her and her household to his church: "Now I lay me down to sleep, I pray the Lord my soul to keep. If I should die before I wake, I pray the Lord my soul to take."

Having Brahmin roots somewhere deep in her, Sushila knew she had buried connections to that higher Self, connections that could be excavated and polished up. She would embark on a revival of her distant past to take control of her present.

For ten years she had been floating rootlessly in the Canadian landscape, not properly Trinidadian (she could not sing one calypso, or shake down her hips with abandon when one was sung—the diligence of being a goodBrahmingirl), not Indian except in skin colour (now, curries and too many spices gave her frightful cramps, and the runs, and in her family a sari had always been a costume), certainly not White and hardly Canadian either. Except in the sense that Canada was a country full of rootless, floating people.

After Sushila's first exhibition, ten years ago, at the N!O!W! Gallery, a reviewer wrote that her style was "delightfully naive," and talked of her "refreshing folksy crudeness." In reaction, out of desire to be an authentic Canadian painter, she removed folksy decoration, borders and patterning from her work, and toned down her naive "tropical" colour. She painted large temperate zone fruit and immense cold-country vegetables, with broad, sweeping, gestural strokes in imitation of the size, depth, feel, colour and temperature of the Canadian landscape. Her heart and shoulders sagged. Colour went out of her life.

She had never touched mendhi before. When it fell out of the pack in a clump of powder, a fine, olive-green dust floated up. It jogged her memory. She recognised the smell, the most powerful of memory stimulants. She couldn't identify it, knew even that her memory was not from this lifetime. Mendhi was not a part of her Indo-Trinidadian past.

That kind of thought would once have saddened her. Now it angers her. From day to day, her skin colour being her primary identifier, she is constantly reminded by certain others of her Indian past. Not by Indians born and bred in India, who insist defiantly that she is in fact not truly Indian (adding to her rootless and confused floating), but by certain others. Brown equals Indian equals India, they had carelessly assumed. So how come, these certain others want to know, she is so ignorant of things Indian? And she becomes angered by the answers. "Indians stem from India, even if they weren't born there, or their parents either. That is where their roots lie." This logic has become inscribed on her fast-obliterating self-image. She wants to know why it is that all that she has of her Indian heritage are her name, Sushila, and her skin colour, both of which are like lies about her identity. She yearns for an understanding that digs deeper than the well-known facts of British Will and Empire.

Sushila's friend Ravi, who lives in Toronto, brought his new bride to Vancouver for their honeymoon. It was her first trip outside of India. She spoke English well but with no confidence. Sushila gawked in awe and curiosity at the bride's yellow hands and feet decorated with brown dots that, when connected dot to dot, formed patterns, borders and flowers: "Mendhi. Pithi. You mix with water, and little oil. Then put on, then take off."

Sushila made a well in the centre of the mendhi lying in a mound on the stretched rice bag, and in an act of bhakti she filled the well with water. She launched her hands into it the way she remembered her grandmother back home in Trinidad beginning to knead flour and water for roti. Sushila juggled the experience of this new sensation and of imitating her Brahmin grandmother (not the action only, but the ritual devotion to family, the preparing of sustenance for their body and soul—fulfilling, according to her father, the duty of woman and mother—that transported her beyond her grandmother to her earliest ancestors).

She poured linseed oil onto the mixture and felt it become smoother under her kneading. The whole consistency began to take a different shape in her memory.

Pundit Maharaj in his white dhoti and kurta preparing for an afternoon pooja at Sushila's parents' home, a shallow square wooden box packed tight and smooth, decorating it with . . . what was it decorated with? She summoned up her early childhood memories and came up with white flour, and coloured rice dribbled to create a border and patterns, the petals of the hibiscus flower, and deep green mango leaves in a bright and shiny brass container. And the swastika! Ah, that swastika, symbol of life and celebration before it was stolen, tipped over and further sullied.

Priests, pundits were men, she thought. Brahmin men, not women. But Sushila was getting wise to a time before his-story wiped out her-story, when women ruled, and were the spiritual guides, and mediums. Sushila became, right there and then, a Brahmin woman pundit kneading and packing earth into a pooja box. Using the mendhi was like having a fine poetic substitute for earth. Suddenly using earth for one's devotion lost its primitiveness and she experienced a moment of completeness, oneness with the universe, a feeling unlike any she'd experienced when she'd tried on Catholicism, or TM, or gone vegetarian in an effort to find a lasting identity and purpose.

She had glimpsed the core of her identity. This act of art-making was itself an expression of her bhakti.

Poly-fix threatened the sanctity of the previous moment, but it was needed for its adhesion quality—otherwise the mendhi would dry, crack and flake off. It also stretched and elasticized the mendhi mixture. The compound smelled like spiced earth.

"The Brits invaded India." She kneaded the mixture more fiercely, more passionately. "Stole its heart and soul. Juggled and shuffled our conquered people all over their empire, disregarding traditions, cultures and souls. The Brits, they invaded Trinidad. My great grands ended up in Trinidad to work the Brits' sugarcane field because the enslaved Blacks ran as far away as their leashes would take them from the vehicles of slavery."

Brown skin, the purest legacy left to Indians generations away from India. And yet, whenever some ignoramus breathed out "Paki, Punjab," as she walked by, Sushila thought how wrong they were. A tame response, but that kind of ignorance simply baffled her into inaction. She had been called Hindu before, too—meant as an insult—but because it was a fact, she was stumped here also, unable to dispute it. People like her were neither here nor there. Roots diluted, language lost. Religion held onto only by the thin straps of festivals.

Sushila took fistfuls of the mixture and squeezed it slowly so that it oozed out between her fingers. She began to spread it smoothly over the rice bag, erasing the blue, red and green design:

DEHRADOON NO. 1, BASMATEE RICE. GUARANTEED BEST.
IMPORTED BY HANIF'S INTERNATIONAL FOOD LTD
RICHMOND, BC

"I want to connect with my point of origin. Not the point of origin as in 'Who-made-me-God-made-me,' nor the point at which we are said to have flipped over from animal to human, but rather the origin of Indian-ness. Where the heck did the Indians in India come from anyway? They were in India, I'm told, for a long enough time that the question is pointless (isn't Hinduism the oldest religion in the world?). But didn't the majority of these Indians originate from someplace else, in the West? This majority, weren't they once themselves White(ish) folks who invaded the Indian continent? So who are the ones that have carbon-datable sediment from the prehistoric soil of that continent gritting up their genes? The Tribals, the ones with pre-Hindu gods and goddesses? (This statement that Hinduism is the oldest religion in the world seems, now, a little wobbly). What is my point of origin? How far back need I go to feel properly rooted? I must be looking for an Indian Cro-Magnon."

METANIL YELLOW K
DADAJEE DHACKJEE & CO. PRIVATE LTD EST'D 1894.

The orange powder floated up and entered Sushila's nostrils. She could taste its bitterness, feel it heavy in her lungs. She gave the deep orange jar a firm shake and about a teaspoon of the dye fell onto the smoothed mendhi mixture. Sushila took a hand cupped full of water and dribbled it over the dye. It turned deep reddish orange. She smeared it over the mendhi surface and watched it change from olive to orange brown. The colours were not her usual bright palette. They were the colours of the earth. She was deliriously transported in her imagination to the soils of her foreparents.

The tall Ismaili man behind the counter at Jamal Foods on Fraser street had been suspicious when Sushila asked him for strong food colouring. "What do you want it for? You can't use it for food, you know. The Canadian government has prohibited its use in foods. What do you want it for?" He held the orange jar in his hand and when she tried to hold it he pulled it back, pointing to the label for her to read:

NON EDIBLE
THE MATERIAL PACKED IN THIS PACKAGE IS EXCLUSIVELY FOR INDUSTRIAL USE FOR DYEING &/OR COLOURING PURPOSE AND AS SUCH EXEMPTED FROM PACKAGE COMMODITY RULE 1977. VIDE RULE 34 CHAPTER V

She explained that she was not using it for food, but as a pigment for painting. And he said, yes, she can use it as a dye, but not in food, he was obliged to make that clear. Actually, he said, people always come to buy it for food colouring and he fulfills his obligation to say that it is banned as food, but he knows what they are really doing with it. After she paid for the mendhi and the metanil yellow K the man said, well you know, he was now nearly eighty years and his mother has been using the metanil ever since he was a boy in Uganda, and nothing has happened to him yet. In fact when she asks him to bring home food colouring (yes she is still alive, almost a hundred years old and still making meethani, oh she is the best!) she insists that he bring metanil, and when he says that it is not good for them to use as food, she says, who says so? The Canadian government? What do they know about Indian sweets? Nothing! Those other colourings are useless. She has used it since she was a child. Bring only metanil. So he does, and look at him, he has never been ill a day since they arrived in Canada in '72.

"If you really are using it for painting you must wear gloves," he warned her. "You won't be able to get it out of your hands and nails for weeks. And don't get it on your clothes, it will never come out."

Sushila's hands were bright orange. There wasn't a hint of white or pink in her fingernails. The dye had trickled down her arm, making a crooked trail to her elbow.

Images from her back-home filled her with yearning. Yearning for accurate details of Trinidad, the substance behind the visuals that left indelible burns on the retina of her memory. Hosay and Phagwa, one a Muslim festival, the other Hindu. The details and their significance were lost to her now, the two festivals blurring into one in her videographic memory. Throngs of people out in the streets, some wearing white T-shirts made whiter by vibrant splashes of coloured dye, buckets full of purple water being elatedly flung (travelling and landing the slow-motion ecstasy of her mind) among, against and over jubilant crowds feverishly dancing to the beat of tassa drums, and chanting in the streets. As she tried to unblur details, to sort out which festival is which, the act of forgetting and remembering and inventing reminded her of her grandmother, who, like so many other Trinidadian Hindus and Muslims she knows, refused to eat either beef or pork because she couldn't remember which one it is that she, as a goodBrahminwoman, wasn't supposed to eat.

The mixture of mendhi and plaster was so thick and inviting that Sushila made fingerprints deep in it. She etched decorative squiggles and patterns and borders over the surface, the cavities and grooves filling up with the orange food colouring. She stood back and watched her painting. It was becoming more full of who she is. She was beginning to recognize in the painting, in herself, an identity of being excavated. She played and fretted and worked and invented until she came to a junction where she could take a turn that skirted needing to be pinned down as Hindu, or as "Indian," or as Trinidadian (in themselves difficult identities to pin down) in favour of attempting to write a story of her own, using her own tools. There were brief moments, brief but empowering, when she felt one with her past. Fleeting. Like a teasing window that opened a crack and instantly closed. But she has become adept at grasping the glimpses, like a hand skilfully snatching flies out of the air. And her delight was transparent. Her finger and hand imprints in the mendhi practically squealed with ecstasy.

Contributors

ELAHI BAKSH (Guyana) is a semiretired teacher now living in Toronto. **MARINA BUDHOS** lives in New York. She is the author of two novels, *House of Waiting* (1995) and *The Professor of Light* (1999). **MADELINE COOPSAMMY** (Trinidad) lives in Winnipeg. She has written stories and poems. **CYRIL DABYDEEN** (Guyana) came to Canada in 1970, and now lives in Ottawa. He is a prolific poet, essayist, anthologist and writer of fiction. **RAYWAT DEONANDAN** (Guyana) lives in London, Ontario. He is the author of a collection of stories, *Sweet Like Saltwater* (1999). **ISMITH KHAN** (Trinidad) has lived in the US since the 1950s. He is the author of three novels, *The Jumbie Bird* (1961), *The Obeah Man* (1964, 1995), and *The Crucifixion* (1987). **HARISCHANDRA KHEMRAJ** (Guyana) lives in New York. His *Cosmic Dance* (1994) won the Guyana Prize for best novel in 1994. **RABINDRANATH MAHARAJ** (Trinidad) lives in Ajax, Ontario. He is the author of two volumes of stories and two novels, *Homer in Flight* (1997) and *The Reluctant Guest* (forthcoming in 2000). **SHARLOW MOHAMMED** lives in Trinidad. He is the author of two novels, *When Gods Were Slaves* (1993) and *The Promise* (1995). **ROOPLALL MONAR** (Guyana) is a novelist, poet, journalist and short story writer. His volumes of fiction include *Backdam People* (1985), *High House and Radio* (1992) and *Tormented Wives* (1999). **SHANI MOOTOO** lives in Vancouver, British Columbia. She is the author of a volume of stories, *Out on Main Street* (1993) and a novel, *Cereus Blooms at Night* (1996) which was shortlisted for the Giller prize in 1996. **SASENARINE PERSAUD** (Guyana) lived in Canada from 1987 to 1998 but has moved to Florida. He is the author of poems, novels and a collection of stories, *Canada Geese and Apple Chatney: Stories* (1998). **RAJNIE RAMLAKHAN** is a researcher and newspaper columnist who lives in Trinidad. She is the author of *East Indian Street Theatre* and *East Indian Artifacts in Trinidad and Tobago* (1991). **NARMALA SHEWCHARAN** (Guyana) lives in England. She has worked as a journalist and editor, and is author of the novel *Tomorrow is Another Day* (1994). **JAN SHINEBOURNE** (Guyana) lives in London, England. She has written two novels, *Timepiece* (1986) and *The Last English Plantation* (1988). **CHRISTINE SINGH** is a graduate student at York University. Her story "The Formal" will appear in a forthcoming issue of *Canadian Woman Studies.*